V L THREE

L M WEST

Copyright © 2023 by L M West
ISBN 978-1-80068-559-8

The moral right of L M West to be identified as author of this work has been asserted by her in accordance with the Copyright, Designs and Patents Act 1988
All rights reserved.

No part of this book may be reproduced in any form or by any electronic or mechanical means, including information storage and retrieval systems, without written permission from the author, nor to be otherwise circulated in any form of binding or cover other than that in which it is published without a similar condition, including this condition, being imposed on the subsequent purchaser.

Cover design and illustrations: © Sandy Horsley 2023

Read more about the books at
www.lmwestwriter.co.uk

PART I

Aubrey

CHAPTER 1

I can barely make out their faces in the louring light. Three figures, ancient hags, sway together, great grooves in their skin deeply shadowed, noses hooked, chins warty. Their heads are covered by grey-mottled rags and they stoop and mumble, pointing bony fingers, then kneel, scrabbling in the ground. One, from beneath her cloak, holds up a noose, its cut edge frayed, and places it in the shallow hole they have dug at their feet. Another fumbles in her apron, then holds up a severed finger, bloodied and ripped, and drops it into the centre of the noose with a crabbed and blackened hand. I gasp in horror and hold my hand to my mouth – I cannot pull my eyes away. From somewhere in the depths of her rags the third witch produces a jug and from it she pours blood, crimson and viscous, as the crones scrabble in the earth, covering up the spell, spitting and cursing. I cannot move for fear. I am frozen, my eyes wide, and I reach out to grasp the hands next to mine, and they grip me tight in return. The hags' faces are bowed as they begin to straighten and moan, and I think to back away, to flee, but then the tallest one turns and it seems as if she is looking directly at me, peering into my soul, dark eyes glinting beneath her hood. My lips form a moan but no sound comes, then the hag opens her mouth to speak and I think my legs will give way with terror.

'When shall we three meet again? In thunder, lightning or in rain?'

There is a cold splatter of water on my face, blown in by a sudden squall from the sea, a taste of salt on my tongue and the spell is broken. I am here, in Dunwich, standing in the crowd, the undercroft of the Town Hall forming the stage before us, and Priscilla and Elizabeth are beside me. I feel as if a ghost has shuffled over my grave and I shudder, grasping their hands tighter, the tension threading through us where our palms meet, and I know I am not alone – we are all touched by it. Our hands remain clasped tight as the moment passes and we watch the play unfold, the King's Men making it seem so real that I truly believe that witches cackle and cavort before my eyes, that death comes quickly, kings become tyrants and queens are haunted by their deeds. But the curtain ripples in the salt breeze that sharpens from the sea, and I can hear the ever-present thrum of the waves breaking on the nearby pebbles and it is that which calls me back. What I see before me is not real, but a play, the kings and queens mere men, players, here to entertain us.

But the thread of malice the play brings stitches into my very being; my fear of the evil of the witches mingles with the smoke from the torches fastened around the stage as I continue to watch with eyes round and mouth open, all the time wholly believing. I feel the pain of the Lady as she washes her hands over and over, the horror of the fighting, the deaths and the sadness. It is brought to life before our eyes and I wonder at the thrill of it.

THE PLAY HAS EXHAUSTED AND EXHILARATED US AND OUR EYES ARE bright, our voices overlapping, as we make our way home, arm in arm, amongst the scattering crowds. The road this summer is dry, and dust films our shoes, powdering our skirts, for we have had little rain for weeks and the land is cracked and blasted. But this is all forgotten as the play is all we can talk about; we are taken up by it, and I wonder at the way it has affected us. We dwell on the very eastern fringes of the country, the sea so close it is eating away at our town; each winter huge bites are taken, houses and livelihoods lost, townsfolk made homeless by the elements, and we need an escape. We are young, excitable and have never before seen players. We have glimpsed another world and we are captivated.

Priscilla looks at me with blue eyes full of sorrow and excitement. Her cheeks are flushed, her pale gold hair flying around a face which sparkles with life.

'Oh, Aubrey, Elizabeth, did you see the Lady? So beautiful, yet so thin and sad; the way she was wringing her hands – and the blood. How did they make the blood?'

'I expect it was pig's blood, for it certainly looked real enough.' Elizabeth is the more practical of all of us, her dark head full of sense, less likely to believe in magic, but I can tell even she was enthralled. 'And when the King's head was struck off...'

'I thought it would tumble at my feet...' I clasp my hands to my mouth in horror. For a moment I had truly believed, shrinking back at the bloodied lump rolling towards me across the stage.

'It must have been made of wood or cloth.' Elizabeth's words are calming, ever sensible, and I know she is right, but it looked so real, and I have long been fearful – my heart still thumps at the memory of it.

PRISCILLA HAS BEEN DANCING IN FRONT OF US, BUT NOW SHE STOPS short at the sight of a nursemaid struggling with her charge, a small boy who is screaming and pulling at her arm. The girl is shaking him, frustration writ large on her face.

'Thomas, stop this. If you do not, I will tell your grandfather...' The boy quietens at the threat but pulls away from her and turns to stare at us. I start back at the intensity of his gaze. He is a thin boy with spindly limbs and a head that seems too large for his body. He bears a ragged red scar that distorts his forehead and he is looking at us with such cold intensity that I shiver. I smile at him, thinking to break his gaze, but the smile dies on my face as his eyes grow huge and black. He raises a trembling arm and points first at Priscilla, then Elizabeth, then me. We watch, frozen to the spot, as his jaw tightens and he begins to make grunting noises that sound as if they are being pushed from deep inside him by an unknown hand. Then his head twists slowly to one side and he falls to the ground. His limbs thrash violently, twitching and jerking as dust clouds around him, his head rolling and banging on the hard track. It is as if he is possessed. A crowd is gathering now, the nursemaid bending to him, so I take Priscilla's arm.

'Come away, there is nothing we can do.' Elizabeth takes her other arm and we pull her on, but it seems as if she cannot draw her eyes from the boy, who is still now. 'Come, Priss . . .'

'Is he dead?' She looks at us, her face tight and worried.

'No, see, they are helping him up. He suffered a fit, I think. Come away.' I pull at her arm until she turns, and the three of us move away from the crowd and stand under a tree, glad of the shade in the heat of the evening. My shift sticks to my back under my bodice and I reach to scratch it away, as a bat flies and swoops in the darkening sky, then I take Priscilla's hand.

'What is troubling you? Is it the boy?'

'It is a sign.'

'He was ill, that is all.'

'It is a sign . . .'

'There is nothing to fear.' I seek to calm her for I see how disturbed she is by the incident.

'I have never seen such a thing . . . and the way he looked at us, pointed at us as if marking us out. Oh, Aubrey, the play has put such fears into me. Are there really such things as witches? Such malice and cruelty?' Priscilla has always been prone to dark thoughts and I reach my hand to her face, sweeping them away with the lock of hair that has fallen across her eyes.

'Priss, the boy was ill and the play was not real. It was a play, a clever play, that is all. Such things are stories, made up, they cannot happen, especially here. There is no need to be afraid.'

Elizabeth nods in agreement.

'Do not dwell on it, Priss, 'twas but a fantasy.'

'I know you are right and I am foolish to imagine such things could happen here, but that play – it seemed so real. And the ghost, how his chains rattled...'

And there we are, back to talking about the play we have just seen, the boy forgotten, and trusting all will be well; three friends who have shared something extraordinary. We are fourteen years old and the whole world is at our feet. We are invincible.

If only we had known. If only we had listened and taken heed. For the words were there, the warning clear.

'... *something wicked this way comes.*'

PART II

Priscilla

CHAPTER 2

It is the death of Elizabeth's mother which drags us sharp out of our childhood. She has no father and now finds herself an orphan at seventeen. None of us had thought of being left alone, how it would be, how we would live. Aubrey and I go to her as soon as word reaches us, to find her bereft.

'Oh, Priscilla, Aubrey, what am I to do?' I guide Elizabeth onto the chair, then sit beside her, rubbing her hands to free them of cold. 'Two days ago Ma was here, lying in the bed, and now they are to take her and put her in the ground. It is so unreal. I keep expecting to hear her call out to me . . .' Her voice breaks and she rubs at her eyes. I stare at her mother's body, which lies still and cold before us on the table, stitched into a rag-tag of cloths which are old and stained.

I hug her tight as Aubrey heats a mug of the ale she has brought with her with the poker from the fire. It sizzles and spits and a sweet burning smell fills the room.

'Here, drink this, it will give you strength. And I have brought fresh bread, butter and cheese, I thought it may be of help.'

'Thank you, Aubrey, I have not been able to . . . ' She takes the mug gratefully but sips the ale too quickly, and it burns her mouth.

She gasps in pain, then grimaces as she touches the sore point with her tongue.

Aubrey kneels by her side.

'Your mother is in God's care, and you did all you could for her. Shall we say a prayer for her safe entry into Heaven?' We join hands and drop our heads as she speaks the words of a psalm, the sound resonant, soothing in its familiarity. As we mouth the 'Amen', Elizabeth looks up at us, her eyes sparkling with tears.

'I do not know what to do now.'

My parents work the land and have no plans for their children except for the same life. I have always helped my mother to bring up my brothers and sisters, and my dream, one day, is to marry and have children of my own. Aubrey is an only child and has been brought up to serve others, her mother and father devout Puritans. She longs for more, as we all do, for she is clever and quick, although her sheltered life often makes her anxious and fearful. But we have family and Elizabeth now has none, so we try to help her as best we can.

'We will think of something, Bess, I know we will. It is too early yet to worry about such things. We should wait until after she has been buried and talk about it then.'

They come for her mother the next day. Snow falls on our small procession as we walk slowly with our friend to the churchyard, white flakes beginning to settle on the ground and on the mound of earth that the men have hacked out of the frozen land. Elizabeth, Aubrey and I stand solemnly, our winter cloaks pulled tight around us against the bitter wind, shivering, as her mother's body is tipped into the dark earth. The funeral is a poor affair, for Elizabeth had no money for a proper shroud, no spare coins to hire the town coffin. No one comes. The churchyard is silent, save for a keening wind and the church bell, which tolls once for every year of her mother's life. It is this grey leaden sound that breaks her. Overwhelmed with grief, she begins to sob loudly, falling to her knees beside the open grave, tears flooding down her already-frozen face.

The minister ends his prayers and hurries away, keen to be out of the cold as we help Elizabeth to stand, taking one arm each. We begin to move away but then turn, startled by a clatter; the gravediggers, their faces mottled with cold, dark hats pulled low, are finishing their task.

IT IS A SLOW WALK BACK TO THE COTTAGE, FOR ELIZABETH CAN scarcely stand, and the snow is now turning to an icy sleet which cuts through us, biting and damp. As she pushes open the door to her cottage I try not to show my concern. She has tidied up as best she can but the room is cold, the fire nearly out. I gaze around numbly as Aubrey goes outside to find wood, then we all kneel, slowly feeding the yellow flames, until a small warmth begins to fill the room. I light a candle stub and place it on the table. A sewing basket sits open, its contents strewn, and I tidy it away in the cupboard, for fear it would remind her of the last task she did; sewing her mother into a makeshift winding sheet as best she could.

The room begins to warm as we sit together quietly, holding out our hands to the flickering flames, each with our thoughts. It is Aubrey who breaks the silence.

'Do you have enough money to be going on with, Bess? Have you had any thoughts about what you will do?' She takes Elizabeth's chapped hands between her own white ones, rubbing warmth into them, her pale blue eyes full of concern and pity.

Elizabeth takes a deep breath and sits up straight, looking at each of us in turn.

'I found a few coins Ma had hidden but I will need to work. So I will carry on as I was, collecting fallen wood for kindling as I did before she died. That should be enough.'

'A chip-girl? But is it not such a hard living?' I look at her. She is strong, yes, taller than us both, with brown soft eyes and dark wavy hair. She is striking and with a good heart, but when I think of the leather straps of the willow basket, the way the wood will weigh her down when the basket is full, the constant stretching and bending that has already begun to take its toll . . . I think of her poor cracked hands, the broken fingernails, the cuts and bruises. And I think of the abuse, the ill-will that has often followed her, for her mother was not always well-liked in Dunwich; some said she was a witch, for she made herbs and simples, but her cures were popular and folk flocked to her, albeit under cover of darkness. I could not bear the ill will, I would hate to be despised so. Some of the townsfolk look at Elizabeth as someone far beneath them; there is rarely a kind or courteous remark, just gruff orders, snapped words, the clatter of coins thrown to the ground where she must scrabble for them in the dust. I have seen it and I want better for her.

'It is all I know. I do not have my mother's skills. I didn't want to learn about herbs and remedies, although she begged to teach me. I did not want to be as she was . . .' Her eyes fill with tears.

Aubrey takes her hand and pats it gently.

'You did your very best for her. It must be a frightening thing to be alone.' Elizabeth is sobbing deeply now and I take her in my arms, while Aubrey embraces us both.

'Hush, hush, Bess, we will help you, you will always have us.'

Elizabeth smiles at us gratefully and forces a watery smile.

'Remember the play? We three?'

We untangle ourselves and step back, our hands still joined, as we smile at each other with love and affection.

'Together we will find a way around this.'

But the death of her mother affects us all. That winter Aubrey is kept indoors, caring for her ageing parents, and I see little of Elizabeth as the months progress. There is not enough work in Dunwich so she begins to travel further, tramping to the outlying villages and hamlets, selling her wood. Summer passes in a heartbeat and it is not until autumn is beginning to bite that she comes home. I hear tell that she is back but I do not go to her immediately, as once I would have done. For I am also changed. Something else has taken me over, something that fills my waking hours, and threads through my dreams. For this autumn is when I meet John Collit.

ONE BRIGHT MORNING LATE IN THE SEASON, WHEN THE FIRST FROST has crisped the fallen leaves and all smells woody and ripe, Aubrey calls on me and asks me to accompany her on a visit to Elizabeth, who has been home for several days. I feel a pang of guilt that I had not gone sooner, and I am eager to hear what she has been doing, full of news of my own, so I unhook my cloak from its peg and, arm in arm, we set off to the cottage on the outskirts of the town.

Elizabeth must have seen us walking up the path for she pulls the door open and hugs us tightly, then sits us by the fire which blazes in the hearth. The cottage is clean and tidy and I am glad to see she is caring better for herself. She passes us mugs of ale as we exchange gossip about the town, remark on who has moved away, who has died, who has given birth, and how our town is still being eaten away by the tide. She is keen to hear what has been happening here but, as we pause to sip our ale, I can wait no longer.

'Oh, Elizabeth, enough of Dunwich. We are so glad to see you. Tell us of your adventures.' Aubrey sits forward on the edge of her chair, her small face bright with anticipation. She has pulled off her coif and her hair curls red around her shoulders.

Elizabeth smiles at us.

'Well, I am no longer selling wood. I have had a piece of luck – I was able to buy stock from a pedlar's widow in Halesworth, she had ribbons, pins, needles and thread, even cloth, so now I make my way by selling these from cottage to cottage. It is an easier life, the women are glad to see me, and times have improved. I travel further afield too. Westleton, Yoxford, and the villages beyond always welcome me and I am relieved I no longer have to deal with the menfolk, for they were often cruel.'

'I am glad you are managing well, Bess, we have been worried about you. I am sorry I have not visited you sooner but, well . . .' I cannot wait any longer, '. . . I have some news of my own.' My friends lean forward, curiosity sparkling in their eyes. 'I am being courted. A young man has asked me to walk out with him.'

I have kept him to myself ever since I first laid eyes on him – I did not want to share him. He was working in the fields with the other farm workers, stacking the corn. It was his dark hair I noticed first, how it fell in soft curls over his face, then I saw his strong shoulders tight under his damp shirt. I lowered my eyes, thinking to be modest as I know I should have been, but I could not resist glancing at him again and, as I did so, he looked at me. I tossed my hair as if I didn't care and turned away, but all the time I could feel his eyes following me and I had to turn back. He was gazing at me, a wide wicked smile on his face, and a feeling came through me, such as I'd never felt before. I pouted at him, trying to be coy, but he threw back his head at my attempts and laughed, then turned back to his task. I'd felt myself blush with humiliation as I walked slowly away but then, the following week, after many a sleepless night, I returned to the field. The corn ricks were finished now and the thatchers were busy covering them, and he was not there. I swallowed my disappointment but as I stood, feeling the loss, there was the warmth of someone standing close, too close, behind me, a tingling on the back of my neck, a smell of clean sweat, ale and hay.

I turned.

'Do you look for me?' His eyes were laughing.

'Why would I do that, Sir?' I lowered my head and looked up at him under my eyelashes as I had seen the other girls do.

'Because you have been here before, because I have seen you looking at me, and because I think you like what you see.' His brazenness should have made me angry, and wary, but my legs were liquid and I just wanted to stay there forever, breathing him in.

'Shall I call for you?' He took my hand and touched his lips to my fingertips and I was lost.

. . .

I sit back on the stool, glowing with happiness, as Aubrey and Elizabeth take in this news. I am the first one of us to be courted. The first one of us to grow away.

'So, who is it? Do we know him? What do your parents say?' Aubrey's eyes are dancing, a broad smile lighting her face. She is happy for me.

I smooth the front of my dress, smiling shyly. Even now I hesitate to tell them, in case it is all a chimera, that speaking his name causes my world to splinter and dissolve. I take a deep breath.

'His name is John, John Collit, and he is a farmhand. You may have seen him in Dunwich. He is a cousin of the Spatchetts.'

Aubrey catches her breath. We all know of the Spatchetts. Robert, the grandfather, holds Dunwich in the palm of his hand, and it is said that his grandson, Thomas, stands to inherit his vast wealth when Robert, now sick in body, passes from this life.

'Was Thomas Spatchett not the boy we saw after the play? The one who had a falling fit?'

'It was. It is said he is a little odd, for his nurse dropped him on his head as a babe. He carries the scar to this day.'

Aubrey nods.

'I saw it, I remember that day, 'twas after the play – he seemed an odd child, menacing somehow . . .' She shudders, 'But no more talk of him. Tell us of John Collit.'

Elizabeth leans forward, smiling, but her eyes are unreadable.

'I know him. He is often at the family farm when I call with my wares.' She hesitates. 'He will make a good husband.' Her words are clipped and I wonder if she has fancied him for herself, but then she softens. 'Oh, Priss, I am so pleased for you. He is very handsome. You will make a fine couple.'

Aubrey smiles in agreement

'I have seen him around Dunwich. He is a fine-looking man with good connections. I wish you every happiness, Priss, I truly do. We all hope to find someone who will love us, and I am glad for you. Such good news. And your parents, what of them?'

'They are very pleased – Mother thinks he is a good catch, Father too. John . . .' Even now I hesitate, his name still unfamiliar in my mouth. '. . . John has spoken to them and has charmed them both. He will suit me well I think.'

'So, will you wed?'

I smile coyly. I dream of him being my husband, but I dare not think of that just yet. Matches are often arranged with speed, I know, and I can only pray that he will ask Father for my hand, but I am not yet certain of him. I have seen the way he looks at other girls when he thinks I do not see. He has a wandering eye, as good-looking men so often do. I know I am said to be pretty but I am not yet sure I can make him mine.

'It is too early to say. But if he asks me I will not turn him down.' I smile broadly at them. 'Oh, Aubrey, Bess, I love him so much. He is handsome and strong and makes me feel safe and desired. I want him so, but I do not know what his intentions are. I cannot tell.'

'You must wait for him to speak of it first, you know this. You must be modest and compliant with your affection, and this may yet make him yours.' Aubrey reaches for my hands and squeezes them, her green eyes filled with love. 'Look at you, how could any man resist you? But wait for him, Priss, let him ask for your hand. Do not let him think you are forward, for men want wives who are pure and biddable.'

It is good advice. But I do not take it.

I ONLY HOLD OUT AGAINST HIS ENTREATIES FOR THREE WEEKS. I cannot resist him. He buries his face in my hair and tells me often how much he loves me, how beautiful I am, and that he wants to make me wholly his. His words are soft and sweet and draw me closer and closer. And when I resist he asks if I do not love him enough, and what can I say to that, for I do, I love him with all my heart. We meet in the silent places and our kisses grow wilder and wilder. He makes me feel whole and beautiful and desired and finally, one evening, in the barn where the hay is stored, where it is warm and dry and smells of summer, I allow him to touch me under my skirts. I think that is all I will do until such time as we are wed, but the next time his breath comes harder as he pulls my bodice down and skims his fingers over my breasts. I do not have the power to stop him. I am water, I am sand, I am the shoreline caressed by the sea. And when he covers me with his body, the weight of him bearing down hard upon me, when he fumbles with his britches, I do not have the willpower to stop him as I know I should, for I want him as much as he wants me.

I think what harm can it do, if, perhaps, this will cleave him to me forever? So we meet and we love and I still think what harm does it do, if two people who love each other this much wish to lie together? I forget my parent's teachings, I forget the words of the Bible, the warnings of my friends. John Collit is all I can think of, all I desire. And even when my courses cease and my bodice tightens I think all will be well, for we love each other.

But lovers are fickle, men are cruel. When the babe begins to stir in my belly and I summon the courage to tell John of my predicament, I think that he will fall upon me, covering my face with kisses, begging me to be his wife, telling me how much he loves me.

He does not. Instead, his face darkens and he pulls away from me.

'Could you not have taken more care?' I do not know what he means and I look at him as a fear washes through me.

'John?'

He runs his hand through his hair, his brow furrowing.

'No, I will not be caught like this.'

I pluck at his sleeve, misery making me beg.

'John, this is just the beginning for us, do you not see? We can marry and have this babe . . .' He looks at me like a stranger.

'Marry? I am young yet. I do not wish to marry.'

'But you said . . . All those sweet words, did you not mean

them?' I can hear the pleading in my voice and despise myself for it, but I am anxious, suddenly afraid, for all know what happens to women who bear children out of matrimony. I grip his sleeve harder and he shrugs me off.

'I need time to think. I will come and see you tomorrow.'

'And you will speak to my father? You will ask him?' He nods, pulls his coat around him and strides off into the night. I go home and make myself ready for bed, ignoring the questioning face of my mother.

The next day comes. But John does not.

CHAPTER 3

It is decided for us. Mother eventually gets the truth from me and my father goes to speak to John's. They agree we should wed, we have no say in it, and I am grateful.

We are sitting around the fire in Aubrey's house when I tell them the news.

'I am to be wed . . .' My two friends look at each other in astonishment. '. . . in four weeks time.'

'You did not tell us John had asked you!' Aubrey's smile fades as she sees my expression.

'So soon? Will you have time to plan it all?' Elizabeth, as ever the practical one of us. I feel myself blush, feel the heat of it cover my face, sink to my chest, and I look down at my lap, my fingers twisting the fabric of my skirt, and then I bring my head up proudly to face them.

'I am with child . . .' Aubrey covers her mouth with her hand. 'I know what you are thinking, both of you, and you are right. I know we are taught that we should save ourselves for marriage, but he was so . . .' I remember our love-soaked tumblings and cannot regret it for a moment – and now I will have everything I dreamed of. 'He was so loving and kind – I could not resist his entreaties. He is so beautiful and his lips on my ear as he whispered his desire for me . . . it melted me so much I could not refuse him.' I smile at the telling. 'And now . . .' I cup my hands over a barely visible swelling under my skirt. 'Please be happy for me, do not berate me. For who is to say what you would have done in my place? And he is all I have ever wanted.' I am smiling as I look at Aubrey and Elizabeth and they smile back, for my pleasure is theirs, but they both seem serious.

Aubrey leans forward.

'And what of your parents? What of his? Are they in agreement to this match?'

'It was they that arranged it. John's mother thought at first that I had done this to trap him into marriage, but he has said he would do the right thing, so I think she is satisfied. The banns are to be read for the first time this Sunday.' I look at them both – their expressions are hard to read and suddenly I am afraid. 'Please be happy for me. This is all I wanted. It will not change our friendship, I promise, but I must know that you wish me well.' I look pleadingly at them and they smile and it is as if the sun has come out.

'We only want what is best for you and if you are sure he is the one, of course we are happy for you. We both wish you the very best of happiness and a long and healthy life together.' Elizabeth stands and hugs me and Aubrey joins her. They circle me with their love and we are friends once more.

I am smiling as I walk home. All will be well. John and I will wed and we will be happy. All will be well.

It is Aubrey and Elizabeth who prepare me for the wedding ceremony, for my mother is faint with worry at the prospect of guests and is scurrying back and forth. It is my two friends who dress me for the occasion. They wash and brush my pale hair until it shines, then thread it with wild flowers. They dress me in my best skirt and a new bodice, blue like the sky, which Aubrey has embroidered with garlands of flowers on the front, as a wedding gift. I gaze at the figure in the foxed mirror that stands in my parent's bedchamber. I scarcely recognise myself, for the coming babe has made my face rounder and my skin glow. I smooth my hands over the bodice, feeling the slubs of stitching under my fingertips, and straighten my skirts.

'Time to leave.' Elizabeth hands me a posy of flowers from her garden and they stand there smiling at me – Elizabeth tall, her brown hair wavy and thick, her dark eyes soft; Aubrey small and wiry, red-haired and pale. My own true friends – we are so different yet we think as one. Suddenly I have a moment of doubt.

'I do not wish to go.' My heart is thudding now and I feel close to fainting. 'I do not wish this.'

Aubrey rushes to my side and puts her arm around my waist.

'What is the matter?' But I cannot find the words. It is just a sudden feeling of foreboding, that this will end ill. 'Priss, this is what you have long dreamed of. Every bride feels frightened on her wedding day. You love John and he loves you. Go now.' She gives me a gentle push in the small of my back and my nerves disappear like a bubble on water. I glance at myself in the mirror once more and smile.

Our wedding takes place in the porch of the church of St Peter. It is a perfect summer's day, the sun gleaming in a pure blue sky, arrows of swifts screaming above us, when John and I step from the shade and out into the bright sunshine as man and wife. I am still smiling as we step into the crowds of well-wishers, John's hand clasped firmly in mine. We both look around, accepting greetings and good wishes from the townsfolk who have come to bless our match. I glance up at the man I have just wed. He stands tall beside me, black hair ruffled by a summer breeze that has struck up, so handsome in a new waistcoat. He shows no trace of nervousness, it is as if he had never doubted us. I see Aubrey and Elizabeth at the back of the crowd, laughing and waving and, pulling away from my new husband and the group around me, I run to them, drawing them into a hug, enclosing and including them in my happiness.

'Thank you for everything.' I kiss Aubrey first, then turn to Elizabeth, and they smile at me, speaking their congratulations, happy for me. 'You know that it will always be we three. Oh, Aubrey, Bess, I am so happy.' I let go of them and return to my husband's side. He glances down at me with pride as well-wishers throw flowers and wave ribbons. We finally leave the porch and form a loose procession to walk to my parent's house for the wedding feast.

IT SEEMS AS IF MY MOTHER HAS INVITED THE WHOLE OF DUNWICH, and everyone is keen to celebrate us and our good fortune. The house is full to bursting, a long table of food set with clean linen, candles and flowers, and everyone eats and drinks their fill. Then the floors are cleared, rugs taken up, and there is dancing, a pipe and violin scratching out merry tunes while dancers whirl and stamp, the ale making everyone bolder.

I dance with John until my back aches and my feet can take no more, then I sit, sipping ale, slipping my heels in and out of my shoes to ease their ache, watching him dance in turn with our guests. He is smiling and happy, a little drunk I think. I watch the envious gazes of the other girls there and I feel so blessed that this handsome man has chosen me as his wife. Then, a hand soft on my shoulder, and I turn to see Aubrey and Elizabeth. They pull up chairs beside me.

'It will not be the same.' I give voice to my fear.

'Oh, Priss, it will not change us. We will still be friends.' Aubrey squeezes my arm in consolation.

'I try to believe it, but I am John's now, and I am frightened of how this marriage will alter me – for it changes everyone.' But my words fall onto air as Aubrey is whisked away by a young man who takes her hand and pulls her into the dancing crowd. I see her smile, her face flushing, as he spins her around, her hair flying in a red cloud behind her as I sit with Elizabeth and watch.

The evening draws to a close, the crowds thin and people begin to stagger rowdily to their homes as a group gathers to escort John and I away. We are lucky – a tied cottage has been given over to us by Robert Spatchett. It is small, but it is in the centre of Dunwich, and I look forward to making it our home.

Elizabeth and Aubrey walk with the others, all calling and laughing through the dusk, as an owl whoops in the distance. I cling to John's arm. He is staggering now, for strong ale and an evening of dancing have taken their toll. As we reach the cottage I turn and fling myself into his arms. He dips down and reaches under me, lifting me high into the air. I scream with delight and mock fear, wrapping my arms tight around his neck as the company applauds and cheers. Stumbling slightly, he carries me over the threshold, dark curls falling across his face, strong shoulders pushing at the stuff of his shirt, and I feel as if my heart will burst with happiness. The crowd is beginning to move away now, the excitement over, chattering and laughing as they make for their own beds. John still holds me in his arms as he turns to shut the door behind us. Suddenly, I shiver. I am sure he must feel it and I look up at him. As I do so, I see his eyes are not on me but on a girl in the crowd, one he has danced with several times tonight. I pull his face to mine in a deep kiss, but a troubling starts up inside me that does not leave me.

THE FOLLOWING SPRING, WHEN BUDS ARE PEEPING THROUGH THE sandy soil and birds sing in the greening trees, I give birth to a daughter. The labour is long and hard, for my body is slight, and by the time it is over I am barely conscious. The midwife brings me the babe, cleaned and wrapped, but I cannot hold her as my arms are weak. She folds the counterpane and places the babe on it, next to me, then bares my breast, squeezing my nipple until a clear fluid beads it. Then, very gently, she holds the babe, pushing her head towards my breast, offering soft words of encouragement, until the tiny mouth latches on. It is a soft fluttering at first then a sharp tugging pain which drags from the very depths of me. My daughter. She is so small with pearl-like fingernails and large blue eyes, closed now in contentment as she suckles.

'A beautiful babe. What will you name her?' The midwife sits beside me, supporting the babe until I am able to fold my arms around her and hold her for myself. She is so tiny I am afraid I will break her, and my tears begin to fall.

'I do not know. I cannot look after her. I do not know how.' The midwife shushes me and strokes the hair back from my forehead.

'Now, now. You are tired from the birth, that is all. You will feel different in a few days when you have regained your strength. It is normal, Mistress, for new mothers to feel like this. You will feel stronger as the days progress, your milk will come and your daughter will grow strong and healthy under your care. The Lord will guide you in this, as in all things. He will show you what to do, for motherhood is a natural, God-given blessing. It is a wonderful thing to be a mother, but many feel just as you do now. Come, do not worry, let us get you bathed and into a clean nightgown and then I will summon your husband.'

She passes me a bowl of warm water and a cloth and takes the babe from me, laying her gently into the carved wooden crib that has rocked generations of Collits. I feel better when I am washed and my hair brushed, but I still cannot look at my babe. It is as if she doesn't belong to me, as if I gaze on a tiny imposter who has been placed in the wrong room.

The stairs creak and voices soften as John comes into the bedchamber, ducking his head under the low beam by the door. He stands at the foot of the bed and looks at me.

'Priscilla?'

'We have a daughter. Fit and healthy, see . . .' and I stretch my arm out to the cradle. He walks over and looks down and, in that moment, I see an expression of pure love in his eyes such as I have never seen before. He stoops and carefully lifts her out, the midwife flapping and worrying at him, making sure he holds her correctly and supports her downy head. Her eyes close and a tiny hand waves in the air. When he looks back at me there are tears in his eyes.

'Thank you, Wife. She is beautiful. My daughter . . .' He pauses and takes a breath. 'What shall we call her?' It is not something we have discussed but I knew as soon as I felt her move in me.

'Bess. She will be called Bess.' He smiles at this.

'Then Bess it is.'

I recover slowly from the birth, often prone to fits of weeping and periods of silence that I cannot comprehend. After a few weeks, John calls the midwife again, and she comes and examines me, but reassures him that it is common for new mothers to be sad and that it will pass.

'The best thing you can do is to make another child, and soon. She will be so busy then she will not have time to dwell.' I turn away, terrified at the thought of another small life to care for. But John takes her at her word and, despite my entreaties, that night he presses himself on me. I am still sore and torn from the birth and I cry out, but he seems to take this as the sound of my pleasure and his movements get faster and harder. When he is spent I turn my face from him so that he does not see my tears.

Aubrey and Elizabeth visit often in the early weeks and help as best they can and, as little Bess grows, the darkness that has haunted me these past months seems to lift a little and I feel happier.

ONE DAY, NEARLY A YEAR LATER, AUBREY COMES WITH NEWS OF her own.

'Do you remember the young man from your wedding feast, the one I danced with?' She and I are sitting on the doorstep whilst my babe crawls in the grass, exploring the garden. 'Well, we have been walking out together since then and – oh, Priss, he has asked me to marry him.' I take her hands and smile widely at her, thrilled at her news.

'What is his name? Tell me about him, all of it.'

'He is called William Grinsett, he is a fisherman. His mother has recently died and he lives in her cottage down by the quay, near Hen Hill. It is tiny, but I can make it homely. And he will teach me to make nets so that I can be of help to him. He says I will be able to earn good money doing this, and I will have a skill to fall back on.' I know that she has yearned to be free of her parents, though she loves them dearly. Her eyes sparkle and happiness pours out of her and I cannot help but be infected by it. I know the houses she speaks of though. They are little more than shacks, built on the shifting sands, tarred and bent, and I cannot imagine her living in such a place. But I think that if this William makes her feel this way, then it is of no matter where she calls home.

I lean towards her.

'And what of your parents, Aubrey? Are they pleased for you?'

'I believe so. I thought Mother would forbid me to marry, for she has often said how I will be there to care for them in their old age, but now it is happening she seems resigned to it.'

'I am glad.' I take her hands in mine. 'Are you truly happy, Aubrey?'

She nods.

He is a kind man, not handsome like John . . .' she looks at me and smiles, '. . . but I know he loves me, as I love him, so yes, I am happy.' She looks at me and her face clouds. 'It will be a very different life. Priss, what if I cannot make him happy? I fear . . .'

'Do not be fearful Aubrey. You once told me that it was normal for a bride to feel nervous. All will be well, I am sure of it.'

HER WEDDING IS NOT THE GRAND OCCASION THAT JOHN AND I HAD, but I am there, little Bess wriggling in my arms. The September sun is low and, out to sea, the skies are beginning to fill with clouds, but here the sun shines on them in blessing as the couple emerge hand in hand from the church porch. I have loaned Aubrey my wedding bodice that she embroidered for me, and she wears it with pride. She and William look so happy and I think of how John and I were, how I thought... well, we are wed now and I do my duty by John as a wife should, but it is not as I imagined. Maybe lovers turn from each other when marriage is done, perhaps this is what other people find. Perhaps it is not just me.

I was sad that Elizabeth was not there to see Aubrey wed, but the invitation found her too late; the summer being a good one, she was too far away to return, but I know she would be pleased to see Aubrey so full of joy.

'I wish you every happiness, Aubrey, and you too, William. May God's blessing be upon you.' William smiles as he tickles little Bess under her chin and she giggles in delight, reaching out a chubby hand to pull at his hair. He seems a kindly man and I think they will be well-suited.

'And maybe, in a while, you will be blessed with a child, as I have been.' Aubrey blushes and takes her new husband's arm as I kiss her cheek and squeeze her hand. 'Be happy, Aubrey.'

I walk home, thinking about my friends. Aubrey, now with William, is making a new life as a fisherman's wife, and Elizabeth is tramping with her wares. We have gone in different directions and I will miss them sorely. Overhead, the sky darkens with a sudden squall and, as I speed towards home, the weight of Bess growing in my arms, fat drops of rain spatter the ground.

CHAPTER 4

Bess is barely two years old, demanding and noisy, when I give birth to another babe, a boy. These days John constantly seeks to ingratiate himself with his cousin, Thomas Spatchett, who, although young, has taken over the running of his grandfather's estates, and John is sure he is the up-and-coming man.

'We shall name him Robert, after Thomas' grandfather. It is a prudent move.'

Little Robert is healthy but I suffer worse than before, my moods strained and erratic, and I can see that I begin to drive John away, but I am unable to cope. I cannot find the love that I should feel for my newborn babe and guilt eats at me. My appetite disappears and I become thin and constantly tired. I do not have the strength to take care of myself as I should. Little Bess is walking now and has her hands into everything, and there is so much noise and clamour with her and the new babe that I cannot sleep. It is as if my life has become one long worry and I find myself crying frequently for no reason. John has little patience with me that summer, and it is Aubrey who shows me tenderness, trying, by words and deeds, to bring me back to the person I once was. And gradually her ministrations work, my old self begins to return, my mind clears and I begin to love little Robert as I should. I am mightily relieved, but my relationship with John is damaged and his moods change like the weather.

I am sitting watching Aubrey one afternoon, sewing untouched on my lap, as her fingers fly, the wooden needle moving swiftly, threading and knotting the twine around the block as the net grows.

'You have become quick with that.'

She smiles.

'William has taught me well. And I like to do it. I like the feel of the twine through my fingers, and seeing the net grow. It helps to keep me occupied, especially when he is at sea, and brings in money.'

'Are you happy with him?'

She stops and looks at me.

'I am. He is a good man, gentle and kind, and the times he is away only makes us love each other more.' She lowers her head but not before I see her blushing. She carries on with her work and we sit in companionable silence but then I sense that she is summoning the courage to speak. I smile at her.

'Say it, Aubrey, whatever it may be. We are friends are we not? I shall not be offended.'

She takes a deep breath.

'Priss, is everything alright?' I stiffen. 'I mean with you and John? I know that it is difficult with the children so small, but you seem worried, not yourself...'

As she speaks I realise how much I have longed to tell someone.

'He is changed, Aubrey. I am not sure what has happened to us.' Now she has opened the gates the flood of words streams out. 'I know the last months have been difficult, for I have been so unwell, but he is not as he once was with me. He sits often in silence and once...' I pause, unsure whether to speak of it. 'He struck me, Aubrey.' I see her face and seek to reassure her. 'It was only the once and he did not mean it, I know he didn't. I was slow, his meal was not ready, and he was over-tired. The children cry all the time and we are unable to sleep, so he gets cross and ... well, I try not to anger him.'

'What of the children – he would not ...?'

'No, no, he is always patient and kind to the children, I have no fears for them. It is me. Everything I do seems to bring on his temper and I find myself continually on edge when he is around. I cannot tell how he will be when he comes home each day for his evening meal. The children dote on him, but with me, in the quiet times, he is aloof and distant.' I hesitate, then take a deep breath. 'We are as man and wife still, but there is no love in the matter, no feeling, he just rolls over when it is done and sleeps instantly. I do not know what to do. I try to please him but nothing seems to help.'

Aubrey clasps my hands between hers and looks down.

'Priss, does he mind me being here?'

My head falls. I had hoped she had not noticed.

'Oh Aubrey. He has said he does not want you to come here so often. He thinks you are a bad influence on me, and that you keep me from my duties. He continually finds fault with my cleaning, my cooking, and he says that the time I spend with you is partly to blame. I do not want you to go, but he says that if I do not tell you soon to keep away, then he will.' Aubrey sits stone-still, her face flushed. 'I have been so afraid he would speak to you himself, but I did not know how to tell you. It is as if he does not want to share me with you, with anyone. He is the same when Elizabeth is home in the winter.' I squeeze her hand but she does not respond and I know she is deeply hurt. 'Aubrey, I am so sorry. You have done so much for me and the children and I do not want to lose you ... I need your friendship now more than ever.'

Tears glitter on her cheeks as she hangs her head, then brushes her eyes with the back of her hand and stands, gathering her tools, and bundling the unfinished net into her basket.

'You are right to have told me. Your husband must be obeyed. I will go now, but if there is anything more I can do, anything, just send word and I will come. I do not wish to stand between husband and wife, so I will not call here again unless you invite me. I daresay we will often meet in the marketplace and we can talk then.' She smiles wanly. 'Go with God, Priss, and I hope things improve.' She bends and places a soft kiss on my cheek. 'I will always be your friend, just remember that. Whatever happens, I will be there for you.'

WHEN ELIZABETH RETURNS TO DUNWICH THAT AUTUMN MUCH HAS changed. I thought she would visit me, but Aubrey must have told her what John said, and so I do not see them often. I miss my friends sorely. I miss the easy days when we sat and chatted about nothing in particular. I miss their good humour, the laughter and gossip we exchanged. I miss hearing about their lives; their worries and their triumphs – all the little things that make up a friendship. I live a lonely life now, save for John. Even though I have given up my friends for him, his black moods become ever more frequent and often he will strike me if something is not to his liking, so I clean and cook and give in to his demands, for I love him still and seek to make things right between us.

I am cleaning out the cottage, readying it for the winter, pausing from my labours to stand and look at the weeds which have grown in my small patch. My hand is at the small of my back, rubbing the pain away. Little Bess and Robert play in the dirt, picking up pebbles and throwing them into the long grass. I smile down at them, keeping a careful eye, for every now and again a pebble finds its way into Robert's mouth. Suddenly, Bess cries out and points and I turn to see what she is looking at. A figure is walking slowly up the lane. I shade my eyes with my hand against the sun to see better and, as I do so, the figure stops and looks at me. To my surprise it is Aubrey. She has not visited me for many weeks, and she is clearly unsure now of how she will be received. But it is early in the day, and John will not be back until evening, so I wave to her and she comes closer. I have much missed her company and I think we can sit for a while with a jug of ale and pass the time as we used to. I smile as I take off my filthy apron, scoop up Robert, and walk towards her, but my greeting fades on my lips as she comes closer. She is moving slowly as if bearing a great weight. I barely recognise her.

'Priscilla, I am so pleased to see you.' She smiles wanly at me.

'Come in, come and sit. I have ale, will you have some bread and cheese, I need to feed the children anyway and . . . oh, Aubrey, what has happened, what is wrong?'

She hesitates, then comes inside and sits heavily at the table, her hands clasped in front of her, head down.

'I am not sure where to start.' I put Robert down, give him and Bess a crust to occupy them, and reach for her hand. I hold it tight, waiting, as tears fall from her eyes and pool on the clean tabletop. At last, she heaves a breath and looks up at me. 'William is gone.' I look at her. She is so pale, her face thin, her eyes have lost their sparkle and her hand in mine is bony and cold.

'Gone?'

'Priss, he is dead.' The sobs come now, wracking her small frame. 'He drowned – three months ago. He was on a vessel bound for the fishing grounds off Iceland and there was a fierce storm. The ship sank. Most of the crew were lost . . . the sea was too cold. They found some bodies, but not his. I only had word three weeks ago.'

I reach for her and hold her close. I can feel every bone under my fingers. She is sobbing harder now, her face against my shoulder and my heart breaks for her.

'I am so sorry. I wish I had known, I would have come to you. I should have been there to comfort you. Oh, Aubrey, I have not been a good friend to you.'

I cannot think of what to do to help her. I want to hold her, care for her as she has cared for me, but John will return soon and I dare not provoke his anger. Then I know.

'Go to Elizabeth, tell her what has happened. I heard she has come home for the winter. She will care for you. I cannot . . . John . . . I dare not . . . you must go to Elizabeth.' She nods in understanding, but grips my hands tighter.

When she speaks again it is in a whisper and I have to bring my ear to her lips to hear her.

'There is something else. You are a mother, you will understand. William was not my only loss. Oh, Priss . . . I was with child, but the shock of losing William . . . the babe came too soon, it had barely quickened, and the midwife said that there was no chance of life.'

I hold her tightly, my tears blending with hers.

'Oh, Aubrey, I am so very sorry.' I can find no more words.

She looks up at me and her expression rends my heart.

'The midwife took it away, said it was not fully formed. I do not even know what she did with . . . Oh, Priss, I could not even bury my babe.' She crumples into my arms and I hold her, feeling the pulse of her heart as pain sears me and the blackness which I have held at bay for so long descends.

AUBREY DOES AS I SUGGEST, AND ELIZABETH TAKES HER IN AND tends to her. I do not see them for several weeks, though my heart yearns for them, for I have troubles of my own. It is as if a curse has been laid on us for, shortly after Aubrey's dreadful news, I too miscarry of a child. Although my own babe has only just quickened, soon, too soon, the movement stops and I know it must be dead. The midwife comes, gives me a potion of herbs to empty my womb, a poultice to lay on my stomach, and, after many hours of pain, the thing is done. I lie in my bed, listless and full of sadness as she covers the bowl, but she is not quick enough and I think I see, lying in the blood, a monstrous thing, ill-formed and lumpen. She tries to reassure me that I am mistaken, tells me that it was too early, that the babe would have no form, but I know what I saw, and I cannot shake the vision of it from my mind.

'It is a punishment from God.' John stands before me as I lie on the bed, weakened and miserable. He is angry and upset and more bad-tempered than ever, berating me at every opportunity. And, as time goes by, I find that this little death affects me sorely – I am the same as I was after Bess and Robert, crying and low in spirits, and it haunts me, for I know not what I did to cause it.

One day Elizabeth comes to see me, pausing by the gate, not coming in. I look around fearfully in case someone should see her and tell John.

'I have news of Aubrey. She has decided it is time to return to her cottage by the quay. She has recovered well and now wishes to be at home with her nets. She says that the work will help take her mind away from all that has happened and she has no wish to return to her parents, so she must look to earning a living. I have done my best for her. But what of you? I was so sorry to hear that you too have lost a child. Are you recovered?'

My face falls.

'In body, yes, but I cannot rid myself of the thought of it, Elizabeth. I do not know what I did to cause it to be born so early, I had no shock such as Aubrey did. I have born two healthy children and there is no reason why this one should not have come into the world hale and whole. John says...'

Her brow furrows and she takes my hand.

'I can imagine what John says. But it is not your fault, Priss, you did nothing wrong. Perhaps this is God taking your child to His bosom...'

'The Devil more like!'

Elizabeth pulls away, shocked.

'Priscilla Collit, do not speak like that. Of course it was not the Devil. You are a God-fearing woman, you go to church, and you heed the teachings of Christ. You obey your husband in all things, and you are a good mother to Bess and Robert. It was an act of God, not Satan. Never think like that, never speak of it. You must get strong again and perhaps, in a few months, maybe...?'

'I feel as if I will never be strong again. I feel tired and my joints pain me. I have grown old.'

'We all have.' She rubs at her face, smoothing the lines that have formed there, seeking to lighten the mood. 'We are turning into old crones.' Then she crosses her eyes and hunches her shoulders, pulling a face. She looks just like the witches we saw in the play and I laugh, then cover my mouth with my hand, ashamed.

'I should not be merry. I have not laughed since...'

'Priss, you are permitted to laugh and it is good to hear it.' She clasps my hand. 'For some reason, God decreed that you should suffer this unbearable loss, but He would not frown at your laughter. He is a kind and caring God, we are told that and must believe it. He would have you mend, as would I.'

She pats my hand and steps back onto the sandy track that leads to her cottage, then turns and looks hard at me.

'It was not your fault, Priss, remember that. And no more talk of the Devil, eh?' She waves and walks away. But despite her words, the thought has lodged there in my mind, and will not be shaken out.

THAT WINTER BRINGS US BETTER FORTUNE. ON THE DEATH OF ROBERT Spatchett, Thomas inherits all, and John is offered the position of overseer. It serves to improve his mood, and for several days he can be heard humming to himself as he comes through the door. He plays with the children and speaks kindly to me, and I begin to think that all will be well, that it will be as it once was and he will love me again. Then, one day, he comes home late, breathless with excitement. The house is quiet, the children are asleep and his supper is bubbling on the fire. All is clean and tidy as he demands, and I greet him with a curtsey as he bends his head for me to kiss his cheek. He smiles down at me.

'Wife. I have news, but first I must eat.'

I place a plate of meat and gravy in front of him, pass him fresh bread and stand beside him as he eats noisily. I remove the plate as he wipes his mouth on the back of his hand and sits back, drawing on his mug of ale.

'Cousin Thomas is to marry. A woman called Mary Back.'

'That is happy news.'

'It is a good match, arranged for him I hear. Now he has inherited his grandfather's estates it is right that he has a wife to support him. And she brings money to the marriage.' He sits back, banging his empty mug on the table. I reach for the jug and fill it for him.

'Have you seen her? Is she fair? Is she from Dunwich, I do not know the name?'

'She is fair enough I suppose, although too plain and pale for me, but a good Christian woman. She will make Thomas a fine wife. It is to be a summer wedding.'

'And what of your new position? Is he finally to pay you more for it?' I feel shrewish for asking him, but the injustice of our situation bites at me and I cannot let it lie. John's eyes go blank and his look blackens.

'We have enough do we not? Surely you are able to manage? I am not paid a poor wage – you must learn to be thrifty ...'

'Of course, I will try to do better.' I lower my head. I know I should say no more for fear of darkening his mood with further questions but, in truth, with the children growing so fast, it is hard to manage with the few coins he gives me. And John is in such a good mood I lose my normal wariness. 'But Cousin Thomas will own half of Dunwich when he comes of age – you know all the farms his grandfather owns here – Mill Close, Calves Close, Raphedowne, Shepherd's Acre, and there are rumours of places in Cookley, Walpole, Chediston ... he will have all of that and be a wealthy man. Surely, now you are overseer, he should pay you more?'

I do not see the blow coming. John's fist slams hard into the side of my head, making my ears ring and the blood in my heart thunder. I muffle a cry, for I cannot wake the children, then he hits me again, my vision blurs, and I sink to the floor. I can barely speak, my voice is trembling and thin.

'John, think of the children...'

'Do not ever question me. How dare you suggest I cannot provide for my wife and children! You have always been careless with money. You spend too much time preening yourself, buying fripperies from that pedlar you deem your friend.'

'Elizabeth? I think only to help her, for she has less than...'

'You forget yourself, Mistress! We do not give alms and you belong here, in my home, caring for our children, keeping house. You are a wife and mother, your duty is to be obedient and meek and you are not. You and your sly friends, I've seen the way you all look at me, no doubt laughing about me while I am hard at work... it seems I must teach you your place, once and for all.' His eyes blaze as he puts strong hands under my arms and pulls me up, pushing me backwards onto the table. It is as if he is possessed. He seizes my skirts and drags them upwards then fumbles with his britches. I struggle, but this serves only to make him more angry and I gasp as he forces himself into me, the dryness burning and intense as he thrusts and thrusts as if he will split me in two. I can feel a splinter of wood catch and tear at the skin on my back as his weight bears down on me. Then it is over. He steps away breathing hard, fastening his britches, pushing his hair away from his forehead in the way that I once thought so endearing. I pull myself to a stand, straighten my skirts, and put a hand to my hair. Then I hold out my arms to my husband, thinking to reconcile, to make my peace, but he storms out, slamming the door behind him.

In the corner, Robert whimpers in his sleep.

CHAPTER 5

Some months later I journey to the marketplace for food. It is late afternoon, the stalls about to close, but these days I prefer to go at this time to avoid being seen. I have shunned all company since that night, seeking to be the good and quiet wife that John demands but now, in front of me, I see Aubrey and Elizabeth, arm in arm, walking slowly, their heads close, deep in conversation. I yearn to join them. I look around to see if anyone watches, then remember that John is in Cookley, so he will not know. Still, I think it safer to avoid them, so I lower my head and pull my hat over my eyes, but it is too late, for Elizabeth looks up and waves. They make their way over to me, smiling, and I am so glad to see them that I forget my caution. As they come close though, their smiles fall, and I can see they are shocked by my appearance. I cannot hide the large bulge under my skirts and I know my hair to be dark with sweat and grime, my clothes unkempt. I am ashamed to have let myself become like this but, in truth, this coming child has sapped all my strength. Aubrey tries to hide a flicker of discomfort when she sees my condition and my mind flashes back to her own loss.

'Aubrey, Elizabeth. I am so pleased to see you. It has been a long time, I rarely go out these days . . . I have not been well. As you can see...' My words trail off as I realise that I am searching for excuses for my absenting myself from them, without speaking the real reason. I move my hands to rest on my stomach and the babe stirs restlessly inside me as my back begins to ache. How much I have missed their company.

Elizabeth is the first to speak.

'You are expecting another babe, Priscilla? You are truly blessed. How much longer will it be?' A smile softens her words.

'I think it will be a month or more. I quickened in the early Spring, just after the snows went.' I look down at the bulge under my skirt. 'But I am not certain when it will come. I feel so heavy with this one, and I am full of fear for it.'

Aubrey puts her arm around me.

'It is common to fear, all women do, but you have been through childbirth before, had two healthy children . . . and you were well.' She hesitates at the untruth.

My face tightens.

'I am not frightened of the pain, that is to be borne with fortitude, it is the lot of women, but – I was not myself afterwards, you know how I was, so quick to tears and to temper. The sadness . . . it was unbearable. And John . . . he gets angry with me often these days, for I am not as I once was – those two births changed me, changed things between us. I am frightened that he will draw even further away from me when this one is born.' I had not meant to tell them, but now I am with them, seeing their eyes full of love and sympathy, the words pour out. 'This time it feels different – I cannot describe it. I am not afraid for me, but . . . I am so fearful that something is going to happen, something bad. It is like a black cloud hanging over me and I cannot shake it.'

ELIZABETH AND AUBREY GLANCE AT EACH OTHER THEN AUBREY HOLDS me close.

'I know that I have not been blessed with a child but I also know that you feel as every mother does. It will pass, I am sure of it.' Her face is creased with concern and I can tell how much it costs her to say this.

'Aubrey is right, all mothers feel doubt and worry. It is natural for you to be afraid, but you will be well. And I am sure John will love you again as he once did.' Elizabeth reaches for my hands. They look small and reddened in her large square palms and she closes her fingers over them. I feel her warmth threading into my fingers, up my arms and through my body. How I have missed them both. They are seeking to reassure me, but we all know that their words have a hollow ring. For many are made ill by childbirth, many die, and I am old to be birthing.

I have a sudden urge to tell them everything, as I used to, for they are my friends and I know they will not judge me. I lower my voice, glancing around, making sure no one else can hear.

'Truth be told, we should never have made this babe. It was not conceived in love and I fear for it.' There, the words are said, and, as they leave my lips, my heartache eases a little. 'But John is pleased, he hopes for another son. And we are doing better, the Spatchetts treat him well . . .' The lies come easy. 'Cousin Thomas has leased our cottage to him, so we are secure enough.'

'But money is tight?' Elizabeth, always practical, senses the truth. She pats my hand and I feel her warmth.

'John has been given more responsibilities, a position of trust, but his earnings have not changed and everything costs more. Times are so hard but he will not ask Thomas for more, his pride will not allow it.'

Aubrey leans in towards us, her face sharp.

'Is it right that Thomas Spatchett fell into the well outside his house not long ago, in exactly the same place as he was dropped by his nurse when. He was small?'

I am relieved that the subject has moved away from me and I fall into the gossip gladly.

'Yes. He was lucky not to die, for he was sorely injured. John said that it was more than a month before he recovered, and since then he has been prone to fits of anger and strange thoughts. He has become more religious too, a true Puritan, full of preaching and ranting, and he is not as good to his workers as his grandfather was. But he is John's kin and so John stays. He has work, we have our cottage and I have to think of the children . . .' It is like old times, the years have dropped away, and we are young gossiping girls again. Then I realise how long we have been talking. The sun is lower in the sky and my back is beginning to ache badly. I need to get home, to sit down, before John comes in. He does not like to see me resting, and this standing is taking its toll on me. I step back reluctantly.

'I am sorry but I must go. I need to put Bess and Robert to bed and make a meal for John, he will return shortly. I must make haste.'

Elizabeth holds my hands and squeezes them, kissing me on my cheeks. 'All will be well, my friend, you will see.' Aubrey hugs me tightly, whispering a few kind words and then I walk away, turning to look back as I reach the lane. They stand there, watching me with concerned expressions. I wonder when I will see them again, maybe when this babe has come, hopefully soon.

But life, and God, have a way of changing our plans.

THE BIRTH IS NOT A LONG ONE AND THE BABE IS BORN SMALL BUT perfect. I watch limply as the midwife passes him to John, whose delight at another son is written large on his face. Little Bess and Robert come to greet their baby brother shyly, then sit and watch over him, gently rocking his cradle, soothing him. His tiny hands wave like sea anemones from his bindings, his eyes are a deep blue, his mouth a perfect pink bud.

John sits beside the bed, watching his new son sleeping soundly in his cradle.

'We will call him Thomas, after my cousin.' He reaches for my hand but I am like stone, I cannot move. Then his words sink in and I try to rise, propping myself weakly on one elbow.

'No, John. Not Thomas, No. I cannot have him named after that man . . .' I know I am being unreasonable, but I have feared that man ever since I saw him as a child and he pointed at me. I see John's face darken in anger at being challenged so I soften my tone.

'I am sorry, Husband, but I would prefer a different name. Please? I know Thomas is your cousin but I wonder if his name will bring bad luck. Consider how he was dropped, how he fell down the well . . .'

'Very well, then we shall call him Edward if that is acceptable? It is a good, strong name.'

I slump back onto the bed, relief coursing through me as if a storm has blown past.

'Edward is a good name and well-chosen. Edward he shall be.'

John looks down into the cradle and brushes his fingertip across the tiny forehead, which puckers under his touch.

'Go in God, Edward.'

I close my eyes, for I cannot bear to see the pure love on John's face, cannot remember when he last looked at me like that, or if he ever did. I have birthed a babe that was conceived in brutality and contempt and I know I should love him but I do not. I cannot bear to touch him or endure his cries. His wailing cuts through me and I just want it to end. I want all of it to end. They bring him to me to feed, his tiny face red, wet and screwed up with screaming, his fists flailing, but I do not want him near me and push him away. The midwife suggests to John that she should find a wet nurse and quickly, for the babe is in distress, tells him that I am unable to feed him as I should. She is careful with her words and I am grateful, for I do not wish John to find further fault with me. I know I should rest, but it is as if I cannot be still, so I rise from the child-bed too early, unable to settle. Sleep deserts me and my mind fills with fear and dark thoughts, worse than ever before, and I am tearful and confused. I watch the midwife carefully now, for each day I become more certain that she is trying to harm me, that she will poison me with her potions and herbs; that she wants John for herself.

I can think of nothing else. There is a commotion in my head, many voices, soft at first, comforting, but then one rises above the other. It is deep, brown like the fallen leaves in autumn. It slinks in the shadows of my mind, slipping and turning, always listening, and it brings with it a smell of ash and river as it whispers to me, filling my head. Soon it is all there is.

'Here, drink this, Mistress.' The midwife stands close, her face creased with kindness and concern, holding out a cup that has brown liquid swilling in the bottom. It smells acrid and pungent and I am certain that she is trying to bring about my death, but I find I no longer care. I drink the contents back in one, their taste lying bitter in my mouth. It takes no time at all before I am drifting down, down, the voice is silenced and my body rests. But all too soon I wake again, to find Elizabeth and Aubrey sitting beside me. For a few moments, I cannot remember where I am, then I start at their presence, looking wildly around for John, as the fear settles back in my chest, ice-cold, heavy, like stone – he must not find them here.

Elizabeth smiles down at me.

'You are awake. The midwife said she had given you a potion as you would not rest.'

'She looks to poison me ...'

'Priss, why would you think that? She has cared well for you. It was for your own good, we are all so worried about you.'

I try to sit up and Elizabeth helps me, and I feel her strength against my weakness.

'Oh, John? Elizabeth, he must not know you are here ...'

Aubrey reaches for me, taking my hand, stroking it, soothing me.

'Look, he is sitting in his chair by the fire. Rest easy, Priss, it was he that sent for us. He thought that seeing us, having our help, will mend you, as it did before. He is content for us to be here, do not fret.'

I lie back in my bed, then start up again, my panic rising to my throat so I cannot breathe.

'I must get up. I must clean the house, John will not like it to be so. . .' I swing my legs out of bed and pull on my shawl, shrugging off their hands, and Elizabeth and Aubrey sit back in shocked silence, watching me. I stagger over to the door and fling it open, blinking at the bright morning. I know I must do something but all of a sudden I cannot remember what it is.

'Priscilla, be calm, we have only come to see you and your babe, and to wish you well.' Elizabeth comes towards me and steers me back to the bed. I lie down, arms held tight by my sides, my fists clenched. My heart thumps fit to burst.

They move to the crib where Edward sleeps.

There is a rustling and crackling deep inside my head and then . . .

'They have come to harm him.'

It is a man's voice, deep and dark, his whispered words are beguiling and soft.

'What a beautiful child.' There are two figures bending over the crib, speaking. I do not know who they are or what they are saying, but one stretches out a long hand to him.

'He is mine, they must not take him.'

I stand and move swiftly to the crib, pushing the figures away, clutching at their clothes, pressing hard on their shoulders.

'Leave him – you shall not have him.' They start back in alarm and I bare my teeth at them. 'If you come any closer I will bite him.' From the corner of my eye, I see a third figure rise from a seat by the hearth, its face white and pinched, its mouth wide with horror. The two move away from the crib, as far as they can, their hands held up in submission.

'We will not harm him, Priscilla, look, we will stand here. No one will take your babe.'

I feel the fear leave me and I turn back to the door, looking out at the clear day. In the hedge outside birds sing and the sound is pure and clean.

But underneath it, the voice in my head is rising again.

I WAKE, AS FROM A DREAM. I AM IN BED BUT I DO NOT KNOW HOW I got there. I do not move but wait and listen. The dark voice is there, I can hear him breathing, but he does not speak.

All I can hear is my husband's voice, low and full of fear, it catches as he talks softly to Elizabeth and Aubrey.

'The birth went well, the midwife was pleased, but since then . . . she is not my wife. She speaks strangely, of unnatural things, she does not sleep but paces around the house muttering. It is as if she is constantly talking to someone, but there is no one else here. A wet nurse comes, for Priscilla will not go near the babe. It is as if she is possessed, the midwife has not seen the like of it . . . I do not know what to do.' I hear him sniff loudly and think that this is the strangest thing all – that a man so full of anger can weep. I want to reach out to him, to tell him all will be well, but the voice swells, bids me stay and listen.

'She has always been fey. Elizabeth, remember how she was after the players – for days after she spoke of fear and doubt?' Aubrey keeps her voice low but her words billow in my head like the ripple on a pool when a pebble is thrown. A vision of the three hags rises grey in my memory, then blurs.

'It is more than that, her mind has gone. She barely speaks, just paces around the cottage. The children are frightened. Neighbours are helping to care for us but this cannot go on. Those children need a mother's love . . .' John glances at Bess and Robert, their playing stilled, their faces pinched with shock. '. . . and I need a wife. It is as if she does not see us. It is as if we no longer exist.'

'*Your husband cannot provide for you. You would be better off without him, without any of them.*' The dark voice comes, clear and sharp as ice and I rise from the bed, clutching my nightgown to my chest, and move around the cottage, looking in every corner, but I cannot see him.

'Who are you?' My voice is cracked and dry and I hear it as if from a vast distance. John stops talking and they all turn to look at me. Aubrey reaches out a hand but I pull away from her.

'Priss, you are not well. You need to rest . . .'

The dark voice is close by now, I can feel his breath on my cheek, smell the dank reek of river as I sink to the floor, my legs no longer working. The voice is all there is now, it swirls around the room, and my mind is filled with a thick thrumming that vibrates against the very walls of the cottage. Faint and distant, I hear Elizabeth call my name, but the voice drowns her cry.

'*Forget them. They will not help you. Only I know what it is you need. You are tired and in want. They do not care for you. Only I care, only I can give you what you desire. I know what it is you wish for. You will have silver, enough for your every need. But if I am to help you, and I will, there must be reparation. I will ask one thing of you, it will be the thing of a moment, and then you will have all you desire.*'

It is as if he releases me from shackles and suddenly I am soaring, cold and fine, above the room. There is a sweet singing, a ringing of bells coming clear, as if across the frosted fields on a winter's morn. Three figures sway below me, grey and huddled, like the witches in the play – I do not recognise their faces, their names are gone. Two children sit quiet in a corner in the sunlight, but I can't remember who they are. Then the grey figures separate and two women who seem familiar speak in hushed tones with a man I do not recognise, and there is a crib, rocking gently. I swoop down from my great height and gaze inside. I hover above it, wondering. The bundle in it is red and misshapen, the noise it makes sears through me, and I speak to the voice.

'Will you help me?'

His voice comes even closer now, filling my head. It is firm and insistent, its tone soothing.

'I will help you and provide for you if you will but follow me and do my bidding. You must wait until nightfall when all is quiet and all sleep, and I will come to you again and tell you the price you must pay. It is but a little thing and afterwards, you will have all you wish for...'

The voice fades and then I am no longer floating calmly but lying on the floor, crumpled and in pain. The sensation of soaring has gone and my heart aches for it. I am ill and muddled, I have been poor for so long. My life is hard and my husband lost to me and I think that whatever is asked of me will be a small price to pay, for I can no longer live like this. If I carry out his wishes I can soar again. He will set me free.

Then the voice tells me what I must do.

PART III

Elizabeth

CHAPTER 6

'Mistress Southerne – Elizabeth. You must come quickly.'

The midwife is red and breathless when she reaches my door. She rubs at her side, grimacing with pain, as she tries to speak.

'It is Mistress Collit...'

'Priscilla? What has happened?'

'She has worsened and her babe is harmed. Her husband asks for you to come with all haste.'

'I must fetch Aubrey – Mistress Grinsett...'

The midwife grabs my hand.

'There is no time... and it is best you come alone, that no one sees...'

I sweep my cloak from its hook and follow her out, wrapping it round me as I walk. We hurry along the lane. The midwife's face is grey with shock and she holds her red cloak tight around her body. I am breathless with fright. As we draw closer to the cottage, we can hear a babe's screams of torment and the midwife lays a hand on my arm.

'You must be prepared, Mistress. Have courage.' Her words set my heart thumping against my ribs so hard I fear it will break out. She pushes open the door.

The first thing I notice is the crib has been placed far away from the bed and the sound that is coming from it sears through me. John sits slumped in a chair, his face frozen in shock, the two children at his feet. Robert is sobbing quietly, his hands over his ears. Bess just sits, staring, her eyes glassy.

'John, I came as quickly as I could. What has happened?' He puts his hands over his face and bends forward, teeth bared in pain, then points a shaking finger at the crib. I move slowly towards it and look down. I have to push my hand over my mouth to block the vomit that rises in my throat as I see what is inside. Little Edward is purple with screaming. His downy hair is burned away on one side, the skin bright red and blistered, the wound shining in the dull light. Deep down, I see the white glitter of bone. The midwife moves forward and gently picks him up but no amount of soothing will calm him. I step back, my mind reeling. The door opens as two women from the town come in with baskets of food for John and the children. They greet him, nod to me, and then speak in hushed tones to the midwife as they look closely at the babe, their eyes sliding between him and the bed. News has travelled fast as it does in this town. Word will soon be out. But the only thought in my mind is how? How did this happen?

NONE SEEM TO NOTICE ME AS I MOVE TO THE BEDSIDE. PRISCILLA JUST lies lifeless, seemingly unhearing of her tiny son's screams of pain and distress. They have not restrained her. I sit beside her on the bed, taking her hand but I have no words. The townswomen move silently around the room, preparing a meal, speaking softly to each other, and I bend to the prone figure of Priscilla.

'Priss, what has happened?' I look back at John, at the crib. 'I am so very sorry. Poor, poor little Edward. If there is anything I can do, anything at all, just tell me.' She does not seem to hear me so I move closer, brushing her hair away from her face. Once so soft and golden, it is now dark with grease, lank and stinking. 'Priss, can you hear me? It's me, Elizabeth.' My tears fall on her face, and the warm wetness seems to rouse her, for she turns to me. Her eyes are blank and dark.

'Elizabeth? Is it truly you?'

I squeeze her hand gently.

'Yes, I'm here. What has happened?'

Priscilla pulls me closer.

'He came to me, I knew he would. He told me to do it . . .'

'Who, who would tell you to do such a thing?' I cannot comprehend what she is saying, it does not make sense. But then her eyelids close and she falls asleep. By the hearth, John stirs. When he speaks his voice is harsh and cracked.

'Elizabeth, she has gone quite mad. She got up from the bed in the dead of night, picked up her newborn babe and dropped him onto the fire. Then she went back to bed as if nothing had happened. I was sound asleep. I heard her get up and I thought that maybe she was feeling better, that she wanted at last to hold our son. She picked him up as if to nurse him and I thought all was well, but then she stooped and held out her arms and . . .' His voice breaks. 'I was not quick enough to stop her. It was my little Bess – my daughter that pulled her brother from the fire, for she was faster than me. For a child to have seen such a thing . . . ' He looks at me with guilt-filled eyes. 'These last few days since the birth have been a torment and I was so tired – I just fell asleep for a moment . . . an innocent babe, to see it suffer in this way. But I am not to blame. It is her. How – how could she be so careless?' He presses his hand to his brow, pain searing his once-handsome face and my heart fills with pity for him.

Beside me, Priscilla wakes and reaches out a bony hand. She pulls at my cloak and I move my head close as she puts her lips to my ear. I can scarcely hear her.

'It was the Devil, Bess. You must listen to me. The Devil told me to do it. He told me I must make a covenant with him, that my child must burn. He promised me silver . . . and I am so tired of living like this, of being poor. It was the price I had to pay.' She falls back onto the bed, the effort exhausting her, as I recoil in horror.

My words come out in a low hiss.

'You must never say such things, Priscilla, do not even think them. Promise me that you will not speak of this to anyone else.' I glance behind me but the townswomen are busy attending to John and the children and are not listening 'Promise me above all things that you will never tell this to anyone else. Not even John. Promise me. It was an accident. You were still weak after the birth and you dropped him. No one told you to do it. No one made you. You were not strong enough to hold your babe and he fell from your grasp. This is what you must tell them. Do you hear me?' I take her by the shoulders and shake her gently, for I need her to understand what I am saying. She nods and her eyes close, but I do not know how much she has heard, if any of my words were comprehended, and I am consumed with fear for her.

For to speak of such things is witchcraft.

WHEN I RETURN THE NEXT AFTERNOON, LITTLE EDWARD HAS worsened. He lies silent, too weak even to cry. His thin chest heaves with the effort of breathing, his eyes are sunken and glazed, his face bone-pale, and the wound has reddened and spread. The cloth the midwife dressed the burn with has come away and I see that the soft spot on the top of his head has hollowed and is no longer moving. His skin is loose and wrinkled on his tiny bones and his breath is shallow and rapid.

'The wet nurse has tried to feed him, but he is too ill.' John's voice is tight with tension. I draw up a chair next to Priscilla and take her hand, but she lies, unmoving, and does not seem to recognise me. She does not weep or wail, it is as if she is dead. 'I cannot sit here, I must get air. Would you stay, Elizabeth, 'til I return?' I nod and John pulls on his coat. I sit watching as the midwife tends to Edward. I try to play with the children, but they are numbed with shock and do not respond. When John comes home later he smells of the tavern, but I do not begrudge him this little comfort. For all his faults, he has lost a child.

It is the following day that little Edward heaves a last shuddering breath and is still. I watch as his soul leaves him. His eyes remain open, and they seem to stare at me in rebuke, but the wet nurse bends to the crib and passes her fingers gently over them to close them, her shoulders shaking with tears. John has sent for the midwife who checks for signs of life and then takes the tiny body in her hands. She begins to wind him in his swaddling clothes, and I stand beside her, trying to help. I hand her a clean cloth to cover his wound, then the stayband for his head, and watch as she gently binds him. When she is finished she hands him to me and I cannot stop my tears as I gaze at his little face. His eyelids are blue-veined, his lashes long and pale, and his mouth a perfect rosebud. He looks for all the world as if he is merely sleeping, but I know God has taken him. I carry him across to Priscilla, where she lies motionless on the bed. John and the midwife have told her of her babe's death but she does not seem to be aware. She is unable to sit, all emotion and feeling seemingly gone, but I hold her babe out to her.

'Priscilla, I have brought Edward, your son, to you so that you may say farewell. He is to be buried tomorrow. Will you take him, hold him, give him your blessing? Please try – for me?' But she turns her head to the wall, and I can only stand, holding that small still body, and weep. The next day I watch over Bess, Robert and Priscilla as John goes alone, carrying the tiny burden, to the church of St Peter where they were married, and lays his son to rest in the cold ground. He has been but three days on this earth and those spent in pain and torment.

. . .

JOHN'S FACE, WHEN HE RETURNS FROM THE CHURCH, IS HAGGARD WITH tiredness, strain and distress, and my heart goes out to him. Everyone has left and I push myself to my feet and go to the cauldron on the fire.

'John, sit, I have made soup, it is good and hot, and there is fresh bread.' He nods and bends to take off his boots, his dark hair flopping over his face then, as he brushes it away, he looks up at me. His eyes glisten in the firelight and I place the bowl of soup before him. He reaches for my hand.

'Elizabeth, I could not have faced these past days without your help. Will you forgive me for keeping you and Aubrey away from this house before? I thought it for the best, but I was wrong...' His eyes fill with tears and I sink into the chair beside him and clasp his hand in return. It is the first time I have ever touched him and his hand lies heavy in my palm.

'I am so very sorry for your loss, John, but God has taken little Edward to His bosom and has freed him of his pain. He is in heaven now, he is safe.'

John's face hardens.

'Safe? *He* may be safe, but what of Robert and Bess? How safe are they? Their mother refuses to care for them, just lies there doing nothing. She does not even weep. It is not natural.' He is furious, it is as if the burial has removed any softness, and I stroke his hand, trying to reassure him.

'I think Priscilla may be improving, but it is slow. She seems so listless, as if she is not of this world, but she did sit earlier and take a spoon or two of broth. I will stay, help...'

'I cannot ask this of you, Elizabeth, you have done so much already – more than you needed to.'

His hand is warming in mine.

'She is my friend, John, has been these many years, and I would not desert her in her time of need. Nor you and her children.'

His face tightens.

'She needs to take charge of her family again. She was ill in her head after the birth of the other two, and the one she lost, I know, but nothing like this.'

'But to have a child die in this way . . . it will affect her severely.'

He nods, but the anger is still there.

'It affects us all. Little Bess still does not speak . . . no, Priscilla needs to get up and return to her tasks, otherwise, I fear she will never heal. I cannot continue to rely on the goodness of neighbours and friends – of you especially . . . ' He pauses. 'These past few days, although I am grateful for the help, it seemed that my house was no longer my own. It was always full of people coming and going.' He takes a few spoonfuls of soup, tearing bread from the nub with white teeth. 'The midwife has said that Priscilla's body is nearly recovered, that she needs to get up and move around, get back to how things were, so that she does not dwell on all this and unbalance herself further.'

'Priscilla is still unwell, her mind is not as it was, and people only wanted to help.'

John's face tightens.

'I do not want their help. I ask that she gets up and does her duty. It is not good for her to lie there unmoving. By taking up her role as wife and mother she will come back to the Lord, and her mind will be restored, I am sure of it. The children need their mother, especially Bess, after what she saw . . . and the neighbours? I am sure they are just here to gossip . . . '

I see he is determined, yet I am certain she is not yet capable.

'She needs more time, John. Maybe weeks, a month or two? Just until she comes back to her senses. You have us to care for your children, Aubrey and me, and they will be well looked after until Priscilla is back to health.'

He looks at me.

'She cannot lie there for weeks. I will not allow it.' I stiffen at the sharpness of his words. 'She must get up and do her duty. Even then, I am not sure whether it is safe for Bess and Robert to be left with her.' He pauses, looking down at his hands, picking at the skin on his thumb, then takes a deep breath. 'I am considering whether to send them elsewhere until I am certain they would be safe. Cousin Thomas has offered to take them in . . . his wife would care for them at his house in Cookley. He says it is the Christian thing to do and that God wills it.'

I look at him in shock. I remember how Priscilla fears that man, I am sure she would not want her children in his care.

'But you know how much she loves them.'

He leans towards me, his body tensed, and the words spit from his lips in anger and frustration.

'Love? Yes, she loves her children so much that she dropped my newborn son in the fire. No, I have decided. If the children are not safe here, they must go to Cookley, to be cared for until she is well. If she ever is.'

I take both his hands in mine.

'John, please reconsider. I will be here when you are not, I will make sure Priscilla cares for them as she should. Please do not take them from her, not now. That would destroy her.' He looks long at me, then nods.

'If you ask it of me, and if you are sure you and Aubrey can manage, then I will see how it works out for a short while.'

I squeeze his hand.

'All will be well, John, you will see.'

AUBREY GOES IN EACH DAY TO TEND TO BESS AND ROBERT WHILE John goes to work, watching over them as she weaves her nets, and I take her place each evening, to cook a meal and see them to bed. When John returns he goes first to look at his sleeping children, tucking the blanket around them tenderly, then glances at the bed where Priscilla still lies. I make him broth and stews, buy good bread, meat and fish, and have his meal ready when he comes in hungry from the fields. Priscilla stirs little. She eats broth and tries some bread but mostly she sleeps. The midwife has left a tincture for her in case she becomes disturbed again, and I give her a few drops each night as directed so that she sleeps soundly. The past weeks have been hard but things seem to be improving.

One evening, after he has eaten, John sits back beside me, looking at me with bleary eyes, his face soft with sorrow.

'The children are fast asleep, praise the Lord. Robert wakes often with night terrors, so sleep will do them good.' He leans forward, his eyes seeking mine. 'Thank you for caring for them so well. I do not know how I would have managed without you.' He hesitates. 'Elizabeth, tell me, has she spoken to you of that night? Told you what happened? For I am not clear in my own mind how it could have come about. I cannot see how . . .?' He shakes his head as if to push the thoughts away.

In the depths of my skirt, I cross my fingers. I know that to lie is a sin, but in this matter, I have no choice.

'She has spoken a little of it, John. She told me that she got up to put another log on the fire. You and the children were asleep, she was alone, and she wanted to hold the babe in her arms. But she was not as strong as she thought and she said that he slid from her grasp into the hearth, and the flames . . . she was weak from the birth . . . it was an accident.' I hope my words are convincing and he does not question her, for I fear she will not remember to keep silent. But she must, for to speak of the Devil the way in which she did is to invite terror. She would be reported, seized, and examined as a witch. All hear of such happenings these days and women must tread gently in the world for fear of accusation. Even a husband may accuse his own wife, to save damning his immortal soul if he does not. I must be certain that Priscilla does not speak of it.

'And do you believe her? You have known her longer than even I.' I can see John is wavering, partly convinced. My crossed fingers tighten.

'I do, John. She is suffering sorely because of her guilt, wracked by the knowledge that she caused Edward's death, and she does not know how to go on, how to put it right. She needs time and love and care. I will help, and so will Aubrey, until she is well again. Your children will be in no danger, you have my word.' His face turns to mine, eyes sparkling with tears, and it breaks my heart to see him brought so low. He wants to believe that his wife will be restored to him. 'Priscilla needs your love now, needs to know you understand and can forgive her.' I reach for his hand. 'I would do anything to help her, John, for she is my friend.'

JOHN TURNS AROUND AND LOOKS AT HIS SLEEPING FAMILY, THEN LEANS towards me and lifts my hand and looks at it. His thumb begins to make small circles on my wrist as his face softens, and I feel such sadness for him.

'Oh, Elizabeth...'

He moves closer, and I look into his eyes. What I see there should make me draw back but it does not. It is as if I stand on the sand-soft cliffs that edge this town, the ground shifting beneath my feet, ready to slide into the sea, taking me with it. I seek a place of safety with my words, for my body is already sliding.

'You have always called me Elizabeth when others call me Bess.'

'That is because you have always been Elizabeth to me.'

His palm is stroking my wrist in small circles, his face softening as he moves closer to me, and I gaze at him. He is beautiful in the firelight, he looks just as he did when I first set eyes on him at his parent's farm, and in that moment all the years fall away.

He bends to rest his forehead on mine and I know I should pull away, but I cannot. He draws me to him.

'I do not know what to do. Help me, Elizabeth. My sweet Elizabeth.'

Pity overcomes me as I watch his eyes swim with tears, and I lean into him and hold him. He smells of the sea, of woodsmoke. His body feels strange in my arms, hard and muscular, as I stroke his back to soothe his tears. I seek to comfort him, that is all I do.

But, without warning, a small flame flickers deep within me, one I do not recognise but one that I know I should put out, and quickly. The night is dark, the cottage silent, his body is close to mine, strong and warm, and my desire for John Collit overwhelms me. He is so unhappy, so troubled, and I cannot help myself as my face moves to his, my lips open. Our tongues touch, the flame rises to a blaze and I am undone.

It is over quickly, the fumbling and rubbing, the thrusting and arching, the thing done in silence. But afterwards, as we straighten our clothing, looking around with guilt-ridden faces to see if anyone has woken, I vow that this thing that has passed between us must never happen again. I try to convince myself that it was done to help John, that perhaps he will now forgive Priscilla, and allow her time to recover, but I know the real reason for my failing. I have long desired John Collit and now I have had him.

CHAPTER 7

Aubrey and I gradually lessen our visits as Priscilla starts to recover. She begins to tend to the house and to John and the children, but she sorely feels the loss of her son. Something has gone from her and she is not as she was. I barely recognise my friend and I miss her company, her happy smile. It has all been taken from her by the tragedy. But there is the other reason for my staying away – guilt lies heavy in me. For a short time, I am in terror that I might be with child, but then my courses come, and all is as it was. I never speak of that night to anyone and, if Aubrey suspects, she never says anything.

As the spring comes in, with shoots of green thrusting through the warming earth, and birds singing to each other in the bushes, I take up my pack, for I must make my way in the world once more. I go down to the quay to say farewell to Aubrey. She holds me close.

'God go with you, Bess. Safe travels. I will miss you.'

I kiss her cheek.

'I will see you in the autumn. Take care of yourself and Priscilla.' The last thing I see of her is a small figure standing in the doorway of her cottage, waving a kerchief.

I pay a last visit to Priscilla, who smiles wanly when she sees me.

'So you are on your travels again? I shall miss you, Bess.'

I reach out my hand and take hers.

'And I will miss you, but I am glad to see you well again.'

A shadow crosses her face.

'I do not know what happened to me. It was as if I became another person. And the thoughts that came to me, they made my mind go to dark and hollow places.'

I put my hands on her shoulders and look deep into her eyes.

'Do not speak of it. You are well again, your children are happy, your husband is content.'

She frowns.

'No, not content, nor happy either. He thinks I have changed, that it is my fault all this happened, but something has changed in him too, and I do not know why.'

Guilt bites at me, its teeth sharp and white.

'You must not dwell on it, Priss, for it will make you sorrowful. You must think of better times and take pleasure in your family. You must enjoy little Bess and Robert now you are able to care for them again ...'

Priscilla shakes her head.

'John blames me for causing Edward's death.' Tears well in her eyes. 'How could I have done such a thing? I barely remember it – one moment I was holding him in my arms, the next he was screaming and screaming, the children were crying and shouting, but it was as if I was underwater. I could not hear them clearly, I could not move any part of my body to go to them and comfort them. I left my baby to burn. 'Twas Bess who pulled him from the fire, she is just a child, and now she will not speak to me. No wonder they blame me.' She is sobbing hard now, her whole body shaking, and I take her in my arms.

'Hush, Priss, hush. Do not think of it. It was done when you were very ill, when your mind was not right. You cannot be blamed.'

'John blames me. Each time he looks at me I can see it in his eyes. I will bear the scars of what I have done for the rest of my life and I will always be reminded of the evil I did. It would have been better if they'd let me die.' Her words make my heart sink, for I had thought she was well. I clasp her to me.

'You are nearly recovered now, do not think like this. And if you feel that things are getting dark, then remember Aubrey – send for her, she will always help you. I will not be back now until autumn, but I will think of you often. So many people care about you, and John loves you. They will help you.' She is shaking her head but I can see her brightening a little at my words. As I turn to go, my heart lies heavy in my chest. It is guilt, yes, but also a sense of bitter foreboding that fills me and will not leave.

BUT PRISCILLA IS NEVER THE SAME. AS TIME PASSES AND THE SEASONS change, I do not stay in Dunwich much, choosing to travel further, selling my wares. But when I next come back, I hear about her, for Aubrey has continued to visit.

'Oh, Bess, I am so worried about her. Priss has become morose and dark, she no longer looks after her husband or herself. She says that John frequently loses patience with her and I have seen bruises and marks on her body which she tries to hide. And John has changed. She tells me that he threatens constantly that he will take her children from her. She is sinking further and further into despair. I have tried to reach her, but she will have none of it. It has been hard, Bess, and I am glad you are home, for I have done my best, but I know not what to do anymore.' Her voice breaks and I take her hand and squeeze it. It is calloused now, shaped by her labour.

'And what of you, Aubrey?' I can see how much this is disturbing her. 'Are you managing?'

'I am making good money, for my nets are in demand. Some of the other net-makers have moved away as the sea nears their houses, so more fishermen come to me. They remember William, you see, and how I am alone ... I am lucky, not living so close to the beach as some, but it is still a worry. Sometimes it is hard to find the time to work with visiting Priscilla as well. I confess, it has dragged me down, Elizabeth, for I see no end to it.'

'I will go and see her, try to talk to her.'

And I do, I visit her several times, and Aubrey comes when she can, but each time Priscilla is more and more remote, seeming to resent our presence. When she begins to ignore our knocks we realise that there is nothing that can be done but to wait, so we stay away, for it is all beyond our understanding. And so we hear and see nothing of Priscilla that summer or winter, and, as spring comes, I pick up my pedlars pack once more, leaving Dunwich and its memories behind.

Stranger tales begin to reach my ears as I travel through the villages and hamlets. Rumours of two men are rife – it is said that they travel around Essex, seeking out witches, and the word '*witchfinder*' is on everyone's lips. As the rumours grow and spread, housewives I have known for years begin to turn me away with apology, saying that their menfolk have ordered them not to consort with women such as me. Everyone becomes nervous and concerned, and callers are no longer welcomed. The growing suspicion disturbs me so much that I come home a little earlier than usual that autumn, thinking to stay safe, for it is hard to be a pedlar in such times. But I am sure it will pass, so I tend my garden, keep my house, and try to make myself quiet and unnoticed. I visit only Aubrey. Of Priscilla, we hear nothing.

I AM PASSING THE FARM ON MY WAY TO SEE AUBREY ONE MORNING when I see John Collit. I pause. He stops his digging to roll up his sleeves and wipe his face with a kerchief. Although it is September, the weather is still warm and his shirt sticks to him. I close my eyes and swallow hard. Part of me hopes he does not see me, yet part of me seeks news of Priscilla. I brush my dress and straighten my coif and the change of movement distracts him and he looks over.

'Elizabeth! You are back. I have not seen you for some time.' His white smile is still the same and it melts me.

'I have been travelling further away this time, and I've come back to spend the autumn and winter here. This trade is taking its toll on me I fear, and I am getting too old for walking through cold and frost in search of a few coins.'

'The life of a pedlar is hard.'

'But it is the one I have chosen.' He nods, tilting his head to one side, friendly. It encourages me. 'I like the walking, meeting strangers, visiting houses I know and those I don't. I talk and listen and hear things, and people look out for my coming. Sometimes they are cruel, but not often. Usually, they are pleased to see me, to see what new things I have brought them. I have come home early this time . . .' I hesitate to speak of the Witchfinder. '. . . for I missed my home, and I have made enough this summer to keep me. But what of you and Priscilla? And the children, are they well?'

His face hardens and I step back in surprise.

'Have you not heard? I thought I was the subject of most of the gossip in this town. She has become quite demented, Elizabeth. She mutters and curses, and nothing I can do will change it.' His expression contorts in anger and I take a further step back. 'I cannot forget that she killed my son – just a babe, so small and innocent. I will never forgive her. She murdered him and now she is gone quite mad. I will not have her near my children; Cousin Thomas and his family in Cookley have taken them in. I see them when I can.'

'You have taken her children from her? But does she not go with you to visit them? Is she able to speak to them?'

John's face is like thunder now.

'No, and she will not, not while I have breath in my body. She is not fit to see them, and I have given instructions that she is to be chased off the land if, somehow, she makes her way there. Not that she is likely to go, for she just sits in the chair or lies in bed. She does nothing. She is an unfit wife and mother. No, she will not see Robert or Bess again, I will make sure of that.' He raises his hand and I flinch, pulling backwards, my hands flying up to protect myself.

John sees my terror and drops his arm.

'I did not mean to frighten you.' He smiles at me, but the smile does not reach his eyes. 'Do not fear me, Elizabeth, I would not harm you.' His body relaxes again as his anger passes. 'I often think of that night...'

'Do not speak of it, John. Ever. It did not happen. Look to your wife.'

'I think to rid myself of her.'

The shock must have shown on my face for he straightens, defiant.

'But you are married in the eyes of God, 'til death do you part!'

'Priscilla is ill, mad, she is no wife to me, no mother to her children. This is a small town, and everyone knows about her. I am determined to start again elsewhere. Plans are in place and I will not be here for much longer. There is another family willing to take over the tenancy of the cottage and Cousin Thomas has offered me work elsewhere. He says that God will favour me if I am no longer associated with such as she. I intend to leave Dunwich shortly, for Cookley.'

My heart is thumping in my chest.

'But what of Priscilla? Does she know? How will she be able to fend for herself?'

'I do not know, but I will have no more of her. She can go to the Devil for all I care.'

I flinch at the word. Does he not know how dangerous it has become to say such a thing?

'So you are to leave her and she is to lose her home after she has already lost her children? How could you do such a thing? It is cruel, John Collit, callous.'

He has hardened, become as flint and I can see he will not be moved on this.

'This is a small town now, Elizabeth, people talk. They stare at me and I know they gossip about me. Every day I see their looks. This is where her actions have brought me. No, Cousin Thomas has offered me a better living on another of his farms and I am leaving.'

'And Priscilla - how has she taken this?' My tone has hardened to match his. He looks at me nervously now, and, with a shock, I realise that she does not know of his plans. He has not told her. He is no longer the person I knew, the laughing, handsome man that Priscilla married all those years ago. He is changed into one that is harder and uncaring, bitter and revengeful, and my heart pains for her.

'Cruel you may call it, Elizabeth, but it is what will happen. They are my children, it is my life she has damned with her mutterings and violence. If you care so much about her, you tend to her.'

So I do.

CHAPTER 8

It all happens swiftly. A few days later John packs up his belongings, loads the furniture onto a wagon, and leaves. Thomas Spatchett sends his bailiffs to remove Priscilla from her home and the cottage is given over to new tenants.

News does not reach me until the thing is done and, as soon as I hear, I go to her. She is standing outside her cottage, all her worldly possessions in an untidy bundle at her feet, confused and frightened. I reach her, out of breath from rushing, and take her arm, but she shrugs me off, looking around wildly. Her hair hangs in tangles and her coif is gone. The front of her bodice shines with stains and the hem of her skirt is black with dirt. Her voice is shrill.

'John, where is John? They have taken it all.'

'Priscilla, come home with me. It is warm there, I will make you some broth . . .' I keep my voice gentle, for she looks like the deer on Westleton Heath, poised and wary, ready to take flight at the slightest movement.

She does not acknowledge me but remains gazing at what was once her home.

'Where has John gone? Where are my children? I cannot find them . . .'

'Come home with me, you can rest a while, then we can look for your children.' It is not the right thing to say, for it may raise false hopes, but it is all I can think of. Still she will not move. Then, the sound of footsteps and I look around, relieved to see Aubrey rushing towards us.

'Aubrey, they have just left her here, I cannot believe anyone could be so heartless.'

Aubrey takes her other arm.

'Come Priss, come back to Elizabeth's house with us. We can have a mug of ale and chat. It will be like the old times. Would you like that?' Her voice is soothing and, to my surprise, Priscilla nods and turns towards us. I shoulder her bundle and we move slowly away, as Aubrey talks continuously, calming and reassuring her.

All of a sudden Priscilla stands stock still and finds her voice.

'Do you remember the play? How frightened it made us? How young we were, how little we knew of the world . . . the Players made it so real, did they not, it was as if we were there. And those three witches, how they writhed and chanted. I hear them still.' Priscilla looks deep into my eyes and the feeling unnerves me. 'My sisters. We were happy that day, were we not, but then that boy . . .?'

I jump in before she can become morose.

'We three are like sisters, yes, together again, as we said we would always be. But let us take you home. First I will heat some water, we will bathe you and wash your hair, and you will feel better for that. Then we will have some food, and sit and talk – or you can rest if you'd rather?'

Aubrey moves closer to me, talking in hushed tones.

'Do you think to take her in, Bess? Will you be able to care for her, for she needs someone there all the time? We do not know what ails her – are you sure of this?'

'Aubrey, there is no choice. She has nowhere else to go – and she is my friend. Maybe, soon, with care and attention, she will be well.'

'I'm sorry I cannot help, Bess, but my cottage is but one room, it was scarce big enough for the two of us when William . . .'

I pat her arm.

'I know you would take her in if you were able to. I am happy to do this. She would do the same for me, I am sure.'

I MAKE SPACE FOR PRISCILLA'S FEW POSSESSIONS IN THE CUPBOARD IN the corner, and she shares my bed, as my mother and I did all those years before. But Priscilla is not my mother. Her thoughts grow wild on occasion, and they cause her to rant and mumble to herself. I begin to believe that John was right to say that her mind has become damaged – his leaving seems to have tipped her over into an abyss. I determine to see how she is over the winter, but I am concerned about what will happen to her when I need to travel again.

As before, Aubrey is my saviour.

'I will look after her while you are away, if she still needs care. If you are willing, I could move into your cottage and care for her here. I keep an eye on it for you anyway, it would be no trouble . . .'

We two are sitting on the step outside, a cruel parody of those years before when we were young and thought nothing could hurt us. Priscilla is asleep inside, her heavy breathing reassuring us that, for now, all is well.

'I cannot ask this of you. It was my decision to take her in.'

'And what else could you have done? But you do not need to carry this weight on your own. We are friends, remember? And hopefully, she will be better by the spring. Maybe with your care and John gone, she will improve.'

But she does not. For, as autumn closes and winter draws in, Priscilla worsens. She fails to eat and wash unless pressed, she has fits of anger and crying, then long days of silence when she lies, unmoving, on the bed. Aubrey and I make her meals which she pushes away; we tell her stories of our childhood, find her seed heads and berries, ribbons and trinkets to try and cheer her. We read the Bible to her and speak to her about the folk in Dunwich, how the sea is taking part of one street then another, for the storms are lashing the shoreline this winter as never before.

As the seasons turn and the weather warms a little, we take her out, walking around the calm of the Abbey, but staying away from the town, not wishing to remind her of her losses. And it finally seems to be working, for she brightens and pays more attention to the world around her. She begins to come with us more willingly, often talks and smiles of her own accord, and sometimes she is almost as she was. We give her everything we can and we begin to hope that our friend is coming back to us and that all will be well.

ONE MORNING, WHEN AUBREY COMES THROUGH THE DOOR, CALLING out her usual greeting, Priscilla grabs at her arm and I see Aubrey flinch at the sharpness of her fingers. Priscilla's face is shining, her eyes bright.

'Sit down, sit down, I must speak to you both. For something wonderful has happened.'

We sit and look at her with curiosity, our hands clasped. Her palm is warm and clammy in mine and I can feel her body trembling through it.

'Priss, are you well? What is it?'

'He has come back to me.' For a moment I think John has returned, that all will be as it once was, but then I look at Aubrey and see the fear in her gaze.

'Who has come, Priss?' Aubrey leans in towards her, keeping her words careful, her voice low. Priscilla gazes at her, rapt. It is as if she has seen a holy vision.

'The man, the voice. He came in the night. He promised me ten shillings – ten shillings! – if I signed his pact . . .' We look at each other in horror as her voice rises and her words come fast. 'I pricked my finger with a bodkin as he asked and he did the same and we melded our blood and the pact was sealed – I have not had the money yet but I know he will bring it. I have despatched him to Newcastle, to destroy one of the fishing boats there, and I have no doubt that he will bring the silver when he comes to tell me that deed is done.' She falls silent, as if the effort of speaking was too much for her, and looks around. Her words are garbled, on the edge of madness, and a cold terror stabs through me.

Aubrey's face is frozen in horror, but she manages to keep her voice calm.

'Priss, who was this man?'

Priscilla looks at Aubrey as if she was a slow and sluggish child that was failing to understand its lesson.

'A man. I cannot tell you his name. He speaks to me at night, a voice in the dark.'

Aubrey's eyes are wide, the centres black and she is shaking as she snatches her hand away

'Priss, you must never speak of such things, you know how dangerous it is in these times.' She is crying with fear now and tears prick my own eyes.

Priscilla looks confused.

'But he will help me, he has told me he will care for me. God has done nothing for me, but the man has said he will help me. I have his word. And when I have the coins he promises, I will be able to have my children returned to me, and we will all be happy again. Ten shillings is all I need to do that. I will have my babes back' She is animated now, her arms waving, her fingers curling and straightening. The clean coif I put on her head this morning is askance, and her hair flies around a face that quivers with passion. She looks quite mad. We try to hush her, soothe her as best we can, helping her to her feet and settling her onto the bed. I fetch a draught of valerian to calm her and we speak softly to her until her eyelids flicker and she falls into a deep sleep, from which nothing can wake her.

'Aubrey, this new madness – what can we do? I thought she was a little better, but to speak like this . . . and we have nothing in the house to eat. I intended to go into town, I had thought to take Priscilla with me to help, but now . . .' I look at the figure curled up on the bed, the valerian doing its work, and I can feel the panic threading through me. 'I dare not take her like this.'

Aubrey grasps my hand.

'I will help you care for her. We will do this thing together and I am sure all will be well, it will just take time.' She nods towards the bed where Priscilla lies breathing heavily. 'The draught has calmed her. We could quickly go and get some food, she is sound asleep and we need only leave her for a very short while. She will be safe enough. We will lock the door to keep her in and we will be back before she wakes. She will not even know we left her.'

I nod reluctantly, then gather my cloak and basket, find some coins, and we step outside, closing the door silently behind us. I turn the heavy key, the old lock grating, resisting through lack of use. We leave Priscilla there, safe asleep, and walk down the hill to the market for food, going as fast as we can, keeping our thoughts close. We do not linger, we are gone only a short time. But when we return she is gone.

THE DOOR IS WIDE OPEN. THE LOCK HANGS JAGGED, THE WOOD THAT held it torn and splintered. We step inside. Nothing has changed, save the bedding, which has been thrown back. Priscilla's cloak still hangs on the hook but her boots have gone. Panic engulfs us. We drop our purchases on the table and then run outside, searching together around the heath and up into the woods.

'Bess, we must separate. I will go down to the town, you check the path to Westleton, she may have gone that way.' Aubrey's face is white and pinched. 'Go – go now, for we must find her before . . .' The words go unspoken, our fear real and solid.

I run as fast as I can along the sandy track, heading west, sick with worry, my heart pounding. But there is no sign of Priscilla on the track so I turn back, intending to join Aubrey. When I reach my cottage I lean against the fence to catch my breath and rub my face with my hands. Priscilla must have used unnatural force to break the lock. But maybe she has found her way back. I step inside to check but the cottage is empty. My basket of bread and salt fish is untouched on the table where I dropped it, along with the jug of ale that Aubrey carried. My heart sinks. I promised to keep her safe and I have failed. I go back outside, my racing heart finally slowing, but just as I start to pull the door closed I hear running feet and the sound of Aubrey calling my name. She is flying up the track, a look of sheer terror on her face.

'Bess, Bess, some men have found her!' Tears are scoring her cheeks, and, as she reaches me, I take her hands and squeeze them.

'What has happened? Tell me.' I put my arm around her. Her whole body is quivering.

Aubrey pulls a sob from her throat.

'Three fishermen...'

'Fishermen? What was she doing on the beach?'

'No, not the beach...' Aubrey is shaking now, '... she was not on the beach. They – they pulled her out of the sea!' I put my hand over my mouth in horror. To try to take her own life – I did not see it coming, did not think her so desperate. 'They are bringing her here now, some local men. They are carrying her on a trestle. Oh, Bess, what will we do?' But I cannot answer her, for my mind is spinning and swirling.

THEN, IN THE DISTANCE A HUBBUB, THE THRUM OF MANY FOOTSTEPS. The crowd stops outside my cottage, men and women, all speaking excitedly, and I take a deep breath and step towards them, pulling myself up straight to face them. I look around – their faces are pinched, their expressions fearful as they murmur and cough, feet shuffling. Then, a man's voice, harsh but full of authority. The crowd grows silent, expectant.

'Mistress Southerne, we have returned this *person* to you. I understand that you have taken her in.'

Thomas Spatchett steps forward. I recognise the child in the man. The jagged scar, the too-big head. Now his face is flushed and damp with exertion. I have never seen him this close before. The damage to his head looks severe, and I think that it is a miracle he survived to become such a powerful man in this town. His voice echoes through the assembled crowd as he stands too close to me, his breath sour, clouding in the chill of the day. He is shorter than me but he radiates power and intimidation, and I take a step back, fear flooding me. This man is dangerous.

'Mistress Southerne. I understand that you have charge of this woman?' I nod, wary. He knows my name. 'You have allowed her to roam free in her madness. I am here to order you to control her. She is deranged, clearly a lunatic, who knows what she will do next? She should be restrained or locked away.'

I want to argue with him, to tell him that she is just ill and cannot help this, but, in the intensity of his glare, the fight goes out of me in a rush.

'I will do my best, Sir. Thank you for returning her.'

'You must do better than that, Mistress Southerne. Ensure you keep her confined. We cannot have her sort running amok in Dunwich, it will not do.' He turns and throws his arm out in a grand gesture. 'Our people would not be safe in their beds.' Heads nod in unison but all remain quiet.

'Has she spoken, Sir?' I have to know if she has incriminated herself.

'She has not, Mistress. I fear her insanity has prevented her.' He waves a hand behind him and four men move forward and bend, resting a trestle on the ground. Two reach down and pull Priscilla to her feet. Her clothes are soaked through and seawater drips off her, leaving a wet trail on the mud-churned track. 'You have been warned, Mistress. Do not let her out again.' Priscilla stumbles as they let go of her, and Aubrey and I move to catch her before she falls. She is freezing, shaking with cold, her teeth chattering, and Aubrey hurriedly takes her inside as the crowd disperses in a flurry of whispers and remarks, their entertainment over. I watch silently as Thomas Spatchett turns on his heel and disappears from view. He leaves behind him an aura of malice so thick I can almost touch it.

AUBREY IS STRIPPING OFF PRISCILLA'S SODDEN CLOTHING AS I GO inside and heap more logs on the fire to heat the room. We rub her dry with rough cloths then dress her in one of my shifts, covering her with a blanket and cloak, and sit her on the bed. Aubrey heats some ale with the poker and passes it to her but she does not move to take it, so Aubrey holds the cup to her lips. Priscilla sips carelessly, the sticky liquid running down her chin. It is as if she is not of this world.

I do not know whether to hold her or slap her. I do not know what to do.

'Why were you in the sea, Priscilla?' Her eyes are blank, and I cannot tell if she has heard me. I try to soften my voice as Aubrey would, but I am scared and angry. 'Why did you go into the water? Were you trying to . . .' I cannot speak of it, for all know that it is a mortal sin to take your own life. Priscilla looks back at me with dead eyes, and I think she is struck dumb, but then I think I hear her say something. I bend my ear to her mouth.

'He told me to go.' Priscilla's voice is small and tremulous.

I look at Aubrey, then back at Priscilla

'Who? Who told you to go?' But as I ask the question, horror overwhelms me, for I know already what she will say.

Priscilla hesitates, her eyes moving from side to side as if seeking someone, her mouth working.

'The Devil, it was he that told me.'

Aubrey gasps, then stands and holds her close, but Priscilla does not fold into her arms. Her body remains rigid and she does not even seem to feel the contact. Aubrey looks over her head at me.

'She does not mean that. She is mistaken. She has just dreamt this. It was not real . . . it was a horrible nightmare that she has had, nothing more . . .'

'She told me before that the Devil spoke to her.'

Aubrey looks at me in horror.

'But when she said about the voices in her head, she was ill in her mind. There was no talk of the Devil. And since then we have cared for her and she is much better now . . .' I hang my head. 'Why did you not tell me?' Her face crinkles in sorrow.

'Oh, Aubrey, I wanted to so much. But no one else heard her say it and she was so distressed I thought it safer never to speak of it – to anyone. I thought she would forget it. But I should have told you and I am sorry that I did not.' Aubrey pats my hand in understanding and forgiveness, but her face is pinched.

'When did she say it?'

'The day after she put little Edward in the fire.' I pause, the memory still too painful. 'She told me that the Devil had made her do it. She said that he had told her that she should make away with her children and promised her money. She said that she did it because she was tired of being poor.' Aubrey sits heavily down in the chair, her face tight with shock. 'I made her promise that she would never speak of it again, that it was untrue and against God's teachings. I thought she would forget.' She starts to cry. 'I am sorry, I should have told you, should have trusted you.'

'But to speak of the Devil now – what if she said anything to the townsfolk that brought her back? In times such as these, with all the talk of witchcraft . . .' Her hand covers her mouth and she sobs gently.

I kneel in front of Priscilla and take her shoulders.

'Priscilla, look at me.' Her eyes wander around the room, but I shake her gently until they fix on me. 'What did you say to the men? Tell us, it's very important. What did you say to the townsfolk, to the fishermen who rescued you?'

She seems to rally a little and looks at me, then across at Aubrey.

'I was afraid to speak in case the Devil was listening.'

She talks so softly I have to lean in to hear her.

'So you said nothing?' She nods. 'Good, that is good.' I turn to Aubrey. 'If she has truly said nothing she may yet survive this. But we must keep her here, indoors. She must not be allowed to go out on her own. It is not safe – for any of us.'

I turn as I feel Priscilla clutching at my sleeve, her nails digging into my skin.

Her voice is stronger now.

'It was my fault, Bess. I went in too deep. The Devil told me that I was to walk to Boston on the waves, that it would take me two days, and that I should take a care not to go into the sea above my knees. But the water was deep and cold, the shingle slipped away and all of a sudden I stepped forward and fell and the water covered my shoulders. The waves – they kept coming over my head and I feared I would drown, but he had told me all would be well and I trusted him . . .' Her eyes are wild now, her grip tightening and I glance at Aubrey. Her face is soft with pity, bleached with fear. '. . . and he did save me, for a boat came by and the fishermen dragged me out. They were cursing as they raised me out of the water, saying how heavy I was, how the Devil was holding me fast down in the water, but it was him who sent them to save me, I know it.' She pauses and rubs her face. Her eyes are wide, shining black, her body restless, then she sways, and nearly falls, and I realise exhaustion is overwhelming her. We lay her down gently on the bed, piling more blankets and clothes on top of her to keep her warm. Once she has fallen into a restless sleep we go and sit at the table, mugs of ale in hand, shaken and quiet.

Aubrey turns to me.

'She truly believes the Devil comes to her.' I nod, my heart heavy. 'But to speak of such things, even in a fever – it puts all three of us at risk.'

I look at her, my heart thudding.

'I do not think it is a fever, Aubrey. I fear she is possessed.'

CHAPTER 9

Priscilla sleeps for two days and nights while we take it in turns to sit with her. When she wakes, she seems much improved and her near-drowning seems to have made her more biddable, for she does not attempt to leave the cottage again. But we dare not leave her alone. I pray that the incident will soon be forgotten, but I should have known better, for when I next go into Dunwich with my pack for the weekly market, it is all people can talk about. I had thought I would be able to quietly sell my wares here while Aubrey sits with Priscilla, that no one would notice me, but the need for gossip is great. They crowd around, buying my pins and needles, ribbons and cloth, but all they ask are questions about her near-drowning. I answer politely, for I do not wish to lose their business, but tell them as little as I can.

Gradually though, as the weeks progress, the gossip settles down and the talk goes back to whose sheep strayed onto whose land, and how poor the fishing is. The rain seems unending this winter and the customers dwindle, those who venture out dashing from stall to stall with hoods pulled low and cloaks high. The winter-sown crops that have pushed up scrawny shoots have been washed from the sandy soil before they have a chance to thrive, so a poor harvest is forecast, and the threat of hunger looms. But as winter slowly turns into spring, and the days grow warmer, there is another subject on everyone's lips, for talk of the Witchfinder is growing. It seems that Matthew Hopkins and John Stearne have widened their net, and now Hopkins is searching out witches in the east of the country while John Stearne takes the west.

HOPKINS COMES THROUGH SUFFOLK LIKE A STORM, BLACK AND thunderous, and women fall in his wake. They say that he carries the Devil's own list of names of those who follow him; that he has been chosen by Parliament and God to cleanse our land of evil. We hear of the many he has tried, of those who are hanged. I still try to tell myself that this will not touch us in Dunwich, as this is a poor place and out of the way; I try to convince myself that the threat is exaggerated by the gossip of simpletons and fools, but the word *witch* sears through me and starts a clenching in my heart that I am unable to shake off.

Priscilla seems to improve as the days grow longer. She says no more about the Devil and keeps her conversation light, speaking only of the day's tasks, as she moves around the cottage, helping with the cooking, lighting the fire, and cleaning the hearth. But we do not dare take her outside. The rumours and talk keep us indoors, living privately, and we quietly settle into our ways. But only too soon I find my funds again running low. There is not enough trade in Dunwich to keep us in food, even with Aubrey's help. I need to travel further afield, but how can I leave Priscilla?

It is Aubrey, again, who decides for me.

'Go, Bess, do what you have to. I can look after Priscilla, and we both know she is much better now and I have done it before . . .'

I am still unsure, but her words make sense.

'I will not be gone for months this time, I promise, just a few weeks, and I am hoping for plenty of trade – I have the new chap-books, and more ribbons which are always popular. But are you sure you are happy for me to go?'

Aubrey reaches for my hand and squeezes it, smiling at me.

'Of course, she is settled and calm now. You go, come back with an empty pack and a full purse.' I smile back at her and the matter is decided.

THE MORNING I AM TO LEAVE, I AM PACKING UP MY BAG WITH MY wares, testing its weight on my shoulders, when Priscilla brings me a mug of ale.

'Here, this is for you.'

She hands me the mug, smiling, and I am so pleased to see her returned to her old self that I beam back at her.

'Sit beside me, Priss, help me sort these ribbons.' I hand her a bundle of tangled silk and she starts to smooth each one free between long fingers, placing them neatly into piles. 'Tell me how you are. We may not get a chance for a little while, I have to go away for a short time, but I will be back before you know it.'

She looks down at her lap, running the ribbons through her fingers.

'These ribbons – they are so pretty.' She looks up at me and smiles.

'Here, have one. Choose a colour.'

'May I? Bess, you have done so much for me already . . .' She looks at the tangled mass of silk in her lap, then pulls out a dark red one. 'This one. It is so pretty. Will you fasten it for me?' I reach over and take it from her, then gently brush her hair to one side and tie the ribbon around her throat. Her fingers reach for it and she smiles shyly.

'It looks beautiful, it sets off the colour of your eyes.' I pass her the pewter mirror that sits on the mantel shelf and she gazes at her reflection, smoothing the ribbon over and over with a fingertip. 'There, you look like you again.' She stands up and twirls around on her toes, laughing at herself in the mirror, then stops and looks at me, and I see the old Priscilla shining before me as she once did.

The moment passes and I turn to her and cup her chin in my palm. 'Priss, how do you feel? Tell me truthfully now.'

'I feel well. I do not have the wicked thoughts that I did, they have gone.' Her grip tightens in mine and her face becomes earnest. 'I never intended to take my own life when I went into the sea, I want you to know that. It was the voice in my head . . . I truly believed that the Devil spoke to me.' She looks up at me. 'Bess, I do not know what came over me, to act so, and I am sorry that it caused you and Aubrey such pain and worry. When John went . . .'

I take her hands in mine. They are warm and soft, but bony. She is thin now, wasted.

'Do not speak of John. What he did to you was cruel, heartless, he deserted you in your time of need.'

'He took my babes.' Her shoulders shake as she starts to sob. 'My little boy died and he took Bess and Robert from me.'

I grip her hands more firmly.

'He did what he thought was best for the children, to keep them safe. He loves them dearly.'

She snatches her hands away. Her mood changes in an instant, her face darkens and the soft smile goes.

'Do not defend him to me. How can a man remove children from their mother, who truly loves them? What sort of husband would do that?'

'He was frightened for them, you were not in your right mind. You do not know how you were. Priscilla . . .' I hesitate, then decide to speak up. '. . . you put your babe on the fire. John thought his children were in mortal danger. They were young, they could not understand. Your husband was cruel to leave without saying, yes, and it was wrong that you lost your home, but he was pushed to the edge by your wildness. I know you were ill, that you did not know what you were doing, but think how it was for us, for John, your family and friends. He did what he thought was best.' I seek to justify his actions, but this only serves to make her anger grow, and her eyes blaze. She stands, her fingers twisting and plucking at her skirts, and begins pacing the floor; all the time her mouth moves, but no sound comes out. Then she pauses, her voice softens, her body relaxes and she is back to how she was.

I breathe again and my heart settles as she comes back to sit beside me. She picks up the ribbons again and begins to separate them and this little task calms her. I help her to knot the ribbons together according to their colour and we work silently until she reaches for my hand.

'What I did to Edward – it was as if a madness came over me, Bess. I heard the Devil tell me to do it, and he was kind, he promised to help me. We were always short of money and I was tired of being poor, and the words made sense to me, he made it sound as if it were such a little thing to do. I know it was not, that it was wrong, against all the teachings of the Church, but his words beguiled me. He comforted me, made me feel wanted again.' Her voice is rising and I fear that her sanity is slipping again. I should never have mentioned it. I reach out and put my arm around her shoulders.

'Priss, you are much improved now, you will soon be completely well and then we can decide what you are to do. Maybe you could go and visit your children in the meantime? Let them and John see that you are healed?'

She pulls away from me and her face tightens.

'He will not allow it. He told me that I was to put my children out of my mind.'

'Who, John? I am sure if he could see you now, see how well you are...'

'No, not John. The Devil. He told me that unless I do away with my children I would always remain poor. And I tried to do as he said... my poor babe... but I cannot put the other children from my mind, even now they are gone from me, and that is why he has not given me the coins he promised me.'

I stare at her in horror. Her eyes are blank. I thought her healed, but now it seems as if she still believes this thing.

'It is not true, Priss. The Devil did not come to you. It was all in your head. You had just given birth, your mind was not right. All know that women can often weep and despair after childbirth and think wild thoughts, but it gets better, time heals it. And that is what happened to you. It was all in your imagination.'

She shakes her head and blonde curls frame her face. The blood-red ribbon looks like a wound around her neck.

'It was real, I tell you. The Devil came to me.' She raises her head and looks at me.

'But Aubrey or I watched over you when John was at work, and then he was with you at night. No one came to you, I promise. You slept most of the time, you were not in the world then.'

'Are you sure?'

'I'm sure.' I smile at her.

'I imagined it all? But there was the other thing.'

I look at her with concern. Her eyes have widened and she seems nervous. Her fingers grasp at her skirts, clawed, nervously pulling and twisting at the linen. She does not look me in the face.

'What other thing?'

'I have never spoken of it...'

'What thing?'

She keeps her head lowered, her eyes on her hands.

'John told me that he... I do not believe it, I never have.' I look at her and know in an instant what she will say. My heart stops in my chest.

'I dreamed that John told me that he had lain with you. That he said I had been no wife to him, that he had found another, willing and lascivious, who wanted him as I did not. That he had broken our marriage vows on many occasions with you. But I did not heed him for I knew that you would never do such a thing.'

Then she lifts her eyes to mine and sees the truth.

. . .

I WATCH THE COLOUR DRAIN FROM HER FACE. I SEE HER AS SHE SLUMPS over and wraps her arms around herself, moaning in pain. I am unmoving as she staggers to her feet and rushes outside, and I hear the sound of retching and vomiting. I have caused this. I have hurt my friend so deeply that there is no way back. I am consumed by guilt for my wrong-doing and would give anything to put it right. But it happened, and now she knows, and our friendship is broken, for I am sure she will never forgive me. She comes back in, shaking, wiping her mouth with the back of her hand. Her face is deathly white.

'So it is true?' I nod. Then the anger comes, and she screams and claws at me and I just sit and let her, for I deserve it. I try to tell her it was once only, not the many times she was told, but she is in such fury she does not listen.

When Aubrey comes to bid me farewell we are as wild women, red-eyed and haggard.

'What has happened? Have you been harmed?'

Priscilla spits at my feet and turns away.

'Ask her. Ask your *friend* what she did.' She is still trembling with hurt and fury and Aubrey turns to me.

'Elizabeth?' I cannot look at her. I reach for her hand and draw her down to sit at the table and sit opposite. Priscilla remains standing by the window, quiet now, her shoulders slumped in misery, her back to us.

'I have made a grave mistake.'

Priscilla spins round.

'Mistake – *mistake*? She lay with my husband! That is the sort of friend we have, Aubrey, it is well you were not married for long else, she would have had yours too.'

Aubrey's face is white with horror.

'Tell me this is not true, Bess. Tell me this is another of her imaginings.'

But I cannot, and I hang my head in shame, my face burning, tears coursing down my cheeks.

'It is true. But it was not as he told Priscilla, it was only once, I thought to help her, help him.' I try the untruth of this in my mouth – it is bitter to the taste.

'Help me? How could this help me?'

I look at Priscilla and Aubrey, their faces thin and shocked. My friends look at me like strangers.

'He was so sad, he had just buried his son and . . .'

'So you thought you would lie with my husband?'

'No. I thought only to hold him, to try and comfort him, but . . . we swore never to speak of it and I took him at his word. I never believed he would tell you.'

'And do you know *when* he told me?' Priscilla spits the words in my face. 'As he took away my children. Have you any idea of the pain? All he could say was that if I'd been a better mother and wife to him it would never have happened and that it was all my fault. But do you know the worst thing? I persuaded myself that I had dreamt his words. I never believed him, not once, for I trusted you. I trusted you with my life, Bess. You assured me my talk of pacts with the Devil were imagined, that my mind was not right, and it was all fantasy, so I took John's words to be spite, said to hurt me, and I began to believe that everything was in my head. His stories got all muddled together with my thoughts of the Devil and his words to me. But now I find that the thing about you – the one thing I did not believe – was true! And I think that if that is true, what of the other things?' She wraps her arms around her head and pulls at her hair with bony fingers, keening, tears pouring down her cheeks. Aubrey sits beside us, her face frozen.

I cannot speak for guilt, sobs forcing hard at my throat.

'Priss, I am sorry. I never meant harm. I did not mean it to happen. He was so unhappy and I . . .'

'You thought to have him for yourself, that is the truth of it. You have always been jealous of me. I have seen the way you looked at him, how you always did. You hoped for him long ago, but he chose me instead, and this is your revenge. Well, now you have it and I hope you take pleasure in it.'

The silence is deafening. Then Aubrey stands, her small frame trembling and puts her arms around Priscilla, smoothing her hair.

'Elizabeth, I cannot believe this of you. We are your friends. We have been as sisters since we were small. We cared for you when your mother died, helped you whenever we could . . .' My head hangs low with the shame of it all. 'I know you have cared for Priss these long months, that it has been hard and hurtful, but I thought you did it from love. But now I see that it was guilt all along.'

I cannot bear that Aubrey hates me too.

'No, you are wrong, it was not guilt. It hurt me to see her in such pain, so damaged. She had nothing and I was glad to take her in, happy to help.' She stares at me. 'It was but one moment, one madness. It should never have happened and I wish it never had, but just for a moment, I fell from grace. Since that night I have prayed for forgiveness and begged the Lord to overlook my transgression. I know you will never forgive me, Priss, nor you, Aubrey . . .' I turn to Priscilla, who is stilled, sobbing quietly now, her anger blown out like a sea-storm. 'Priss, I have cared for you, taken you in, nursed you as best I can, all the time you have been unwell. I have tried to do my best because I love you. It was never through shame or guilt, it was because you and Aubrey are my dearest friends. I have to leave today, for I need the money, but before I go . . . I know it is a grave hurt I have caused you but can you ever find it in you to forgive me – please? I would travel easier knowing that you would try, at least.'

Priscilla looks at me and I see her face tighten, her anger returning.

'Never. Go if you will, I do not care. You are no longer part of me or my life.' Through my tears, her face is a shimmering mask of grief and bitterness. 'You betrayed me and I hope one day that someone causes you as much hurt as you have caused me. I can never forgive you.'

CHAPTER 10

I stay away for the whole of that summer and well into the autumn, for I cannot face them. I walk and walk, further than ever before, every step heavy with guilt, but, as winter begins to close in, I know I have to return. My purse is full, my pack nearly empty and I am tired, so very tired. I miss my cottage and my friends, so I turn around to go home. Days of tramping later and the path becomes familiar. At the sight of Westleton Heath I falter, for I do not know how I will be received, but, as I walk towards Dunwich on the damp leaf-sodden path, I can smell the sea, feel the chill air and it gives me courage, for I know I am nearly home. I walk quicker now, down the sandy lane, round the bend, ready to face my friends. I am thinking of what I will say to them as I catch the first glimpse of my cottage, but then I pause. There is no smoke coming from the chimney as I expected. As I draw closer, I see weeds and tares in the small back garden. It is untended and deserted, and I go cold at the thought that Priscilla may again have tried to take her own life, and that Aubrey has been left to deal with this on her own.

I push my front door open hesitantly. It is unfastened, the lock still broken, and it creaks on its hinges through lack of use. A gust of stale air wafts across my face as I look around, sliding my empty pack to the floor. Ash, cold and grey, mounds in the fireplace. My cups and plates and bowls are resting tidily on the shelf but they, too, are shrouded in dust. No one has been here for some time. I swallow my disappointment but pull myself together – I need to buy food and ale, wash my clothes which have become grey and filthy from the long roads I have travelled. The cottage needs cleaning and the fire laying. Things will seem better with a warm blaze and a mug of good ale in my hand.

The afternoon is still sunny so I prop the door open to air the rooms and move my pack into a corner as I look around. Spiders have been industrious as always, their silver strands sticking to my hands and hair as I waft them away with a cloth. A thin layer of dust covers everything. I pull the coverlet from the bed and take it outside, shaking it thoroughly, then spread it over the hedge to air. I plump up the mattress and pillow and brush the ash from the hearth into a pail, then come back with kindling and logs and lay the fire ready. It is only then that I realise Priscilla's few belongings have gone, and a sharp pang of guilt stabs me. It is as if she was never here. I must find out what has happened to my friends. The purse I brought home with me lies heavy in my palm and I open it and take out a few coins, then tie the leather bag tightly and move to the hearth. There is a loose brick, and I prise this out with my fingers, putting the purse in the space beneath, then replace the brick and wipe ash over it with my boot. It will be safe there. Tucking the coins into my pocket, and picking up my willow basket, I walk down into Dunwich.

THE TOWN LOOKS MUCH AS IT DID WHEN I LEFT IN THE SPRING, although I can see that more of the cliff-side has crumbled and more buildings are edged nearer to the sea. The market square is bustling even this late in the afternoon. I hurriedly buy a loaf of bread, some cured fish, a little meat and a small piece of cheese. There are some apples in a barrel by the cheese stall so I take two of these as well, placing them carefully in my basket, handing over coins to a nod and a muttering of thanks. Next, I buy a jug of ale from the alewife and, holding it with care, turn to go home.

Aubrey and Priscilla stand staring at me. I flush red, unsettled, unsure what to do, but I am saved by Aubrey, who walks over, holding Priscilla's hand, smiling warily.

'Bess, you are back.'

I feel awkward, still bitterly ashamed.

'I got back a short time ago. I had no provisions . . .' It is tense, awkward. Then I set the jug on the floor and step towards Aubrey at the very moment she reaches for me.

'Aubrey, I am truly sorry . . .'

My friend stops my lips with a finger.

'It is done now, let us try and forget. I have missed you, so much.'

'Priscilla, will she . . .?' I look across at her now and am shocked by the change in her appearance. She is standing motionless watching us, her face blank, and she has aged in the months since I last saw her. Her coif is askew, her fingernails bitten and grimy, but, despite this, she looks cared for. I turn back to Aubrey. 'I have missed you both – and our friendship – so very much. When I saw the cottage was empty I feared . . .'

'I thought it best that she stayed somewhere else. She can still be . . . difficult at times, and so I have cared for her myself as best I can.' It must have been hard, Aubrey's house is small and ill-served, but she has always been kind and this kindness has always overcome any practicalities.

'And what of Priss – how has she been?'

Aubrey's face drops and she glances back at our friend then looks around warily as she brings her face close to mine.

'She is worse, still speaking of the Devil and her pact with him. She swears that it was he that made her hurt the babe, and I have to keep her indoors for fear she will repeat this in company. We only go out together when I can be sure she is safe.'

'And has she seen her children – or John?' I hesitate to speak his name.

Aubrey's face darkens.

'No, he has not been near. I have sent messages asking if I could take her to see them, but he sent back refusing, saying that they would never see their mother again and that she was not fit. He said they are all happy, Robert and young Bess are growing strong and healthy and they are better off without her. That man has no heart. The message fair destroyed her, she sat in the house for weeks after that, not moving. I had to help her eat and wash, for she would not care for herself. It was the same as when she was ill after little Edward.'

I clasp Aubrey's hand firmly.

'I am back now, I will stay until next spring at the earliest and it may be that the money I have earned will last the whole summer if I am prudent. I am getting old for this travelling, truth be known, it becomes harder each year. Maybe I can stay.'

All the time we are speaking Aubrey has been keeping a careful eye on Priscilla, who has moved to the shingle to watch the boats on the beach. The fishermen have just landed their catch and I can see this has caught her interest, her eyes following their every movement. She starts to walk slowly towards them and I snatch up my jug as we follow, Aubrey running to catch up with her and clasp her hand.

'Priss, where are you going? We should be getting back.'

Our friend turns and her eyes are bright.

'I wanted to see what they had caught. I thought to have a herring for my supper.'

'That is a good idea.' We walk together down to where the fishermen are unloading their catch into sour-smelling willow baskets and we peer into one. Creamy-brown claws writhe and clasp at the air as the creatures fight for their freedom, not knowing that their movements are in vain.

'Crabfish! It is full of crabs!' Priscilla's eyes shine. 'I should like to taste crabmeat again, it has been so long. I cannot remember when I last ate it.' Her pleasure is infectious and I reach into my purse, passing coins to the fisherman, who selects a large brown crab, binds its claws and wraps it in a cloth, giving it to her, his face set.

Aubrey smiles at me.

'Thank you, that is kind of you. I can't remember the last time she was so interested in something.'

I smile back.

'It is the least I could do, and I am pleased such a small thing makes her happy.'

We turn to walk back, Priscilla holding tight to her parcel, and I grasp Aubrey's arm, unable to keep the question from my lips.

'Do you forgive me? It would mean so much to me to have your forgiveness, and Priscilla's too.'

She lowers her eyes and sighs.

'For my part, there is nothing to forgive. You made a mistake and are repentant of it and that is enough for me.' I squeeze her arm in thanks. 'But I am not sure how Priscilla is now, for she has not spoken of it since you left and she came to live with me. I do not know what she is in her head – I don't even think she knows herself. But she is here now, and she is talking to us both, so maybe, with time, it will heal.'

I smile and move to take Priscilla's arm as we used to, but she frowns and pulls away.

'Priss, it is me, Elizabeth. Shall I help you prepare that crabfish – it looks so nice?'

Her frown becomes a scowl and Aubrey looks worried.

'I should take her home. She is becoming unwell, I can tell by her face.' We start to walk through the narrow streets, up Hen Hill and down to Aubrey's tiny house. As we do I look around. The town is much as it has always been but I can sense something has changed. It is not just the sea that has come closer, people are pulling away when they see us, turning their backs. No one greets us as they used to, there is no friendly face to be seen. And once or twice I think I see fingers curl around thumbs in the age-old sign of protection.

WHEN WE REACH AUBREY'S HOME SHE USHERS PRISCILLA INSIDE, glancing about her to see if anyone sees. I am concerned by her actions, I have rarely seen her as nervous as this.

'Will you come in, Bess?'

'Thank you, just for a moment. Here, I have ale, we could sit on the step . . .?'

Aubrey shakes her head.

'Dunwich is not as it was.' She finds three mugs and puts them on the table. 'It would be best to sit in here.' I lift the jug, remove the cloth cover, and Aubrey pulls Priscilla down beside her as I pour generous measures, passing the mugs around.

'To friendship.'

We touch mugs and take deep drags at the ale. It is sweet and flavoursome and I feel some of my old self return. We sit together saying little, then Aubrey begins to tell me what is happening in the town, how more and more people are moving away as the sea encroaches.

'The life is going from it, Bess, the days of us being a powerful sea-port are long gone. And you remember Thomas Spatchett?' I nod. 'He has become wealthy and influential in your absence, a man to be reckoned with, although he is still young. People listen to him more and more.' Priscilla spits at the mention of his name, a wet yellow gobbet darkening the floor. I look at it, then at Aubrey. 'She will not have him mentioned. That business with John moving away, she blames Thomas Spatchett. He was responsible for her having been thrown out of her home. And he stopped her in the street not long ago . . .' Aubrey's face is dark, '. . . told her she is not welcome in the town, and her born and bred here. I am convinced he is watching us, I seem to see him whenever we go out, and he makes certain to tell me to keep Priss indoors.'

'Is that why you looked around you, just now, when we came in?'

'He has had men out watching the house, I have seen them.' I wonder if she is imagining it all, if Priscilla's nervousness has rubbed off on her, although she has always been a little fearful. But if she is worried, then there must be a cause. She hesitates.

'He has enquired after you too, Bess.'

I STARE AT AUBREY.

'Me? Why me?'

'He has asked when you will return, where you go, what you do. He knows you are a pedlar but he still questions me about your movements. I tell him that I do not know, that I have seen little of you, which is the truth. I try to steer clear of him.'

I take a long pull of my ale.

'I am of no concern to him. Does Thomas Spatchett think that all should fall to his will because he is the rising man in Dunwich?' Aubrey nods. 'Then I will steer clear of him also. I have heard too many tales of witchcraft – it is not wise to draw attention to ourselves in times such as these.'

Priscilla has been sitting quietly all this time so I turn to her and smile.

'And you, Priss, how have you been?' She looks at me with blank eyes, so strangely that I am not sure if she even recognises me. I take up her hand which lies limp on her lap. She does not respond. 'Aubrey, why does she not come to live with me for a while? If she is willing? There is more space and it will be quieter there, out of the town . . .' I squeeze Priscilla's hand. 'Would you like that Priss? To live with me for a while?' It is as if we talk to a child. Priscilla lowers her gaze and I meet Aubrey's eyes over the top of her head. 'Does she hear us?'

Aubrey shakes her head.

'She hears, but I am not sure how much she understands when she is like this. Her moods come and go and I do not know how long they will last. It has been difficult, I will not deny it. She has shouted at some of the townsfolk, even spat at Thomas Spatchett, so I keep her close, keep her safe here as much as I can.' She hesitates, clearing her throat. 'This talk of witches – it is a great worry to me, Bess. I have seen neighbours who have known us for years avoid us, especially if Priscilla is in one of her strange moods. She often mutters and talks to herself, she looks wild sometimes, although I try to keep her tidy, and she can shout out loud at the slightest thing. I am becoming afraid for our safety. Many know what she has suffered, losing her children, her husband, her home, and they have made allowances up 'til now, but the tide seems to be turning. Fear is coming.'

But still we do not heed the warning, still think this thing will pass us by.

CHAPTER 11

It is a golden evening, happy. We dine together on crabfish and vegetables from Aubrey's garden, eat the apples, finish the ale, and laugh at tales from our past when we were young and carefree. Priscilla sometimes joins in and I feel a glimmer of hope that all will be well. And, as the sun goes down, we return to the question I asked earlier.

'Aubrey, you have kept Priscilla safe these past weeks. Let her come and live with me for a while. My cottage is tucked away on the edge of the wood, not many pass that way. She may be safer there.'

She hesitates and then nods her agreement. 'That would be a relief to me, I confess, for times are difficult with her here. I would be glad of some help. I am tired, Bess, so tired and it would be good to have my little house back as it was for a while. But are you sure?'

I squeeze her thin shoulders.

'I am. It is settled. Together we will look after her.'

So Priscilla comes home with me and I try to keep her safe. But I fail. I fail.

. . .

I TRY SO HARD TO PROTECT HER. I KEEP HER CLOSE, LET HER HELP ME weed the garden, plant herbs and roots for the kitchen. As the days pass we settle into a quiet contentment, but still she does not smile, and rarely speaks, and once or twice I catch her gazing at me with an expression of confusion. She never mentions John, of what has passed, and I hope, pray, that she is beginning to forgive me. Aubrey comes to see us most days, bringing food and ale to help out, and I can tell that Priss is glad to see her, for her face brightens.

But then, as spring turns to summer, Priscilla's mood lowers again. She spends her days sitting in the chair, staring into space, and all of her lightness leaves her. I keep her indoors, do not let her out of my sight, but one day, when I see she is sleeping deeply, I go to pull a few vegetables from the back garden for our dinner. The day is soft, the air clean and fresh, and I stretch and breathe, looking around me. Birds sing, leaves rustle, and all is calm. I bend to my task, enjoying the labour, then straighten up. I take another look around, smiling to myself, and then go back inside.

The front door is wide open and my friend is gone.

I RUSH OUTSIDE, AROUND THE COTTAGE, CALLING HER NAME, FOR SHE cannot have gone far, but she is nowhere to be seen. I pull at my hair – I was only away for a short time, I am sure of it. I run to the gate and look both ways, then shade my eyes with my hand and look farther up the lane towards the heath. There is no sign of her, so I walk swiftly towards Dunwich, looking wildly from side to side, calling out to her, but it is as if she has disappeared into thin air. When I reach the edge of the town, I turn and retrace my steps, trying to swallow the feelings of panic and fear. In truth, I do not know how long I was in the garden. It seemed but a few moments but maybe time slipped away as it is wont to do, maybe I took longer than I thought. Perhaps she has gone back to the cottage. I will start my search again and be more thorough this time. I must have missed her. She cannot have gone far.

Then, a commotion behind me, the sound of running footsteps and shouting, and I spin round to see Aubrey sprinting up the lane towards me, her hair wild about her face, her skirts flying, her apron torn. I run towards her, my arms outstretched, and she falls into them, panting, unable to draw breath to speak. I hold her close and then look up at the clamour that follows in her wake. A crowd of men and women are rushing up the track after her, some waving staves; their faces are red, their eyes wide and their mouths black and open. They are shouting and screaming foul abuse and I realise that it is Aubrey they are chasing.

I look down at her as she struggles to speak.

'Run, Bess, run!' Her voice is broken, her breath coming hard. 'They have taken Priss. Save yourself. I will try and delay them. If I stop running they will seize me, and you may yet escape. Go!'

She pushes me away as the crowd draws nearer. I look into her eyes, see the terror in them, and make my decision. It needs no thought, not really, for she is my friend. I smile at her, though fear floods through me, clasp her hand, and we turn, standing together as the baying mob reaches us, as, rattling and booming like the incoming tide on the pebbled beach, they overwhelm us.

MEN CLAW AT US WITH UNRELENTING HANDS, BIND OUR ARMS TIGHT to our sides with hemp rope and begin to drag us back towards the town. They are quiet now, silenced by the enormity of what they are doing, the only sound that of heavy breathing, heavier footsteps, and the occasional grunt and mutter. Sharp fingers prod and pinch us as we try to keep our feet and not stumble over the rough hard ground. The crowd moves as one, sweeping us down through the town, past the harsh faces and stern looks of townsfolk, until we find ourselves standing before the church of St Peter, towering over the marketplace. A group of men are waiting for us, standing stern in the porch – two bailiffs in their black robes of office, constables with staves, and a thin, noble-looking man who I do not recognise, but who looks menacingly down his long nose at us. And in front of them all, standing straight as a mast, shoulders back, formal in his severe black suit and crisp white collar, is Thomas Spatchett. The long scar furrows his forehead under the brim of his perfectly aligned hat.

The crowd separates and we are pushed and shoved to the front. There is a sudden release as our bindings are cut, and I bring my arms round and rub at the red rope burns on my wrists. Next to me, Aubrey is doing the same. We must make a poor impression, for our clothes are covered with dust, my coif has gone, and Aubrey has lost her apron, but we straighten up, make ourselves look less unkempt, and try to regain our dignity. The thin man steps forward, a lace-edged kerchief to his nose.

'Elizabeth Southerne? Aubrey Grinsett?' We nod. 'I am the magistrate for this town.' I have heard he is strict and lacks compassion – I can see it in his face and shudder. 'There has been a laying of information against you. You have been accused of consorting with the Devil, of making a pact in blood with him some years since. What say you?'

I can feel Aubrey shaking beside me and I move closer to her, pushing my arm against hers for courage, then stand tall and look him in the eye.

'It is untrue, Sir. We are good Christian women. We would never countenance such a thing.' Aubrey nods beside me as the magistrate speaks again, an eyebrow raised in disbelief.

'But there is one who says you do, that you are witches who are used by the Devil for his own purposes, and that you have become his creatures. That you have formed a covenant with him, practised spells, summoned spirits, for many years, against the teachings of the Lord and the word of his ministers. Well, what have you to say?' Behind him, Master Spatchett smiles.

Aubrey finds her voice.

'It is all untrue, Sir. We would never do such a thing. Who accuses us?'

The magistrate turns and nods to the constable standing next to him.

'Bring out the witness.' There is a scrabbling as the constable enters the church, the crowd murmurs and shuffles, and then the minister of St Peter's, Reverend Browne, comes out, holding his great leather-bound bible before him like an offering. I draw in my breath – for a minister of the church to make such an accusation would damn us both, but I cannot think why he should say such a thing when we have done nothing. Then, behind him, comes the constable, dragging what looks like a grey bundle of cloth.

I stare and stare until a shape unfurls itself from the cloth and the light catches blonde hair, a pale face, and eyes blank with madness. I catch my breath as, beside me, Aubrey's legs give way and she falls to the ground. It is Priscilla.

THE CONSTABLE CLINGS TIGHT TO HER ARM FOR FEAR SHE MAY ESCAPE him, as the magistrate addresses her.

'Priscilla Collit, you have accused these two women, Elizabeth Southerne and Aubrey Grinsett, of the crime of witchcraft. You have said they consorted with the Devil himself and . . .'

Priscilla's head jerks upright and her face contorts with distress.

'No. Not Aubrey.' She looks across at Thomas Spatchett for help, but he stares intently at the floor. 'You know she has not harmed me. She has done nothing save care for me. No, it was Elizabeth, before . . .' The magistrate turns to him.

'Did you not tell me that this witness had accused both these women, and said that they were her accomplices?'

Thomas Spatchett shuffles his feet, defiant, but I can see guilt in the shape of his shoulders. He clears his throat and looks at the magistrate.

'All three are known to be witches, Sir, I myself have seen them coming and going at all hours, I have heard their foul words, heard tell of their malice . . .'

'But has this witness actually accused Mistress Grinsett? You noted down the accusations, has she been accused or not? We cannot try someone if there is no information laid against them. The law is very clear on this matter.'

Thomas Spatchett reaches into his gown and pulls out a parchment. He brings it to his face but I can see he is not reading the words on it, for his eyes do not move.

'She is not specifically named, Sir. But all know that these three are...'

'Then we cannot proceed with our investigation of this woman. She does not stand accused. It would not be right in the eyes of God, nor would it be correct in the eyes of the law.'

Thomas Spatchett hides his fury well, but I see it. I see him. He thought to condemn us all, and his anger is great that he has been thwarted in this.

'Sir, you are correct and I apologise for the confusion. Mistress Grinsett must, of course, be released.' He nods to the constables. 'Let that one go.' They move to Aubrey and pull her roughly to her feet. She stands, still rubbing the red-raw burns on her arms, then looks up at me, confusion in her eyes. She edges closer to me and goes to speak, but I catch her eye and give a small shake of my head, praying that she will say nothing. Her eyes fill with tears but she sees and makes a small movement of her head in understanding. Thomas Spatchett moves close to her.

'Well, be gone, Mistress Grinsett, it seems you have escaped justice this time. But I will be watching you, have no fear of that. I know you to be a witch and I will have you.'

The magistrate hears also.

'Master Spatchett, that is enough. We stand before the Lord's house, you had best remember that. We carry out His wishes here and it is clear that no information has been laid against that woman; she has not been accused in the eyes of either God or the law.'

He nods to the Reverend, who turns to Aubrey. 'God in his

goodness has found you to be held unjustly. Go, woman, be thankful, praise Him for His mercy.' He moves as if to place his hand on her head in blessing, but his fingers do not touch her and his mouth pinches with distaste. She keeps her head low as she moves away, pushing through the crowd amidst an increasing rumble of discontent and anger. I follow her with my eyes, praying that she will be safe. She turns once to look at Priscilla and me, her face twisted in anguish, before the crowd closes behind her.

THOMAS SPATCHETT MOVES FORWARD. 'SIR, INFORMATION HAS BEEN laid against Elizabeth Southerne, there is no doubt about this. And, in addition, and by the very nature of her accusations, I believe that the witness herself has proved that she too is involved in terrible acts of witchcraft. I respectfully request that both are detained, pending further interrogation. We will get to the truth of the matter once they are questioned, I have no doubt.' I see the magistrate consider, tapping a long finger against his lips as he glares at both of us in turn. His eyes are hard, his mouth pursed, and I know at that moment that we will not escape. Time stretches, then he nods.

The constables seize Priscilla and me and man-handle us to the town gaol, throwing us inside as if we were animals. And, like animals, we are frozen with shock, dumb and resigned. The thick iron bars over the window give a view of the church; the cell is dark and cold and smells of piss and worse. We slump down onto the packed earth floor, which is softened only slightly by a mound of filthy straw, and we sit there, listening, as people pause outside to shout curses and abuse at us. Then something warm and stinking flies through the bars to spatter on the floor before us; dung from the road, fresh and shining, and we shuffle back to avoid its foulness. Rotting vegetables and fish heads, left over from the market, follow, and we keep our heads bowed, our eyes closed, trying to shut it out. It is as if the whole town has come to abuse us and vent their rage and fear. We do not speak. When the worst of the shouting seems over, Priscilla leans sideways and stretches to lie full out on the dirty floor, muttering and keening to herself, pulling her apron over her face.

'Priscilla, are you hurt?' She is staring at me, her face scratched and bleeding, her teeth bared. I go to hold her, but she growls like a dog at my touch. I pull back sharply and look at her. Her hair, which she was so proud of, hangs in long greasy strands over her face and she hammers with her fists on her breasts, so hard I think she will damage herself. I reach for her hands to still them and, finally, she allows this small gesture, seeming to calm a little at my touch. I close my eyes and begin to pray.

CHAPTER 12

It is as if the gaol absorbs us. The stink and cold become part of us and we can only sit and endure. There is silence now, save for the slither and drum of pebbles on the shore as they are constantly pulled and released by the sea. It is so familiar and ordinary. I listen to its rhythm, trying to still my pounding heart and settle my thoughts. I will need all my wits about me for what is to come, but I give thanks to the Lord that Aubrey was freed – at least she is safe. I do not speak to Priscilla. This woman has accused me of witchcraft – I do not know her anymore, she has become a stranger to me. She is looking at me as if she is trying to say something, so I pause and wait, thinking she may offer some explanation, some reason for what she has done, but at that moment, we hear a great growing grumbling. I think at first it is the sea, rising up for one last time to finally take our town in its embrace, and I feel glad, for drowning seems an easy death compared to what we must face. Then the noise widens and expands into that of many voices. It is the sound of a mass of humanity, a huge crowd coming together, their voices joining in anger and condemnation. It is a wall of noise and Priscilla puts her hands to her ears, her distress rising. Outside, the voices still and a thick silence falls, only broken by the bark of a dog and the wail of a child. Heavy footsteps, the jangle of iron, a grating as the lock is released and the door thrown open. For a moment we are blinded by light. It is still day, the sun still high and the air that wafts into the cell is warm and salt-tinged. I lick my lips and taste it. We have been shut in here so long that I had thought night was nearly upon us. I am already losing track of time.

Men pull us to our feet and we stumble outside, shading our eyes, trying to make sense of the scene. The constables are standing to attention in two lines and we are pushed along between them.

'Are they the witches?' A child's voice rings out from the crowd. He is hurriedly shushed, but his question has broken the spell and now voices rise again, shouting and screaming abuse. I look around at the crowd, their mouths drawn in anger, as they press forward, spittle flying as stones and dirt are thrown. A sharp flint breaks the skin on my cheekbone and I can feel blood, warm and wet, running down my face to my neck. The constables push the crowd back, staves brandished, as we are taken back, under the porch, then shoved forward to the door of St Peter's church, and pushed inside.

THE INTERIOR OF THE CHURCH IS DARK AND STILL, SMELLING OF MUST, flaking plaster and damp. The windows soar high above us, plain and dull since Dowsing's men put them out two years before. The church is not as it once was now the images and statues are gone, there is no colour here now, no life. St Peter's is the church where my parents married and where my mother is buried – I wonder if she is watching me from her place in Heaven, and I am ashamed. Two constables push Priscilla and I to the nave and there we stop. In front of us is a large oak table, and behind sit the Reverend Browne, the magistrate and Thomas Spatchett, hands clasped before them on the table, their expressions severe. At the end of the table crouches a black-gowned clerk, paper ready, quill poised. I can smell the copper and soot tang of his ink.

The magistrate gazes at us, his long face hawk-like.

'Elizabeth Southerne, Priscilla Collit, you stand accused of the crime of witchcraft. We are here to examine the legitimacy of these accusations and note all that is said. If found guilty, you will be sent for trial. Do you understand?' We say nothing. 'It will go easier for you if you confess now, and fully. Priscilla Collit, you have accused this woman, Elizabeth Southerne, of consorting with the Devil, and in doing so have, yourself, confessed to acts of witchcraft. You must now tell us fully what you have seen.'

Priscilla stoops, her hands limp by her sides, her head bowed, and I think she will not speak, but then the Reverend rises and comes around the table to stand before her. His voice is soft, smooth as a snake, sermon-sharp.

'Sister, you came to me, telling me that you wish to confess your sins, that you cannot live with the guilt of what you have done any longer. You came here, to this very church, to find me and confess this, did you not?' She nods but does not look up. 'So why not tell us now what these sins are, that are so unbearable, and ask the Lord's forgiveness in this, His house? Speak, Sister. Unburden yourself and receive the grace of God.' He stands back from her, brown teeth shaded by thin lips, and waits. But Priscilla says nothing. 'Sister, will you not speak?' Priscilla is silent, unmoving. The Reverend's smile disappears as he returns to his place behind the table, shaking his head in apparent sadness.

The magistrate looks us over as if we were something he had on his shoe. His voice is harder – he is not here to wheedle, he is here to gain our confessions, and I go cold.

'Elizabeth Southerne, do you have anything to say?' I want to fall to my knees, to plead my innocence, to wring my hands and beg for mercy, but I know that there will be none, so I say nothing.

'Very well. Priscilla Collit, Elizabeth Southerne, you have been accused of witchcraft and you have failed to confess. You will be searched.'

They return us to the gaol, give us stale bread and oily water, and we just have time to eat it before they come for Priscilla.

. . .

IT IS QUICK. IT TAKES NO TIME AT ALL BEFORE THE GUARDS BRING Priscilla back and drop her into a heap on the floor. Her body is covered in flecks of blood, her skirt untied and her bodice is laced all wrong. My heart clenches in pity and I move towards her to tend her but, before I can, strong hands seize me.

'No, you don't. You are next for it.' The guards laugh as I am dragged outside. They take me to a small room in a decrepit building a few streets from the gaol. I know the place, for it once formed part of the church of St John, before that house of God was threatened by the tides. Now all that remains are the few stones which have not been taken by townsfolk to repair their own houses, and this building. It has long been used to hold malcontents, foreigners, and those who are too far gone in drink to be allowed to roam, a dismal place, with a heavy oak door, battered and bent. As I am pushed inside I see, in the darkness, two women waiting. I recognise one – the town midwife, a round woman with beefy arms, who looks at me now with contempt. The other is thin and pale, shaking, looking as if she will fall to the ground at any moment, her face as white and stiff as her plain Puritan collar.

'Mistress Spatchett, are you ready to proceed?' I start at the name. This must be the wife of Thomas Spatchett. I gaze hard at her but she does not lift her eyes to meet mine, and I wonder what her husband has said to persuade her to do this thing. Then the midwife nods for the guards to leave the room, and they shuffle outside. I can just hear their voices as they talk quietly to each other, the sound almost drowned by the screams and calls of seabirds circling high above.

The midwife steps forward and closes the door firmly, then rounds on me.

'Remove your clothes.' There is no escape. I unlace my bodice and drop it to the floor, loosen the ties on my skirt and let it fall, then stand in my shift, shivering, for although the day is warm, this room is icy cold.

'Get up on the table.' I do as she asks, sliding my body to lie along its length.

'I am employed to search your body for the marks of the Devil. If I find one I am to prick it to see if blood comes. If it does not, then that is deemed the mark of a witch. If you are no trouble it will be over quickly. But you can save yourself this pain. I can call Reverend Browne to hear your confession.' I shake my head. I dare not speak for fear my voice would fail me, I am so afraid. The midwife pulls up my shift and I lie naked under her gaze.

'Mistress Spatchett, you are to bear witness as you did with the other one. Move closer, you will not be able to see from there.' The midwife's voice is impatient and harsh. And the last thing I see, before the pain comes, is the face of Mary Spatchett, white and pinched, as she passes a sharp metal bodkin to the midwife with a shaking hand.

WHEN IT IS OVER THEY HAVE TO DRESS ME, FOR MY HANDS TREMBLE SO much I cannot manage for myself. My body is stinging and raw, the shift spattered with blood, and I feel dizzy and light, as if I am no longer secured to the ground. When I am dressed the midwife opens the door and the guards enter, Thomas Spatchett hard on their heels. He does not glance at his wife, who stands nervously, biting her lip but stands at a distance from me, hope written large on his face.

'Did she confess?'

The midwife drops a brief curtsey.

'She did not, Sir, and I could find no marks of the Devil on her body. Those marks that were there bled, as is natural. I have found no evidence that she is a witch.'

His grunt of disappointment rattles loud in the damp room.

'Very well, she will have to be watched, for a confession I will have. And what of the other one? Any marks on her?' I prick up my ears.

'No, Sir, her neither. No evidence there.' The midwife stands uncomfortably, waiting for his reply. His wife keeps her head bowed, subservient and respectful as a good Christian wife should be, but fear seeps from her. I despise them all. Thomas Spatchett pulls himself up and turns on his heel. He does not offer his wife his arm, it is as if she doesn't exist. She follows meekly behind him, but he is so tied up with this matter, his mind so focused on this one thing, that he does not even acknowledge her. Nothing will stop him now, he is not a man to be defeated. There is worse to come. It has all been done with ruthless efficiency. As I am returned to the cell, faint and bleeding, Priscilla is taken away. I do not see her again for three nights and three days.

Priscilla is broken and raving when the guards return her to the cell. They have left a jug of brackish water and a stale loaf. I trickle some water into her mouth to try and revive her, soaking the hard bread before putting it to her lips, but she is unable to eat. She does not look at me, does not speak, and I dare not ask her what they have done. Very soon she closes her eyes and falls into a troubled sleep.

Then they come for me.

THE GUARDS TAKE ME BACK TO THE SAME ROOM WITH THE OLD OAK door. The table has gone and a chair has been placed in the centre of the floor. There is a large pool of wet under it and, as they push me closer and the stench fills my nostrils, I realise what it is, and terror engulfs me. I try to push against them but they are too strong. I am forced to sit. My hands are tied behind the back of the chair and my ankles bound to the legs with ropes, so tight they burn. They pull my skirts up above my knees and I shudder with fear and humiliation. Then, footsteps.

'Elizabeth Southerne . . .' I look up through unkempt hair.

Thomas Spatchett stands before me, the town bailiffs on either side, the Reverend Browne a few steps behind, a bible under his arm and a spotless white kerchief to his nose. Master Spatchett's face is shuttered and hard and his scar twists red in the half-light that filters through a plain glass window. This room was once a place of God. It is now a place of suffering. '. . . you have been brought here to be watched. You are accused as a witch and we search for proof. If found, you will face the full might of the law. The Lord will judge your innocence or guilt. We look to see if – when – your imps come to suckle from you. The pain will be severe and it will give me no satisfaction to see you so troubled, so I give you the opportunity to confess, in order that you might avoid this ordeal.' His words sound kind but he lies. This does give him pleasure – I can see it glitter in his eyes.

I look hard at him and he pulls back.

'I confess nothing.' He sighs dramatically and glances down at a paper he holds in his hand – it is trembling, whether with fear or anger I know not.

'Elizabeth Southerne, you have been accused by Priscilla Collit of witchcraft. Her statement, made under oath and in the sight of God, is that you and she fell out around one year ago. That two nights after this falling out she sent an imp in the form of a crabfish to torment you and that she knew it had nipped you and drawn blood, for the imp told her that you used this blood to seal a pact with the Devil.' He pauses and draws a breath which whistles slightly through gapped teeth. 'She claims the Devil speaks to her. She says that he went to you in the night and lay with you as a husband. That he promised he would help you and guide you home, you being a pedlar, and wont to roam around the countryside. Mistress Collit says that she witnessed you meeting the Devil again this midsummer last, on the Heath, by a whitethorn, as you walked to Westleton, and that she heard him promise you two shillings and sixpence the next time you came by, but that he did not give you the coins, instead complaining of the hardness of the times. She has confirmed that you made this covenant with Satan four years since, but that it was to last fourteen.'

I look at him in confusion and anger. These accusations make no sense, they are the ramblings of a madwoman. But then I think of Priscilla, of what she must have endured. Three days and three nights – she would confess to anything. And I can see some elements of truth in what she said, how her mind had retained things, then twisted them. The walks to Westleton, the crabfish we bought on the beach. My lying with her husband...

'Do you confess? Come, woman, speak.'

I look him full in the face.

'I have done nothing wrong. I will not confess.'

Twenty-four hours was all it took to break me.

YOU CANNOT KNOW THE PAIN OF THE WATCHING. YOU THINK IT TO BE a little thing, that you will endure, but your arms and legs stiffen quickly and the burning of your joints becomes all you can think about. The guards watch your every move and if you should sleep they prod you, stand you up and walk you. Sometimes they just kick the chair and shout at you. The Reverend Browne and Thomas Spatchett are there at the start, when I am still defiant, still believing I would be able to bear it. But soon they and the bailiffs go, leaving the guards alone, and we all know how cruel men can be when they have all the power and no one to watch their actions. One guard is worse than the rest. I see him looking at me, watching my every move, and the look on his face warns me. After a while he moves across and grips my breasts, laughing, squeezing them so tight that tears fill my eyes. Then he rubs his hand between my legs, hard, all the time touching himself through his filthy britches. His face is flushed with ale and lust and he keeps coming back, the others merely smiling and nodding as if this was right and just.

Then, over the pain and humiliation, I feel a griping in my stomach and the more I fix on it the worse it becomes. I was determined to ask them for nothing, to show I could endure, but the cramping is too much.

'I need to relieve myself.' The men laugh and mutter to themselves. 'I beg of you, loosen me so that I may relieve myself.' They gaze at me with stony faces. I sit, sweating, as the feeling grows and takes me over. Then my bowels can hold out no longer and, face red with humiliation, I soil myself. I feel it soaking into my skirts; the stink of it fouls my nostrils and the shit burns my skin, and I have to endure the oaths and complaints from the men about the smell. My tormentor does not approach me again. But after many hours of sitting in one position, I no longer care about the smell or the humiliation, for the pain is everything. A woman comes in with food and ale for the men, but there is nothing for me, no one tends to me, save to untie me and walk me if my head lolls. I am so tempted to confess, to give them what they want, but then I think of Aubrey, of Priscilla, and our times together. I remember sunshine and showers, the sound of the sea, the wind in the marshes, the familiar smells of fish and tar and salt. I try to conjure it all in my mind, to take myself out of this place. And it works, for I fall into some kind of dream, floating above my body, trying not to look down, instead searching back into my memories for goodness, laughter and light. Then a stirring, a scrape of a chair on the packed earth floor brings me back into the room, my dream fractured. The guard is coming at me again, swaying in drink, this time fumbling with his breeches, and I think he intends to force me and I cannot bear it. I have never known fear like it and I scream in terror. Laughing, he gets his pintle out and pisses on me.

Within moments the door creaks open and Thomas Spatchett and Reverend Browne stand before me. The guards quieten immediately and they have the grace to look shamefaced as Master Spatchett looks around. He does not seem to notice my tormentor hurriedly tying his breeches, or if he does, he chooses to ignore it. The Reverend moves forward and cups his hand under my chin, his gaze soft as if with understanding, although his mouth is pursed in distaste.

'Does the Devil torment you, my child? Such screaming . . .' I want to tell him how the men have abused me, but I know they will deny all. I will not be believed, so I stay silent. 'If you have done wrong, tell us now, clear your conscience. Was it the Devil who ordered you not to confess?' My head slips from his grasp and he turns to Master Spatchett. 'There, a nod of the head I think. Satan has commanded her not to speak. So she must remain here – we must have her confession.' Thomas Spatchett nods grimly. And then, a pain so severe it takes my breath away. I twist in my chair as my hip goes into spasm, sharp stabs of agony causing me to rear up, my chair nearly overturning and taking me with it. The Reverend pulls back, clapping his hand over his nose at the stench that rises from me.

'See, the Devil moves in her!'

And his words, the smell, and the agony of my twisted limbs, the humiliation, the terror and the thought of further watching are more than I can bear.

So I confess.

CHAPTER 13

They bring in the clerk to take down my words. His nib flies, black and spidery, as the lies tangle the page. When it is all recorded and they are satisfied that they have me, the guards carry me back to the gaol, for my body fails me. I am dragged across the marketplace, the crowds stopping to stare at me. There are a few muttered curses, one man spits at me, another throws a stone, but there is no roaring or screaming as there was before. It is as if they know what has been done to me, and feel some slight shame and fear. As if they realise that if I can be accused then so could they.

The cell, when they push me back in, is cold and dark and I sink to my knees, the pain in my joints screaming in protest. My whole body is shaking. I slump sideways onto the straw, trying to straighten my arms and legs, my shoulders and knees searing at the slightest movement.

I hear a rustling and see Priscilla crawling towards me, pain etched on her face. She pulls the jug of water carefully towards us, cupping her palms and moistening my lips. It is hard to drink from her hands, and water soaks my chin, but enough goes in to begin to revive me.

I nod my thanks for I cannot speak. I take more water from her and it gradually eases the dry, burning roughness in my throat and I find my voice again. It is harsh and croaking.

'Thank you. Oh, Priscilla, I do not know how you survived for three days and nights.'

She closes her eyes, her face blank. I do not expect her to reply but she does.

'It was as if I was not there, I was floating above my body, watching, and there was no pain. I thought I was an angel, I could feel my wings beating, hear the heavenly trumpets. There was light and peace and it was wonderful, and then, coming towards me I could see an angel bearing a babe. It was my Edward, swaddled all in white, but just as I reached out to hold him he called to me again and I fell back down to earth.'

'Who called to you?' I know how she will answer.

'Satan. He is my protector now.' She is matter of fact.

'They read me your evidence. Why did you say such things? None of it is true, you must know that. Was it to be revenged on me for being with John?' The speaking of his name freezes the dank air and she looks away. 'Priscilla, it was one moment of madness that I regretted as soon as it was over. I will never forgive myself for it. I wronged you in the worst way possible, but to accuse me like this, and of such wicked things . . .'

But my words are like water on stone, sliding off her, for she has gone into herself again. She no longer knows me. Then, as I watch her closely, something changes in her, and the old Priscilla appears again behind her eyes. I clasp her hand tightly.

'Priscilla, why have you done this?'

'Elizabeth?' She touches my face with her hand, gently, and I cover hers with mine.

'Why did you confess?'

'I confessed to nothing. I just told them the truth.' My heart sinks. 'I told them how the Devil said I must do away with my children, else I would always remain poor. I had to tell someone.' She is on the verge of tears and my heart goes out to her 'So I told them what I did to my little Edward . . . about the fire. I had to. You do not know what it has been like, Bess. I see his tiny face and hear his screams every night in my dreams, the torment never leaves me. I could bear it no longer. So I confessed all, and the relief is great.' She grips my hand hard, her face earnest. 'Now they know. I have passed the burden of it on to them and they must do with me what they will.'

'And when you tried to drown yourself? Did you speak of that?'

She looks at me in horror.

'I never tried to drown myself, Bess. To take your own life is a sin, all know that, I could never do such a thing. It would be wrong in the eyes of God.' She is genuinely shocked by my suggestion. 'Is that what you thought? I told you before why I did it all – 'twas the Devil ordered me to. It was my own fault that I did not follow his words, else I would have walked to Boston as he commanded.'

'Only our Lord walked on water – what you say is blasphemy. And to Lincolnshire . . . no one can walk that far.'

'He told me I could, and in two days. Why would he lie to me when I had sworn to serve him and carried out his wishes? I sent him to destroy a boat in Newcastle, for that Master Ward looked at me hard when I bought the crayfish from him, and I thought to have my revenge. The Devil said he had done it for me and promised to give me money, said he would leave me the shillings in a whin bush, and I looked and looked but I never found them. But you were there too, Elizabeth, you were with him, I saw you. Did you find them? Did you take my money from me?' Her hands begin to shake and her face twists in anger.

I back away, for I can see her rage growing.

'I never spoke to the Devil and I would never take your money. You have imagined this. Priss, we were friends, we shared everything

She laughs coarsely.

'We did – you think I have forgotten? I imagine nothing, nothing, d'you hear me?' She turns to me, mouth twisted in anger, eyes blank, and I see her wits are gone again.

'Is that why you have accused me? Because of John?' But as I say it I know it is not the reason. Priscilla truly believes that the Devil is protecting her and guiding her. In her mind, she flies like a witch, free and unharmed, safe in Satan's care.

THE FOLLOWING NIGHT, AS DARKNESS FALLS, THERE IS A SCRATCHING at the bars of the window. Priscilla does not look up but I do, waiting for a torrent of abuse, a mess of nightsoil to be pushed through the bars, but there is just silence. I move slowly to the window. The stone is cold as I lay my face against it and listen – I can hear breathing, just the other side. Then, a hiss that forms my name and I take a chance, pushing my face to the bars. In the gloom, I make out a small figure pressed hard against the flint wall by the window and fear falls from me.

'Aubrey, is it really you?'

'Elizabeth, yes, I have brought some cheese and meat for you both. I did not know if they would feed you. How do you fare?' She comes close to the bars and I see her face, pale and drawn in the twilight, hear a rustling sound as a small package, wrapped in cloth, is pushed towards me.

'You should not be here, it is not safe. If they see you here they will seize you too.'

'I had to come. Is Priscilla . . . ?'

'She is well . . . in body, anyway.' I glance over my shoulder. Priscilla sits gazing blankly into the darkness of the cell. 'Oh, Aubrey, her mind has completely gone. Sometimes she is herself, but then . . . She has told them all manner of things, made mad accusations, confessed to wild imaginings that no sane person would believe.'

'But they do believe it, Bess. I have heard that you are both to stand trial at Bury St Edmunds. There is to be an assize, where others accused as witches will be tried, you are to be taken there.'

'Then we are damned. How can we survive such a thing?' My heart sinks. 'Aubrey, you must go. Please do not get caught on our account, I could not live with myself if I thought you had also come to harm.'

'The guard is sleeping soundly enough. This is the first time he does, though. I came yesterday but he saw me, so I thought it best to wait. Is there anything I can do for you?'

'Tend my cottage while I am gone and if I do not come back...'

'Do not speak like that Bess. I will pray for your safe return, and who knows what will happen?'

'If I do not come back, then my cottage is yours. There is brick under the hearth – coins are hidden there. Have them. You have been a good and faithful friend and you deserved better from me. Take it all as my gift and remember me favourably.'

She glances behind her at a creaking and shuffling.

'I must go, the guard is stirring. Oh, Bess, be brave and look after Priscilla, for she needs you now more than ever.' Her voice breaks and I push my cold fingers through the bars. She entwines them in hers and I draw strength from her.

'God go with you, Aubrey, and thank you for everything. I am sorry I have not been a better friend, but I will care for Priss and it may be that we will all be together again sometime.'

'God go with you too, Bess, and my love to Priscilla. I will not forget you, either of you. Be brave, be strong and...'

'Hey, what are you doing there?' Aubrey's fingers pull away sharply, and I hear the swish of her cloak as she disappears into the darkness.

I divide the cheese and meat between us and we chew slowly, unspeaking, I with my thoughts, Priscilla deep in her own darkness.

. . .

Another day passes, then another, light falling to dark, the sounds of the town rising and falling with it. Stale bread and water are brought to us each day by the guard, who slams the dish down onto the hard-packed floor, spitting on it as he leaves. We eat and drink only from habit, our appetites gone. Terror has seen to that. Then, when I have lost count of the days, a rattle of keys as the door is flung open and the gaoler comes in.

'You are to be taken to the assize.' I look at him in terror. 'The magistrate has your confessions, it has all been taken down. You're to be taken to Bury. Cart comes tomorrow. I've been told to make you ready.'

He steps forward, reaching into his jerkin and, to my horror, produces a small sharp knife – its blade glints as it catches the morning sun that cracks through the bars. Priscilla's eyes widen in fear and she pushes herself back against the wall as he moves towards her.

I reach out an arm to stop him and he pulls away from me with a shudder of disgust.

'Whatever you are here to do, do it to me before her.' He pauses, then nods and I stand with my head bowed, waiting, breath held, heart pounding. He looks at me with contempt then moves behind me, and I brace myself. His hand grasps my hair and pulls on it, holding it tight in his fist and I feel my scalp burning as, with a fast sawing motion, he hacks away. The pain is so intense I jerk, and I feel the knife nick me, a warm trickle of blood running down my neck, so I try to keep myself still as he does his work. He throws handfuls of hair to the floor then turns.

'Now you.' I see Priscilla flinch as he grabs her. I have a flash of memory, her hair flying out behind her, so thick and fine, shining gold in the sunlight, as we danced together on the beach, hand in hand. Priss, Aubrey and me – young and free, lithe and happy. So long ago. Now he saws at her hair and it falls in sheets to the damp earth as he cuts close to her head. Splatters of blood mingle with the gold as she bucks and struggles under his grasp. Then it is done. Hair litters the straw, dark under blonde, and we look at each other in disbelief. I have never been vain, have never cared overmuch for my appearance, but now I feel naked and inhuman. I put my hand to my scalp – it is sharp with bristles, sticky with blood, and my head is cold and light, the constant weight of my hair now gone.

I look down at the pile of hair and then up at the gaoler.

'Why?'

He holds his head up, self-important, superior.

'To keep the crawlers to a minimum. And anyway, what would you want with hair where you are going? Not like anyone will look at you again.' He wipes the knife on his jerkin and puts it away. 'I am to clean you up. The carter comes at dawn tomorrow. They want rid of you while the town is quiet – can't afford any more upset than you have already caused.'

He is gone a short while, then comes back with a pail of water, a cloth for washing, and clothes that have clearly been stored in the damp, for they are sticky and smell of mould. But they are better than the soiled garments we wear and, when I am sure he has gone, I strip off and clean myself, then turn to Priscilla. She does not stir so I remove her clothes and rub her body with the damp cloth, careful with the bruises and welts where the ropes burned her during the watching. This act seems to revive her a little and we take it in turns to rub the cloth gently over each other's heads to rid ourselves of the dried blood, then put on the clothes. There are two shifts, spotted and yellowed with age, but clean; grey linen skirts, two old bodices, stained under the armpits, and crumpled coifs. We dress as best we can. The coifs cover up our scabbed scalps but my head still feels light and unfamiliar, as if I am not myself anymore. We look down at our reflections in the brown water. We are drab and drained where once we were full of colour and laughter. We look old and haggard, our bodies pained by the searching, stooped by the watching.

We look like witches.

CHAPTER 14

The cart is empty when it arrives just before dawn the next morning. Priscilla has said nothing since our heads were shaved, just stares into space, seemingly unaware as they tie our hands in front of us and lift us into the back, like hogs taken to market. We sit side by side on the bench, trying to keep our balance, as the cart pulls away from the gaol door, lurching wildly. The carter is flanked by two guards, large cudgels in their belts, who stare ahead, saying nothing. A few bystanders have assembled, even at this early hour, and they throw muck and jeer at us as we move away, the horses clopping along the cobbled streets until they reach the lane where sand softens the sound. The sun begins to come out and dew sparkles on the branches and leaves. The air is warming fast and the smell of dust promises the heat to come. A perfect summer's day, except that we are being taken as witches to meet our deaths. The horses heave and snort as the cart pulls up the slope towards the Leper Hospital and then speeds up as it moves along the lane. I close my eyes in case I catch sight of my cottage, for I could not bear to see it.

Then, from below me, on the path, a voice.

'God be with you and protect you. I will pray for you.' I open my eyes. Aubrey is trotting beside the cart, her face tear-stained.

I nudge Priscilla.

'Look, Priss, Aubrey is here.' But she does not stir, her eyes stay blank, and I turn back to Aubrey. 'You must go, keep yourself close and safe, there is still danger here for you. Folk will remember how you were seized, how we were friends.' The guards are turning in their seats now, alerted by our voices.

'I will look after your cottage, Bess, for when you return.' I smile my thanks and reach towards her outstretched hand, but one of the guards leans forwards and I pull back hurriedly. He turns to Aubrey, his cudgel raised above her head.

'Go on, get out of here, lest I use this on you!' He glares at her and her face tightens in fear. She drops back and stands still, small and slight in the morning sunshine, and the last thing I see is her arm raised in farewell as her shape shrinks and blurs.

I look around me as the cart moves across the heath towards Westleton. I have trod this road so many times, it is as familiar as my own hand and I try to imagine myself free, as I was, walking with my pack on my back, off to sell my needles and thread on a bright summer's morn. I never thought of any danger then, save pickpockets and rogues on the road, and they saw me as one of their own and left me alone. I never imagined the danger would come from my own home, my own friend, that it would be from words rather than deeds. I try to remember better times, the pull of the wandering, meeting new people, being welcomed, as the movement of the cart lulls me gently back into my memories and my eyes close.

A LOUD CRY FROM THE CARTER MAKES ME JUMP AND MY EYES FLY open. There is a grinding of wheels on earth and the cart suddenly stops. My mind is muddled and slow with sleep as I watch another woman being pushed up into the cart. She is small and gnarled with a brown, sun-wrinkled face and a cloud of white hair. I look around in confusion, thinking I had been asleep for a longer time, but I see we have only reached Westleton, its houses clustered around the village green. I have been here many times, and always welcomed, but now the faces of those who stand silently watching are hard and grim.

The old woman looks at us, sharp as a bird, as she is hefted up onto the back of the cart. She settles herself opposite us. Her hands are bound like mine and she is strangely composed. I look at her, then look again.

'Mistress Tooley?'

She peers hard at me with pale eyes dull, then her sunken face lightens in recognition.

'Mistress Southerne? The pedlar-woman?' I nod. 'Well, I never thought to see you in such a sorry state.'

'Nor I you, Mistress. These are hard times indeed.'

The guard at the front turns in his seat.

'Quiet! We will not have you gossiping and spreading your evil here.'

We both look down in silence and the cart rattles on. When it is safer, when our voices are drowned by the rumbling of the cart and the guards are talking, she speaks softly to me again.

'Mistress Southerne.'

'Elizabeth, please call me Elizabeth.'

'And I am Kathryn. What have they done to your hair?' Her eyes are piercing and I put my hand to the grubby coif self-consciously.

'They said it was to prepare us . . .'

She puffs out a breath of anger.

'It was done to humiliate you, is all. This is what men do when they are given a little power over such as we.' Her voice is educated and precise. 'And what of your friend? Is she not well?' I hesitate, not wishing the men sitting up at the front of the cart to hear, but then realise that they will already know of our supposed crimes.

'She is Priscilla Collit. She has been unwell.' I hesitate. 'She is not always in her wits, and she has not taken this well.'

Kathryn laughs roughly.

'Few have my dear, few have. What do they say you have done?'

I look around me and lower my voice to a whisper.

'Witchcraft. It was Priscilla, her mind is gone since her babe died, and she told them that we had both signed a pact with the Devil, but the things she spoke of did not make sense.'

'None of this makes sense, my dear. It is all madness.'

I look at Kathryn Tooley. She was once a smiling friendly woman, who always had a good word and a few coins for me. There was no harm in her and I wonder why she has been taken. I lean forward.

'And you – how are you accused?'

She purses her lips and laughs.

'They caught me talking to my pups. I'd not had them long, Jackly and Pybold I called them. They were about to be drowned, the farmer had no need of them, but I rescued them, thought to have them for company.' Her voice softens. 'And they were such good companions. Never had any children of my own, and those little dogs were so loving, so loyal. I would cosset them and talk to them and I'm sure they knew what I was saying. I could see it in their eyes. Such soft little things they were. But fierce too, sometimes – they would bark like Old Nick himself if they were roused.' She laughs at the memory then her face darkens. ''Twas our minister, Reverend Driver . . .' She pauses and spits over the side of the cart. 'He came across us as he rode on the heath, raised his whip to me, and Jackly set to howling and barking so hard, snapping at his horse's hooves, that it reared and the minister was nearly unseated. I couldn't help but laugh.' She smiles, remembering, then her smile fades. 'It was the undoing of me. He followed me home and had me seized – him, a minister of God. He told them that poor Jackly was an imp that I had sent to strike him and his horse dead, that I was in league with the Devil, and that I made a pact in blood with him. Such nonsense and I told them so. Then the Reverend made up some tale about Jackly telling me that he would steal some money for me and that was it, they took me. And those poor creatures, they did no one any harm...'

'Who cares for them now?' She looks at me and her mouth quivers.

'Hanged. They took them out and hanged them before my eyes. Two innocent pups that were only protecting me. I cannot forget their expressions at the last, when the men grabbed them – they looked at me to save them, but I could not, for I was hog-tied and held fast. All I could do was watch, and the men even held my head to make sure I did not look away.'

I reach out my bound hands to hers.

'I am sorry.'

She brushes tears away with the back of a wrinkled hand.

'Nothing to live for now they have gone. I am too old and tired of life. They searched me and found nothing so they watched me. Six hours and the pain was too much. So I told them what they wanted to hear and I am glad, for death will come now, but at least it will be quick.'

'We may yet be acquitted...' My voice lacks any conviction.

'We may, and my pups may still be alive, and the world may still be a good place for women such as us.' She rubs her eyes with bound fists and falls silent.

THE DAY WARMS. DUST LIFTS FROM THE ROAD IN CLOUDS AS WE trundle on. Flies buzz around us and we swipe them away as best we can but, as the heat grows, more and more come, drawn by the smell of us. The sun is high in the clear blue sky when we pull to a halt in Yoxford and I watch as swallows dart and dive overhead. A group of townsfolk wait for us outside the inn, holding fast to a thin woman who has her hands bound behind her back. She is unable to climb up into the cart, so two men seize her shoulders and ankles and throw her into the back like a sack of grain. She flinches as she falls to the hard wooden floor but says nothing, making no sound.

The carter and guards jump down, take mugs of ale that are proffered by the crowd, and drink thirstily. One guard comes forward with a jug of stale water and passes it between us. We drink greedily then slump back into our places, wiping our mouths with the backs of our hands as best we can. It is midday, the air hot and not so fresh here inland. The guards clamber back up onto their bench as the carter picks up the reigns and clicks the horses forward.

The cart rumbles on as we sit and stare at the new woman. I think I have seen her on my visits to Yoxford, but my mind is so muddled now I am not sure. She slowly pulls herself upright and looks around at us.

Kathryn is the first to speak.

'What is your name, my dear?'

The woman looks at her hesitantly.

'Maria Clowes.' Her voice is high-pitched and childlike, and she has one of those faces that is ageless. She is neat and tidy and seems unharmed, unlike Priscilla and me.

'Are you also accused as a witch? How did it happen to you?'

She chews at her lip.

'Worse. They accused me of murdering a neighbour. They say I will certainly hang.' Her voice catches and she begins to shake. 'I did not do it. She was old and ill and fit to die anyway. I just tried to help her with herbs and simples, but none worked, so they seized me. When I heard of what they do to get a confession I knew I would not be able to bear it, so I told them that the Devil came to me in the shape of a little boy, and that he sent imps to me, but that I did not use them. I was so afraid. I confessed to save myself the pain.' She lowers her head. 'I am ashamed of it.'

I turn to her.

'Have I not seen you before? I am Elizabeth Southerne, the pedlar-woman.'

Her face lightens with recognition.

'Yes, I remember. Last summer. I was going to buy ribbons from you, but my husband saw you off. He thought they were frivolous, ungodly. I remember...'

'And what of your husband? Did he not speak up for you when the men came?'

Maria looks hard at me.

'He did not. He believed all they said, told them that he had suspected I was a witch, but that I had cast a spell over him so he could not leave. He has long hated me. Nothing I could do would please him – I tried to be a good wife – but to be accused by your neighbours, those you considered your friends, and then your own husband – it is so shameful.'

Kathryn leans forward.

'There is no shame there, my dear, no shame at all. We all do what we have to do to survive, to avoid pain and suffering. It is the natural way. You are not the only one to confess to things they did not do.' Maria nods, but drops her head, still biting at her lip. As the cart goes over a bump in the road, her teeth jar and a trickle of blood flowers and trails thinly down her chin.

IT IS LATE IN THE EVENING, BEGINNING TO GET DARK, BUT THERE IS still warmth in the air. This August has been so very dry, and dust is everywhere. We have been travelling since dawn, with stops to load more women into the cart, and we are filthy, thirsty and hungry, but the guards have told us that it will be a further day before we reach Bury St Edmunds.

Some hours later the cart stops at a tavern. We are taken to a poor place at the back, next to the midden heap, a dark barn with no window, that has been used for cattle judging by the stink of it. But there is a pail in the corner where we can relieve ourselves, and the straw is fairly clean. I help Priscilla to lie down and we all settle as night falls. The guards have untied us and given us ale and stale hard bread which we swallow gratefully, for our stomachs growl. But all night they pace outside, the creaking of their uniforms, footsteps and muttered comments keeping us from sleep, until, through the wooden slats of the barn, I see the sky lightening. Then, footsteps, a rattle, as the door is unbolted and a man brings a jug of water and some more stale bread. We scuffle to eat, use the pail, and straighten our clothes before we are pushed outside, our hands re-tied, and we are lifted back onto the cart.

Villagers have gathered to peer at us and they walk round and round the cart, staring at us in silence. Their faces are frozen, expressionless, but I see, down by their skirts, some of the women move their fingers and thumb to make the old sign against witchcraft. Then, a gathering of reins, a clicking noise, and the horses pull away, drawing us towards our fate. The guards sit up beside the carter, alert and stiff as the miles roll away under the wheels. Today is even more hot and dusty than yesterday, and we no longer have the strength to speak to each other, so we just gaze around dully as the farmland passes. They stop the cart at midday to give us small nubs of bread and some dusty ale, then let us relieve ourselves behind a bush. We are all aware of the guard's eyes on us, the cudgels held ready, but we are too tired and weak to run. As I clamber back up onto the cart I look at Priscilla, who seems not to care as the guard pushes her roughly up beside me. Her eyes are glazed and I realise that she has not looked up and has barely eaten. And she has not spoken a word.

THERE IS ANOTHER NIGHT, ANOTHER TAVERN, ANOTHER FILTHY BARN before Bury St Edmunds emerges from a soft morning mist, high church towers pointing heavenwards. It promises to be a beautiful day, the sun warming on our backs, the sky a limitless blue; the sort of day that brings hope, but we on the cart have none. I expected them to take us to the centre of town, but the cart makes a sudden turn on the outskirts, taking a narrow track onto farmland, then grinds to a halt outside a large barn.

'What is this?' Maria looks around in fear, we all do, for this is not as we expected. 'Surely we are not to die here?'

The guards jump down from their post, cudgels brandished, and start to pull us off the back of the cart. I land hard on the packed earth, jarring my ankle, as a guard moves behind me and, with an efficient sweep of his knife, cuts the ropes that bind me. I rub at my wrists which are raw and bleeding, then pull myself up and turn to help Priscilla. She takes my hand and struggles to a stand, but there is no recognition in her eyes. The guard cuts her bindings and I squeeze her hand and wait.

When we are all assembled, our arms untied, a guard turns to us.

'You are to be kept in this barn until your trial. Town gaol's full. Witches everywhere it seems.' He cackles with laughter as they drive us along, harrying us with their cudgels if we do not move quickly enough for their liking. There are many more people outside the black wooden doors of the barn, and more carts arriving as we are pushed into the barn. It is immense. Beams arc hammer-like high above our heads, strips of sunlight quivering through the wood-slatted walls. Dust eddies in shafts of yellow light, rising and falling as the barn fills. High above my head all is beauty and peace, but here on the ground the sunlight only serves to highlight a grey-brown mass that ebbs and flows like a summer river, slow and dark. People. Mostly old, mostly women, a vast throng of humanity dressed as we are, in filthy clothes, rags and castoffs. Many are already slumped around the walls, and few talk; most just groan or are silent. The four of us walk close together and find a space, and I support Priscilla, helping her down to sit. Kathryn and Maria flop down beside me.

'I did not expect this.' Kathryn looks around.

'So many . . .' Maria gazes, horror written on her face. 'Are they all accused as we are? Surely this cannot be right?' I look around at the faces. A few meet my eye but most sit, heads bowed. We are all the same, women of middle years, some much older. We are ordinary, the type of woman that you would not chance to look at in a marketplace or church. We have been taken in various states of dress. Some are still in shifts, some huddling into cloaks, most, like me, are dressed for the house, not outside. And as I look around I see that many, many bear the scars of the searching – the tell-tale pinpricks of blood on wounds not yet healed, bruises, some yellowing, some fresh-made. Most move awkwardly, with bodies that are stiffened and bent by the watching and a few, like Priscilla and me, have had their hair shorn away, scratched scalps shining pink through the tufts. I reach for my coif and pull it down tight over my head, then turn to Priscilla. I gaze at her in sorrow, this little bird so broken and damaged, and I slide my hands from her coif to smooth her cheeks, brushing away the dust and grime. At that moment, her face clears and her eyes, once so blue and sparkling, hold mine. She holds her hands to her mouth as she coughs, the air pricking her throat.

'Bess? Bess, is it you? What are we doing here? Who are all these people?' She clutches my arm, terror tightening her grasp, and my eyes fill with tears. I cannot answer her, for how can I explain this? I hug her to me, so pleased to have her back, if only for a moment, and we sit and wait as the barn heats up and the groaning grows.

CHAPTER 15

It is nightfall before the carts stop arriving. More women, a few men, all bewildered and confused, are pushed into the already-full barns. There is no food, no water, and nowhere to relieve ourselves, so we all manage as best we can in the corners of the barn, which soon begin to reek. The heat rises, the sheer number of bodies making it hard to breathe, and the stink of all that humanity thrust together in a small space becomes all-pervading. We find it best to sit with our aprons or skirts covering our noses, breathing slowly. It is quiet now, apart from the occasional sob, and it is that silence that frightens me the most. For it is a sign that we have all given up. We have no control; we have assumed hunched positions as if waiting for the next blow to fall. After a while, I seem to drift into a fitful sleep, Priscilla's head on my lap, but I am aware of every movement, the shuffling, shrieks or groans. Priscilla's cough seems to have worsened with the lack of fresh air in this place and I rub her back to soothe her, then drift off again when she quietens.

August nights are short and the morning soon dawns, showing slivers of pink and gold through the slats of the barn. There is a knot hole just behind where we are sitting and I push my nose to it, pulling at the fresh air like a newly-landed fish. Kathryn and Maria still sleep but Priscilla is awake.

'Look, Priss, it's morning.' I put my arm around her shoulders and guide her towards the knot hole. 'Push your face there, see, the air is fresh and clean. That's it, take deep breaths, it will ease your chest.' She leans into me, resting her face against the rough-hewn wood, her thin body rising and falling as she breathes deeply. She coughs and I feel every movement of her ribs against mine – it is as if she has become part of me. When I release her she sits upright, her back against the wooden wall, then turns to me, her eyes clear.

'What is happening to us, Bess?'

I swallow and take her hands in mine.

'We have been seized as witches.'

She looks around in horror.

'All these? Everyone one of us?'

'They have brought us to Bury St Edmunds where they are to put us on trial. They will hear the evidence against us and they will decide what to do with us.'

She pulls back her hands.

'They will hang us.' It is not a question. 'And it was my fault. I told them how the Devil came to me... how you met with him... but what of Aubrey – what has become of her?' She looks around wildly.

'She is safe, she was not seized.'

'How could I have told them that after you have done so much for me? I am so sorry, Bess.'

I put my fingers to her lips to silence her. Her eyes are full of fear as she gazes back at me and, all of a sudden, I wish that she was *not* in her right mind, that she did not know what was happening, for I do not know how she will be able to bear what is to come.

'Hush, speak of it no more.' I look around but no one is listening. No one seems to care, all are buried in themselves, waiting resignedly. 'Priscilla, say nothing more. Whatever you are asked, say nothing, for any mention of *him*...' I cannot bring myself to say the name, even in this place. '. . . it will make matters far worse for all of us. You will damn us all if you talk of him in this place. You must never speak of him again.'

She nods and squeezes my hand.

'I am glad we are together, Bess.'

There can be no escape from a place such as this, not when matters have gone this far. But now I have one thing, a thing which I thought was lost to me forever. I have my friend back again; for that, my confession was worthwhile.

People around us are just beginning to stir when a loud clattering and shouting outside brings us to our feet. The whole room stands as one, fear etched fine on every face. We cling to each other, holding hands with strangers, joined by terror. A sliding of bolts, a clashing of metal and the huge barn doors grate open. We all blink against the light that floods in and we hear the men outside coughing and swearing at our state. The stench dissipates slowly as the barn is flooded with fresh air and we all gasp gratefully, breathing deeply.

A burly man steps into the doorway, flanked by guards, his stave of office held firmly in his hands. He looks over the crowd, an expression of distaste curling his mouth, then, without moving his head, he clicks his fingers. A clerk in a black gown, a white kerchief held to his nose, appears from behind him, clutching papers. The burly man snatches them and glances down, then throws his head back. His voice is loud and deep with authority, his face stern and unbending.

'You are to come forward when I call out the name of your village or town. Other than that, no one is to move or speak. The barn is surrounded by armed guards, and you cannot escape, so no point in trying.' He looks down at the parchment in his hand and begins. 'Stowmarket, Framlingham, Halesworth, Metfield . . .' He pauses as people begin to shuffle slowly to the doorway, pushing their way through the crowds, shading their eyes against the bright light. Guards move forward and they are taken away, I cannot see where. There is a pause as the bodies in the barn thin a little and then the list of names starts up again. I turn to Priscilla and grip her hand firmly in mine, then feel Maria and Kathryn at my side, gripping my arms. We stand there, frozen in fear, holding each other and waiting. And then it comes. 'Yoxford, Westleton...' The names are so familiar, the villages so close and I hold my breath. 'Long Melford...'

Priscilla and I look at each other in confusion.

'Did he say it? Did he call Dunwich?'

I think that, in my fear, I have missed it, but she shakes her head. 'He did not.'

I look at Kathryn and Maria who are stepping away from us, trembling and clutching hard at each other. We seem to have been together forever, although it is only two days, and their loss comes sharp. I clasp their hands then loosen them and their fingers slip cold and trembling through mine.

'God be with you both. I will pray for you, pray that you are acquitted.'

Kathryn laughs grimly. 'Save your prayers, my dear, keep them for yourself.' She moves towards us and clasps us both against her scrawny chest. 'God be with you too. I am glad that we met. I am glad to have known you.' I see her eyes fill with tears as she pulls away, clasping Maria's arm tightly as they move into the sunlight. The last I see of them, through shimmering vision are two small bodies surrounded by men who spirit them away.

As the carts rumble away one after the other, we look around, confused. There must have been near on two hundred people here overnight, but they have only taken half away. Surely we are not to remain here? We are all thinking the same thing, the silence turning into a susurration of whispered questions, then the burly guard steps forward, his figure tall and black against the sunlit doorway.

'Silence! You are not to speak. Those taken are for today's trial. You will be tried tomorrow.' I look around in despair – another day and a night in this place, in this heat, will be unbearable. But he hasn't finished. 'You remaining prisoners are to be taken to the gaol in town where you can be held securely. That way they can bring you up to the courtroom quickly, for there are many cases to be heard.' It does not make sense – why move us, when this barn was thought to be secure enough yesterday? But there is a different sense today, the air tight with urgency and worry, and I wonder what has happened. I do not have time to think on it for guards appear from nowhere, move forward, and we are pushed towards more waiting wagons. It is done quickly and efficiently. They handle us with no care, old or young all treated with the same disdain and cruelty. We are packed into the wagons like fish in a barrel, barely room to breathe, and I hold on tight to Priscilla for fear we become separated. Her eyes have glazed again and, as I hold her hands, I see her brow is sheened with sweat, her cheeks flushed with fever. I can do nothing for her save stay with her and hold her, and I do not let her go.

Finally, the procession of wagons begins to move away and the barn slowly recedes into the distance. The farmland around us shimmers with heat, and the horses swish their tails and flick their eyes at flies, their shabby coats constantly twitching. It could be an ordinary day at home, everyone waiting to bring in the harvest. People would be arriving in the fields with tankards, jugs of ale, bread, meat and cheese wrapped in clean cloths; men stripping off to harvest the barley, shouldering their scythes, women and children readying themselves to follow and collect the gleanings. It could be any summer. I have seen many and each seems more glorious than the last. But this one is in another time and another place, it is full of fear and resignation. It is not a field that we are headed to but a town of tall buildings, densely packed, and thick with people. It is a place of walls and gates, of confinement. And the scythe that will sweep through us, through this town, is one of death.

BURY GAOL IS WORSE THAN EVER I FEARED. IT IS PARTLY BELOW ground, the steps to it so green and slippery that, as we are pushed down, we have to hold on tight to the walls and each other to stop ourselves from falling. The grey stone walls run wet, while black mould plasters the cracks. The floor is damp earth and the cells feel bitterly cold, despite the heat of the day. We are pushed inside until each cell is fit to bursting. A narrow window high up in one wall, at eye level, gives a view of the road outside, and we can see the feet of people passing, their steps quick and hurried. The women in the cell push towards it, stretching their hands through the bars to the passers-by, begging for food and help, but their entreaties go unnoticed, save for the occasional oath or spray of spittle. For once we are glad of the proximity of the others packed into this place, and we huddle against each other seeking warmth and strength.

Priscilla is shivering constantly now, I do not know whether through fear or fever. It seems an age before a gaoler brings baskets of coarse burned bread with a pail of stale, fetid water, and it is as if we suddenly turn into rabid dogs, tearing at each other in our haste to get to the food, shovelling it into our mouths as fast as we can before it is snatched from our grasp. I manage to pass some to Priscilla, but it falls from her hand and is scooped up in an instant by an old woman who has failed to reach the baskets. Punches are thrown, curses and obscenities exchanged, and the cell becomes a mass of bestial humanity, everyone struggling for their very existence. When the bread has gone, the last of the water licked up from the ground where it has spilt, we look at each other, shame-faced at what we have been reduced to, but each knowing full well that we would do it again in a heartbeat.

. . .

GRADUALLY THE CELL SILENCES AS THE DAY LENGTHENS INTO NIGHT. It is quieter outside too, the noise of the market and carts halted by the darkness. But there is still a sense in the air, a feeling of tension, and it is not just us here in the gaol, it is outside too. It's in the voices of the men who walk briskly past, the footsteps of guards and soldiers, in the hushed whispers of the women who are returning home to their families and menfolk. Dragging Priscilla in my wake, I push my way through grey hunched figures, ignoring the mutterings, and thread my way to the window to peer through the bars. Someone is stood with his back against the wall outside, right in front of me. A man. I can only see his dusty boots, cared-for but worn, the heel lifting slightly from the upper, the stitching frayed. I reach out and carefully, hesitantly, tug at the leather. He kicks at my hand and I hear him snarl, but he does not move away.

'Sir? Please, Sir?' My voice is cracked but I raise it so he can hear. Inside the cell, all goes quiet. 'Sir, what is happening?' I see his ankles bend, then his haunches as he crouches down to the bars. I cannot see his face but I feel his breath. It is warm, sour and tinged with ale. His voice is hushed.

'It's the war. It's coming close and an alarm has been raised in the town. The King's army has taken Huntingdon, and they say King Charles himself travels down the Great North Road to join the coming battle, so they have decided to suspend the assize. It is not safe.'

'But what of us? And what of those tried today?' He spits forcibly and I see the yellow wetness splatter to the ground close to my face. I try not to pull away in disgust, for I must hear what he will say.

'Condemned as witches, most of them. The judges saw fit to reprieve some, not sure why, given their crimes, but eighteen will hang tomorrow. They cannot afford to wait around, in case the army arrives, so the gallows have been built already. No, a hanging tomorrow.' He stands at a rattling of wheels on cobbles and moves away.

And that is when I see them. The others, those who were named and taken from the barn. Those whose cases had been heard today. They are being led out of the building opposite and loaded onto carts. Their heads are down and many are wailing and keening. I look through the group, searching for the two familiar faces, and then I spy them. Kathryn's head is held high but Maria is sobbing into her apron. I open my mouth to call to them but then they are gone, pushed by the guards up and into the cart and it pulls away. They do not look back. They do not see me, do not even know I am there – that I am praying for their souls.

CHAPTER 16

The world turns on a pin. The fear of war washes over Bury like a sea surge, and the judges and jury hasten away before they, too, are borne up in it. But they wait long enough for the hanging. We cannot see it from the gaol window but we hear it. The rattle of carts bringing the condemned. The jeering and shouting of the crowd, the reedy voices of the ministers, exhorting repentance and confession from the prisoners, begging them to cleanse their souls before they meet their Maker. The intake of breath from the crowd as each prisoner is pushed up the ladder, the cheers and shouts as they drop.

Afterwards, when it is all over and the crowds have dispersed, we in the cells sit in stunned silence as we wait for the guards to come for us. But they never come. Instead, as the day warms, a loud rumbling of carts, and the shouts of many men. Orders are barked, metal bolts drawn, keys turned in locks and, in a gust of clean air and a burst of sunlight, we are pushed back up the steps and out into the square. We stand there, shaking and confused, expecting to be taken to the courtroom. But the burly guard is there again, ordering his men, telling us to get into a line quick-smart as he doesn't have all day. Don't we know the King and his army are coming?

We scramble into the waiting carts. I try to pull Priscilla up behind me but she is a dead weight now, too ill and weak, I cannot lift her, and she falls to the ground. A guard sees her, pulls at his colleague's sleeve, and they step over, hauling her between them like a sack of grain, throwing her into the cart. She lands hard on the wooden floor and groans as the other prisoners push and kick at her in their haste to find a seat. I try to pull her up next to me, but she is motionless now and I do not have the strength to do it alone.

'Let me.' The man's voice is rough and low. I hesitate, all my trust in others gone. 'You cannot move her on your own.' He puts two strong hands under Priscilla's arms and lifts her to sit beside me. I put my arm around her to hold her upright and look at him. He is grimy, light hair lank, and younger than he sounded. I nod at him.

'Thank you. Not all are as kind.'

He smiles at that.

'I have reason to be kind. I have just escaped death.'

'How so?' A glimmer of hope lights inside me.

'I was in the first group that was tried yesterday.'

'So why are you here . . . are you to be freed?'

He shakes his head.

'No, not freed, but not hanged yet either. They said my case was to be carried over to the next day, God only knows why. Some cases were, some weren't. There was no reason behind it. It was all so quick. Only a few minutes to hear each case then sixty of us were approved for trial.'

'Two trials? How can this be?'

'The first is before the Grand Jury who decide whether you are to be tried, then you stand before the Petty Jury, in front of all the good and the great. It seems it is the system.'

'But what of witnesses? How can this be right?'

The man snorts in derision.

'There was no shortage of witnesses. Even the Witchfinder, Hopkins himself, and that devil who accompanies him, Stearne, stood and gave evidence. At first, the jurors seemed as if they would be willing to consider each case, although some began to query the sheer numbers of those accused, and whether their trial was just, but they were told to speed up, for more news of the alarm had arrived. The justices were shaken, you could see it in their eyes, but they still carried on hearing cases. A few cases were thrown out, some were deemed unsure, and the other poor souls were pronounced guilty and sentenced to hang. Afterwards, they took us back to that barn, those who were to die, and us whose cases were to be re-heard. Then they came back this morning and took the condemned away to be hanged. The rest of us were secured on another cart, waiting ready to go back to court. We followed them into Bury . . .' His head drops. 'We had to watch them die. And it was not a good death. It was rushed, see, they had too many seen off at once, the halters put too close together. It was a slow death for many, dreadful. I will never be able to forget their faces . . . it will haunt me forever.' He drops his head, silent, remembering.

A thought strikes me and I turn to the man, pulling at his sleeve.

'Were there many hanged?'

He looks at me, his round face full of sorrow.

'Sixteen women and two men. All convicted of witchcraft.' His eyes glisten with sudden tears and he bites his lip. 'Amongst them my sister and brother-in-law. My poor sister – the rope tightening at her neck, her face turned as red as blood, and her eyes . . .' He shakes his head at the memory. 'It took so long. Brutal it was, pitiless. It was not done proper.'

'I am sorry for your loss.' He nods. 'Where did you come from?'

He looks at me, then at Priscilla.

'Metfield. My sister and husband were from Halesworth. At least their daughter, my niece was cleared, though what will happen to her when she goes back home . . .'

I clasp my hand to my mouth. Those places – so close. My blood beats fast and hard in my ears.

'There were two women taken yesterday, from Westleton and Yoxford?' Do you know what happened to them? They were with us on the cart coming here.'

He tilts his head to one side, his face solemn.

'Hanged.'

I hold back the tears that spring to my eyes. I must not cry for Kathryn and Maria now, there is no time to mourn them. I must remain strong for Priscilla, but the man's words knock the very heart out of me.

The guards have finally loaded all the prisoners onto the carts, and now they come with chains. They shackle us with heavy iron bands which cut into our skin and weigh us down, joining us together so we cannot escape, even if we had the strength.

The man from Metfield is chained next to me.

'It seems we are to be companions.' He smiles briefly. 'James More.'

'Elizabeth Southerne.' He nods in acknowledgement then sits, head bowed, deep in his own thoughts as, all around us, men scurry and run. I keep glancing at Priscilla, who is chained to my other side, but she seems no longer conscious, her head is down and her eyes are closed. I reach my shackled hands to her forehead – it burns with fever.

'Priscilla... Priss? Can you hear me?' Her eyelids flicker but she makes no sound, and I move my shoulder against hers to support her. Her coif has long gone and her shorn head gleams in the sunlight, like a field after harvest – it is alive with lice, and I shudder to think of how she would feel if she knew, her always so clean and tidy. She would hate this, hate what she has become. I am used to a hard life, to sleeping under hedgerows and in barns, but Priscilla has been used to better. I am grateful that she does not know what is happening, but I am worried too, for I fear that she is ill, very ill, and I don't know what to do.

Then a shout and the cluster of wagons begin to move. The procession starts to wend its way back out of Bury and onto the

Ipswich road, and the prisoners begin to mutter. One of the guards sitting at the front turns towards us.

'Be silent!'

One brave voice carries above the murmuring.

'Where are we going? What is to happen to us?' Others join in the clamour and the noise rises. The captain bangs his cudgel hard down on the wagon's rear, and the sound shrivels.

'Be SILENT!' He pauses, considering, then sees it would be better to tell us. 'You are being taken to Ipswich Gaol.' There are groans and cries of horror as the words pass from wagon to wagon – we have all heard of the fearful reputation of that place. 'It is no longer safe in Bury with the King's army approaching, so those in authority have deemed it better that you be imprisoned safely in Ipswich, then brought back to the assize here once the alarm is over. Don't worry, you will still be tried and face your punishment.' He cackles grimly and sits back down to watch the road and we are left in fear, trying to digest this news.

JAMES' FACE HAS DARKENED AT THE GUARD'S WORDS.

'I will not be held in Ipswich Gaol. It is a foul place, known for disease and death. The fever will see you off there if the hangman does not. And look how many of us there are. The prison will be overflowing, they will pack us in. Few will survive, especially in this heat. I will not have it.' He clenches his fists hard, nails biting white against sun-browned skin– the hands of a labourer. He looks hard at Priscilla, his brow furrowing. 'You know her well?'

I nod.

'She is my friend, Priscilla. We were seized at the same time. We are from Dunwich.' I cannot tell him that it was she who accused me – that I deserved it for the wrong I had done her.

'She looks ill. How long has she been like that?'

I hear the concern in his voice and I turn to her and look closely. Her face is deathly pale, shimmered with sweat and, as I pull back the neck of her shift, I see red spots have started to appear on her chest. I look back at him in horror.

'She seemed unwell days ago – she had a cough – but it was hard to tell, and it was so dark and dusty in the barn and the gaol. But this rash is new. It was not there earlier.' I wonder if this is right for, in truth, I had not paid her much attention, not looked at her fully, I was just trying to keep us both alive. It is only now, outside in the sunshine, that I can see the extent of it. James looks hard at her, then back at me.

'Gaol fever.' His brow is furrowed.

I put my hands to my mouth in horror.

'Are you sure?'

He nods.

'Seen it before.' I wonder where, but my worry for Priscilla overwhelms me.

'But she has not been confined for long.'

'Doesn't matter, it comes quickly. Depends where she has been, who else has it . . . runs through gaols like fire. I heard say that a quarter of prisoners die from it.'

'Maybe now we are outside in the fresh air it will . . . ?'

'In this heat with this many bodies around us? It will spread, and quickly, mark my words.'

I think of the gaol in Dunwich, Priscilla stepping out of the church into the light when I was accused. She looked ill then, but never as bad as this.

'What can we do?'

He looks at me sadly.

'Nothing can be done. It is in God's hands. But she will not be the only one, for many have been held for weeks in cells all over Suffolk, before being taken to Bury. Contagion spreads fast. If she has it, you can be certain there will be others. You even.' I shrink away from him, holding my breath. I had not thought of that. I do not think I am feverish. I put my hand to my forehead. It is sweating in the August sun, but it is not burning and I do not feel ill. I breathe again, but my heart races.

James is deep in thought now, his eyes shifting from side to side, his lips moving silently. I think he is praying, but then he looks up and moves his mouth close to my ear.

'There may be a way out of this horror . . . we may be able to make our escape.'

I look at Priscilla and then back at him.

'How? It is impossible.' I hold up my wrists, heavy with iron shackles. 'And I cannot leave her, not when she is so ill.'

He shrugs and our chains clink.

'Up to you. But she will die, it's just a matter of when. Now she has the spots, death is certain. But we could use this to save ourselves.' His face is turned away from me, but I can feel the excitement radiating from him.

'Why would you help me? I have nothing to give you.'

He looks me up and down with a wry smile and I shrink inside myself.

'I do not want anything from you, but I cannot do it alone. I will need your help, and need your friend too. I am certain I can do this and it will look better if there are more of us.' For so many days I have feared death and lived in the shadow of the noose. I am not certain if I can trust this man, this stranger, but I do not want to die.

'What is your plan?'

So he tells me.

THE WAGONS GAIN SPEED AS WE PASS THROUGH THE COUNTRYSIDE, THE horses pushed and whipped to cover the miles between Bury and Ipswich as fast as they can, the guards glancing back in fear. We see groups of Parliament's soldiers marching towards Bury, pikes gleaming. They begin to jeer as they see us, but a snapped order from their commander turns their heads to face the front, and they pull back into formation and continue on their way. Of the Royalist army we see nothing.

When the sun has moved overhead the wagons trundle to a stop and the guards jostle us from our places, shouting at us to relieve ourselves where we can. All shreds of dignity have been ripped from us, and women crouch by the side of the road, skirts hoisted with manacled hands, as the men chained close beside them fumble with their breeches. It is humiliating. There are sobs and groans, but the deed is done and we all take the opportunity to have a few moments respite from the intense heat, finding patches of shade under the few trees and bushes. Skins of water are passed along the lines and we drink thirstily, then pass them on. There is no food. The guards stand over us with cudgels raised to stop any escape, but no one has the strength or will to run. We are broken. We just sit in the shade, panting like dogs, and then we are loaded back onto the wagon. As we move through the Suffolk farmland, dust is thrown up by the wheels and billows around us, filling our clothes and hair, drying our eyes and throats, and coughs stop our speech as we trundle on towards Ipswich.

It is late afternoon, the sun passed overhead and beginning to sink, when our procession stops for a second time. The guards bustle around, banging the wooden sides of the wagons with their staves, manhandling us to the ground and telling us to relieve ourselves again. But this time James, Priscilla and I do not move. Priss lies on the bottom of the wagon as if already dead, her hands clutched to her chest. She is barely recognisable. James and I have kept our faces to the sun all day; now they are burning, sweating and red, as we lie beside her, our eyes narrowed, watching, waiting.

'Off the cart – now!' A guard reaches for us, his cudgel thumping the boards next to my head, but we do not shift. I can hear the captain swearing under his breath as he strides, heavy-footed, towards us.

'Why are these prisoners still here? You have your orders. Get them off now, we do not have time for niceties.'

'They do not move, Sir, and there are two dead in the other wagon.' I hear the captain's footsteps coming closer, then his shadow falls over us. The skin on my chest and neck is raised and red where I have been pinching it hard these last miles, and I move my body and groan as if I were dying, as James directed – he lies beside me, rigid and unmoving, and I take courage from him. Through eyelids flickering with fear, I watch the captain's face freeze as he hurriedly covers his mouth with his hand.

'Move back, men. It is gaol fever.'

The guards slink away and I feel a sudden surge of power. They are afraid of us. They form a huddle, unsure what to do, then break away and begin to tie kerchiefs and cloths over their faces, as the captain barks his orders.

'We cannot have those few infecting the rest. Take them off the wagons, quickly now, roll them into that ditch. I cannot deliver dead prisoners to Ipswich. We are nearly there, this job must be done properly. If we get rid of them now we may yet escape the spread of the contagion to others. And they will die anyway, either in the cells or by the noose.' He rubs his nose with his hand. 'They will not notice a few missing. No count was done at Bury. No one knows how many we are transporting. A few less will not be noticed.'

'Should we not bury the dead, Sir?'

The captain's face darkens.

'They are witches, man, if they were hanged it would have been the lime pit in the gaol for them. They are not worthy of God's forgiveness, for the Devil is their master and they will go to greet him in Hell. Just get them off the carts, quick, before anyone comes.'

There is a clump of boots and the guards move towards us. The chains rattle as our shackles are taken off, and I feel the sharp sting of opening flesh. Then a crashing and swearing, my arms and ankles are grasped firmly and I am flying through the air to land heavily by a ditch. The breath is knocked out of me and my body contracts in pain as the stones and ruts of the road cut into me. It is all I can do not to scream. I roll to one side, into the long grass, watching cautiously through slitted eyes, as the guards move along the row of wagons, listening to dull thumps as more bodies are thrown to the earth.

I FIGHT THE URGE TO MOVE, TO CHECK MYSELF FOR INJURY, I LIE AS still as the grave, as James instructed, eyes closed, breath flickering, listening to the shouts and cries of men and prisoners. I do not know if he is here, or what has happened to Priscilla, and I dare not move my head to look. I will myself to stay perfectly still. The wait seems eternal but finally I hear the grating sounds of the wheels as the wagons start to move. I go to draw in a breath, to lift my head, but then a tramp of feet stops me. Strong arms grip my side, then a huff of stale, foul breath, a hard push, and I am rolling over and over, my vision blurred, trying not to cry out in terror; I am sliding, the smell of mud pricks my nostrils and then I am falling. A shallow splash and all is silenced as dank ditch water closes over my face.

CHAPTER 17

I hold my breath for as long as I can, and then, when my lungs are bursting and my chest is on fire, I cautiously move my head upwards, bit by bit, until my nose is free of mud and silt. I breathe as silently as I can, raise my head a little further so that my ears are clear of the water, and I listen hard. The only thing I can hear is the sound of larks calling high above me and the rustle of trees in the breeze. It is beautiful. No footsteps, no voices. There are no sounds of movement, no crying or groans. The noises that have accompanied me for the past days are gone, and it is as if I am left alone in the world, reborn. I reach my hands to my eyes and wipe them. The mud stings and I blink rapidly to clear my vision, then I lie watching, strangely at peace, waiting for the end as, high above me, white clouds drift in a perfect blue sky.

The silence is shattered by a squelching noise, then a grumbling and groaning.

'Elizabeth?' I raise my head further, every bone in my body complaining, and look around. James is lying nearby, black with silt and stinking to high heaven. 'Elizabeth Southerne? Are you alive? Can you speak?'

'James, yes, I am here.' I pull myself half-up on the grassy bank and look around me. We are in a deep ditch at the side of a field, the type that is built for drainage in these parts. We are lucky that this summer has been so hot and dry, for normally it would be full of water, and I shudder as I think how, but for that, I would have drowned. I watch as he pulls himself up cautiously and looks over the top of the ditch. His head turns slowly from side to side as he watches warily for any movement, then he beckons to me. My skirts weigh me down, they are full of mud and water, but I struggle up beside him, my mind spinning. He turns to me with delight in his eyes, grinning, teeth white against his mud-grimed face.

'They thought us dead. They did not look close enough . . . they took us for dead!' His voice is full of amazement, he had not thought his plan would work.

I look at him in wonder.

'So we are free?' All of a sudden I have the urge to laugh, for the situation seems so unreal.

He nods.

'It seems so. But we need to leave, now, before anyone else comes this way.' He struggles out of the ditch, then reaches out a blackened hand and pulls me up. It is strong and firm and an image of John Collit comes into my mind, inexplicable, unexpected.

'Priscilla!' I look around me frantically. 'Where is she?' Three more bodies lie further along, face down in the dark water, clearly dead. I move towards them, bending to look closely at each one, and then I see her. She is lying on her back, pale as a ghost in the black mud, glassy eyes open, looking at the sky. Her face is clear of the water and it is smooth and calm. 'Priscilla . . .' James reaches out a hand to stop me, but I scramble down the slippery bank towards her, crouching on my haunches above the water line as my joints complain. 'Priss, can you hear me?'

From above me, James hisses.

'Keep quiet, we must not make a noise, we are not free yet. Does she live?'

I put my hand to her chest, feel the fluttering glimmer of life.

'She lives. James, we must save her.' I do not need to turn and see his face, for I know what he will say.

But it is not him that speaks.

'ELIZABETH? BESS, IS THAT YOU?'

'Oh, Priss, I feared you dead. I am here, I am still with you. I will help you.' Priscilla reaches for my hand and I realise how little strength she has left. Her fingers are thin and bony, her body too, and I do not know how she is going to be able to clamber up the bank, let alone get to her feet and start walking. I do not know how we are going to do it. Then I see her eyelids flicker and she pulls me closer, her voice a cracked whisper.

'Go, Bess.' A sob rips my throat as my eyes fill. 'You must leave me behind. I am near to God now, I can see Him beckoning me, and I have made my peace with Him. Now I need only make my peace with you. I am truly sorry for all I told them, for what I did. I should never have accused you, it was wrong of me. Please forgive me, and do not mourn me, for my pain in this life has been great and I will be glad to leave it.'

The tears spill down my cheeks and my throat tightens with grief but I know I must speak.

'Oh, Priss, of course I forgive you – but it was all my fault. I confess I wanted John and I tried to justify it by using your illness and...'

'No, Bess, no more. You wronged me perhaps, but it is as nothing to the harm I have done you. I truly believed that the Devil was helping me – I could see him so clearly, hear his every word, and I had faith in all he said. It was that which caused this, which has brought us to this place. But it is done, and I can change nothing...' Her eyes fill with tears. '... oh, but I would have so loved to have seen my children again, just to hold them once more, to have their forgiveness. For losing my babes has been my greatest pain. But I go to God now and little Edward is waiting for me, and he is made whole again. I have glimpsed him and soon I will be able to hold him in my arms, be a proper mother to him as I was not in this life, and I will never let him go again. And when their time comes, I will meet with my beautiful Bess and my sweet Robert and we will be together for eternity.' Her voice is fading now, her breath coming quick. She squeezes my hand tightly. 'Go, Elizabeth. We will meet again in the next life, God willing. And give all my love to Aubrey when you find her.' She pauses, her chest rattling as she struggles to draw breath. 'Remember the Players? It was the happiest day of my life. It seems only yesterday . . .' I am blinded by tears, wracked by the pain of her words. 'I have loved you and Aubrey as sisters, and I always will. Elizabeth – you have my forgiveness. Do I have yours?'

'I forgive you with all my heart, Priss. I hope you find peace in the next life.' I bend to kiss her forehead and the glimmer of a smile crosses her bruised lips. She squeezes my hand once, then pulls her arm away and lays it across her chest.

'Go in God, Elizabeth Southerne. Be safe.' Her chest rattles one last time, and I watch her face lightening as her soul departs, all pain blown away like dust in a breeze. I pass my hands over her eyes to close them and bow my head.

IT TAKES ALL I HAVE TO LEAVE HER BUT I KNOW I HAVE NO CHOICE. John pulls me to my feet. I cannot see his face for the tears, and I fall against him, sobbing as if my heart would break. He puts an arm around my shoulders and I lean into him.

'Elizabeth, she is gone. There is nothing more you can do, and we must move on. It is not safe for us here.' He shakes me gently, trying to bring me to my senses.

'We must bury her. I cannot just leave her there . . .'

His grip tightens on my arms.

'No, there is no time. I am very sorry for your loss, truly I am, but we must go, and quickly.' My body is heavy and my mind numb, and it is all I can do to listen to his words. I look beseechingly at him but I know, deep down, he is right. It was his plan that freed us, and I cannot endanger him now. I take one last look at Priscilla, lying as if asleep in the silt, before he manhandles me away from the ditch and along the road to a nearby copse. I try to settle myself as I walk, wiping my face with my sleeve and taking deep breaths. My wrists burn raw where the shackles bit and my joints ache from the unaccustomed movement. James pauses for a few moments, then takes my arm and guides me through the trees, away from the road. We begin to walk slowly under the canopy of dusty leaves and all the while he talks.

'It is not safe for us here.' I still cannot think straight, grief searing me. 'Elizabeth, we need to keep moving. There will be a village nearby and we have to find food.' His voice is more kindly now and, as I compose myself, I realise that we are not fit to be seen. Someone will suspect us, for we are filthy and we carry no belongings. I look at James and then down at myself. The mud on our clothes has dried hard and I brush my hands over my clothes, faster and faster, rubbing the coarse fabric between my hands as if I were washing it, trying to remove the grime and filth, trying to make myself look half-human again. James does the same, and then we stand and inspect each other.

'Look at us. We still look like beggars.'

I see a light spark in his eyes.

'And that is what we will become.'

I look askance at him.

'Beggars?'

'The King's army is marching, people are fleeing with what they stand up in. What better way to disguise ourselves? We have nothing, we need food and drink.' I know he is right. Then I think of something.

'Are we to go together?'

He looks at me shrewdly.

'A man and wife, fleeing the soldiers? It is believable. And when we get nearer to home we can see what is best to do.'

'Home? Surely that will not be safe. We were accused as witches, what would the townsfolk say if we were to return? All will remember that we were sent to the assize...'

He stops abruptly and turns to me, his face set.

'Elizabeth, you must do what you will, but I intend to go home. I have lost my sister and her husband, but my niece is alive somewhere. As they were taken away to be hanged I promised my sister that I would find my niece and care for her, and I am a man of my word. So for now, let us pass as man and wife and see how we go on.'

I look at him and see he is serious. I still do not fully trust him, or trust any man, but there is no alternative. It is a good plan, but then a thought strikes me

'You do not expect me to...'

'Lie with me?' He laughs. 'Have you seen at yourself recently? I am not likely to be lusting after a hedge-witch, and a grimy one at that!' I am stung by his rejection. I have always felt my body to be too big for me, ungainly and clumsy, but men have found me attractive in the past. And John... I banish the thought as quickly as it came. James is right, that was the past and I am no longer that person. I look at him; his eyes are bright with elation and merriment and my hurt flies away, for his happiness is contagious. A smile loosens my face and I cackle loudly, the sound just bursting out of me. 'See, you even sound like a witch. But I suppose I must play my part, difficult though it may be.' He folds my arm over his, patting my hand, and his courage and determination flow into me. 'Come, wife, let us see what begging can bring us.' I smile at him and he grins back at me and we walk on, arm in arm, to find a place where smoke curls from chimneys, chickens peck and cluck in gardens, pigs grunt in sties and washing dries on bushes – back towards the civilisation that we had thought lost to us.

. . .

IN THE FIRST VILLAGE WE COME TO JAMES FINDS US CLOTHES, LEFT TO dry on a hedge. I worry that he has stolen them from a family in need, but then he asks me who could be needier than us, so I speak no more of it, for he is right, though the guilt is sharp. He bundles the clothes under his arm and we keep walking until we come across a wood with a stream running through it. We pause and look about. It is quiet, no noise save the trickling of water and the song of birds.

'James, I must rest. I cannot walk another step.'

He nods in agreement.

'We are far enough away from the road, and we have seen no one for several hours. I think it will be safe to stop here, but only for a short while, then we must keep going.' I sink to the grass gratefully. 'We need to wash and change our clothes, cleanse our wounds. It may be some days before we can do so again. Here . . .' He throws me the bundle of clothes he stole and I undo it and sort out a pair of britches and a shirt for him, then a skirt and shift for me. He has found an old bodice too, stained under the arms and frayed in places, but clean –it will do.

'Well, are you going to sit there and watch me?'

He laughs.

'You are my wife, remember, why so shy?' I narrow my eyes at him and he sees my look. 'I jest, Elizabeth, preserve your modesty by all means. I will turn away.' I make sure he does before peeling off my clothes, although I find myself smiling. My old shift is stuck to my skin with sweat and filth, and I grimace as it falls to the ground. I wrap my nakedness with my arms and, glancing behind me to make sure James is still not watching, I step carefully into the stream. The biting cold that wraps itself around my ankles takes my breath away, but I walk in deeper and begin to wash the stench of imprisonment from my body, rubbing harder and harder until my skin stings and glows. I crouch down and splash water over my head, my hair sliding in soft stubbles under my fingertips, then I remember the lice crawling on Priscilla and I dig my fingernails in, scouring every inch of my scalp until it feels clean again. I cover myself in the stolen shift and walk back up the grass, eyes averted, and lie in the sun while James takes his turn. My skin dries quickly and my whole body glows – how good it feels to be clean again.

The clothes do not fit well. The skirt is too short for someone of my height, so I tie it loosely, wearing it low on my hips for decency. When James is done and dressed I take our old things to the stream and scrub them against a rock, washing them as best I can, then we spread them out onto the grass to dry in the August heat while we rest and try to regain our strength. We share a nub of bread given to us by a kindly villager and take water from the stream, cupping its coolness in our palms, drinking deep and long. Water has never tasted so sweet. James looks better in his new britches and shirt but he says nothing about my clothes, and I catch a smile of amusement as I kneel beside him.

'Why do you smile like that? Do I look strange?'

'Well, were you truly my wife I would beat you for looking so slovenly but, as it is, I suppose I must forbear on this occasion.'

I slap his shoulder with the palm of my hand and smile.

'If you were truly my husband I would seek another.'

He grins back at me and I notice how his eyes crinkle in the corners as he does so. He is a handsome man, his tow-coloured hair shining now it is clean, curling round his neck. He is kind, too . . . I catch my thoughts and stop them dead, taking my mind elsewhere by folding the now-dry clothes into two bundles. James finds a couple of branches nearby and ties the bundles to them, then passes one to me.

'Now we truly look like beggars.' He holds out a hand to me. 'Come, wife, it's time we were moving on.' I feel better than I have done for weeks as I take his hand and he pulls me up.

'Husband. Where you lead I follow.' I drop a mock-curtsey and he laughs then we move away, rested and refreshed, with more confidence than we had before.

We begin to believe we are free.

. . .

WE ARE LESS CONSPICUOUS NOW, CARRYING OUR BUNDLES OVER OUR shoulders, but we keep moving. We walk miles every day, and the rhythm and exhaustion help me to push the memory of Priscilla lying in that ditch to the bottom of my mind. But I cannot forget her and I do not want to. As we tramp on I find that my anger at the manner of her passing, of the way she was treated, grows to a ball of rage, black and roiling inside me and my silence grows. James notices the lowering of my thoughts and seeks to cheer me with his plans, which grow ever bigger and more ambitious. He has decided he will return to Halesworth and take over his sister's brewing business. We have long discussions about the sense of this for it seems that the Everards were accused of witchcraft, not only for supporting the King but for the poor quality of their brew.

'I warned them about the ale many times. The townsfolk were becoming angry, some had become ill, but my sister would not listen, said her husband knew what he was doing. He insisted on buying poor barley and over-watering the mash to save the expense. People will put up with many things but to serve bad ale is unforgivable.' He smiles at this but I can see he is serious.

'But how will you be received in that town? You are related to hanged witches and were accused alongside them. Are you sure it will be safe for you?'

'I do not know, Elizabeth, but I was not one of those hanged. I will tell people that many were acquitted, me with them, which is nearly the truth. I do not need to tell them how I came to be free. I hope that things will have settled down and that I can find my niece and perhaps, together, we can work the brewery. I seem to have the luck of the Devil, so long may it continue.'

I shudder.

'Do not speak of him, James, not even in jest. The Devil was how we came to be here. Never say his name in my hearing. If it had not been for him, Priscilla would still be alive and I would be . .

.' My voice breaks and I bend forward, wrapping my hands around my body as if to hold myself together. After all we have been through I am suddenly overcome with grief and the pain of it bites at my guts.

James sees my distress.

'Elizabeth, I am sorry, I was thoughtless. I forget myself sometimes. You are right, and his name will not be mentioned again, you have my promise. Come here. I am sorry.' He puts his arms around me and I sink into him gratefully, my sobs slowing. It is so good to be held and I close my eyes and feel a pull towards him, a spark of something long pushed down, and I know he feels it too. We spring apart as if burned. He clears his throat. 'Here, take this.' He passes me a grimy kerchief and I blow my nose loudly.

'Where did you find this?' I offer it back to him and he screws his face up in mock disgust.

'I do not remember, but I do not want it back, not in that condition.' Laughter crinkles his eyes and I stand upright again. His good spirits are always infectious and I wipe my nose, cheered, this time tucking the damp kerchief in my bodice. He nods in approval and we walk on as he regales me with his ideas and plans for the future.

'I am hoping their brewhouse lies empty still. It has not been that long, so it may still be lying idle. I plan to claim it as a relative, find my niece and try my hand as a tavern keeper. There is always money in ale.'

'It is a good plan, and I hope it works. All your plans have so far, wild as they may have seemed.'

He looks at me.

'Come and work with me, Elizabeth. I could teach you . . . we seem well together.' He is solemn now and, for the first time, I sense he is hesitant.

'It is a kind offer, and I thank you, but I have no skill at that kind of work. And there is another thing – oh, James, I want to go home.' I did not know how true this was until I spoke the words. The longing is a dull ache, the land and sea call to me. Dunwich was where I was born and lived with my mother – it is the only place I have properly known. I need to go back. And I need to see Aubrey, to tell her about Priscilla, and take time to mourn, as I have not yet been able to. James may be right, townsfolk may yet have forgotten, but I have to find out. He nods and smiles at me.

'I do understand.'

'Thank you.' I clasp his hands in mine and smile back at him. In the air between us, something quivers and is lost.

CHAPTER 18

As summer turns into autumn we keep tramping, stopping at towns and villages, begging for a few coins, a husk of bread, and then moving on before we are heeded. We take our time, hoping that, when we reach our destinations, we will have been forgotten, that something else will have filled the mouths of the town gossips.

As winter approaches we reach Framlingham, the castle rising tall above the town, moated and strong. It is market day and the town is bustling. Cattle and geese are being driven along the busy lanes and all around are the cries of street sellers and hawkers.

James and I are unrecognisable now. Our faces are weather-beaten, our clothes grimy, and the cloaks that he stole for us when the weather got colder are dusty and splattered with mud. But we have been lucky these past few weeks, for I remembered how I had first made a living collecting and selling dry wood for kindling, and so that is what we have been doing. It is the best time of year for this and our enterprise has been successful.

'Let us eat.' James takes my arm and steers me through the crowds. 'We will find a place and have a hot meal. We have earned it.' The town seems full of inns but we find one that is quiet, away from the bustle of the market square, up by the castle gate. The landlord takes one look at us and will not let us in, but agrees to serve us ale and a hot pie outside, for, after all, our money is as good as anyone else's. I mutter at him and James grasps my arm tightly, his fingers digging in.

'Be careful, Elizabeth. Do not mutter under your breath, do not curse, it is too dangerous. As you tell me, you must think before you act. The threat of witchcraft is still around, and you must consider how others will see you. Best to say nothing, do nothing that may cause attention.' I drop my eyes in shame for he is right, I forget myself. I have become used to just the two of us, have forgotten how it is to be amongst other people. I will have to be far more cautious.

We slump down on the rough grass outside the inn, pies warm in our hands, tankards of ale beside us. I take a bite and the warmth and taste flood through me. The pastry is light and crisp, the meat dark and flavoursome, and thick brown gravy trickles down my chin.

Beside me, James is groaning with pleasure.

'Is this not the best pie you have ever tasted?' He finishes his mouthful, pulls hard at his ale, then sets his tankard down and attacks the rest of his pie. I do the same, and we eat in companionable silence until we are full. It is the first time we have eaten this well since we were imprisoned, and it restores me. We finish our ale, then I brush the crumbs from my skirts and make to stand up. He reaches for my hand and pulls me back down.

'Elizabeth, wait, there is something I must say. We have spoken of this I know, and I was not sure when . . . well, I am trying to tell you that I think this is where we must part.' He sees my face and smooths a finger along my cheek – it is warm and calloused, the gesture tender. We have talked about this moment many times but my grief over Priscilla has made me rely on him more and more. I knew this would come, that I would have to fend for myself once again, but now it is here I find I do not wish it to happen. I look full at him. He has become my friend, maybe more. We have come such a long way together, been through Hell and back and I owe him my life, for, without him, I would be hanged by now, or be dead of fever in Ipswich Gaol. Without his good humour, I would have laid down at the side of the road and died weeks ago.

'And you are still set on Halesworth?'

He nods.

'It is the only way forward that I can see. If I keep my head down, keep myself close, then maybe people will forget.' He reaches for my hand. 'Please come with me, Elizabeth, there is a place for you by my side if you wish. We could marry. We make a good pair, you and I.' I hear the hope in his voice. I must decide. I wanted to go home. I wanted all that I left behind; my cottage, my own bed, my garden, evenings on the step with Aubrey, a mug of ale in hand, hearing all the news, exchanging gossip as we used to do. But James is offering me another life, a different life. I would not be known in Halesworth, I would have a home and work to occupy me, and a husband by my side and I would feel safe. The temptation is great, every part of me is saying 'Yes', but then I remember Priscilla and John. I have seen what happens in a marriage and seen how someone can be brought down by it. I cannot take the risk. And, above all, I must see Aubrey. I turn to him and he knows in that moment what I will say, for his face falls.

'James, you have been so good to me and I wish you luck. We do fit well together and I think we would make a good couple. You have become so dear to me but . . . James, I am sorry, but I will go home to Dunwich.'

WE PART AT DAWN. WE HOLD EACH OTHER TIGHTLY AND I WONDER IF I do the right thing, but then he kisses my forehead.

'Goodbye, Elizabeth, take care. Be happy – and if you ever change your mind . . .' He smiles at me then his face softens. He tilts his head, lifts my chin with his finger and moves his mouth to my lips. His kiss is the sweetest I have ever tasted and, in that moment, I feel my resolution slipping, but then he steps back, shoulders his pack and, with a wave of farewell he is gone. I stand there for a long time, bereft, resisting the urge to run after him, then I lift my pack, turn in the opposite direction and begin to walk eastwards, heading towards the sunrise.

After only a few miles, I am already losing faith in this journey, the absence of James an ache in my heart. By the evening I am tired as death, cold and thirsty, and I think how easy it would be to lie down and let life leave me, as Priscilla did. In the shortening days and colder nights, I reach my lowest ebb. Although I keep trudging along, I feel ready to stop, give in, and face whatever end the Lord intends for me. Then, from the grassy verge beside me, a scurry and rustle, and a hare leaps onto the road. I stop perfectly still, watching, as it twitches brown silky ears, then turns and runs along the road in front of me, disappearing across the field. Its dancing lightness reminds me of Priscilla, something in the movements; the twitch of its nose, the arc of its body. I remember the dark thoughts I was having at the very moment it appeared, and I know it is a sign, sent to me to give me courage and strength. I set down my pack and stand beside it, breathing steadily. All is quiet, save for birdsong. I can smell the dampness of rain-soaked leaves, the tang of mud – autumn is here. I must not allow my thoughts to bring me down any more. So I make myself like the hare. My ears stretch for the slightest sound, I sniff the air for impending danger. I do not know what makes me do it, but I crouch down into the damp grass by the side of the track and feel the spirit of the hare pulse through me. It makes my aching bones feel supple and lithe again. It clears my mind of thoughts of the past, makes me look to the future, and I feel stronger and lighter. I look around. Nearby is a large branch, blown free of a tree, so I reach for it and pull out my knife, using it to fashion a staff, then I push myself up and stand tall, shoulder my bundle, and walk on.

 I take my time. James and I divided up the coins we had earned when we parted, and with them I buy some chapbooks and pamphlets, and, for a while, I go back to my old life, selling these from door to door, as I slowly wend my way home. People are still hesitant, the fear of witchcraft on their lips, but I am less afraid, for I am no longer as I was. James had suggested I change myself for safety, and so now I bind my breasts beneath an old shirt, wear a cracked leather jerkin and britches and a man's leather boots, bought from a street trader. My hair is short and curled, it never properly grew again after it was shaved, and it sits tousled under a wide-brimmed felt hat. My skin has been burned brown by the sun, my face is wrinkled and thin, and my hands are worn and strong. A man I have become. And it is safer on the road than being a woman so I travel onwards, pack on back, staff in hand, transformed.

Westleton, when I reach it, is as it always was. In one or two places I fear I may be recognised, but I am changed so much that it does not happen. No one looks at you when you are poor and homeless, and now I am grateful for it. There is no word spoken here of witches or the war, and my long-held breath comes a little easier. No other pedlar has come that way for some time it seems, and everyone is eager for news, so I am welcomed and my purse fills along, with my stomach, as my pack empties.

THE TRACK TO DUNWICH IS BARE AND HARD, THE SAND UNDERFOOT scuffed and muddied in places. It seems narrower, as if few have passed since I was last here and, as I draw closer, I finally begin to feel a twinge of fear at what I will find. Winter is coming in fast now and the air is chill. I know that I will not be able to last on the road for much longer, my aching bones will not take it, so I trudge on. As I do, the way becomes more and more familiar. I recognise the trees, the dips and hillocks, even the smell is the same, brine and leaves, and I know I have made the right decision. I pause by the whitethorn, where Priscilla said that I had spoken with the Devil, and I shudder. But even the bush is diminished now, its leaves gone, its white-star flowers sleeping until spring comes again. There is no Devil here, never was, just the madness of one poor woman tormented by her thoughts and the pain and cruelty of her life – and the obsession of one man. My eyes fill as I remember her, myself and Aubrey, as we once were, when the Players came and our lives stretched long in front of us and the sky was blue and birds sang.

I walk further, to the end of the track, gaze to my left and there is it. My cottage, still standing, though overgrown and poor. I push at the wooden gate and it falls apart under my hands, so I kick the wood to one side and walk hesitantly up the weed-edged path to the front door. It has been closed up, wooden planks nailed over it. I use my staff and prise them away with shaking fingers until the door is freed. I open it and step inside.

The air is cold and damp but it smells of home, of lives lived and lost. I half-expect my mother to greet me, turning from the pot on the fire, a smile of welcome on her face. But there is no one here, there has been no one for a long time, that much is clear. Perhaps the house of a witch is too frightening for people, the very air it contains scaring them away. I drop my pack to the floor and straighten my aching shoulders, I look around and think about what must be done. I must make a fire to warm the place through. I remember the planks of wood, and the broken gate, and move outside, bending to pick up the pieces.

I do not hear the footsteps behind me. The first thing I know is the icy sting of a blade on the back of my neck.

I KEEP MY HEAD LOWERED, NOT DARING TO BREATHE IN CASE THE blade is pushed deeper. Slowly, I put out my hands to show I am unarmed.

'Who are you?' It is a woman's voice, sharp and frightened.

'Do you think to rob me? I have nothing.' I keep my voice low and gruff, hoping I may be able to reason with her – it is a man they must see, not Elizabeth Southerne, witch.

'What are you doing here? This is not your cottage.' Relief

washes over me like a summer squall and I start to straighten. But the knife pushes deeper, there is a sharp pricking, and I feel blood warm my skin. I tense, then find my old voice, the one she knows.

'Aubrey? Aubrey, it's me, Elizabeth.' The knife does not move from my neck, the figure behind it standing stock-still. I pull away a little and turn my head carefully to look at her, still fearing the plunge of the blade. Her face is tight with shock and confusion; she is a little older, a little thinner but as dear to me as my own. 'It is Bess. I have come home.'

The blade leaves my neck and I raise my hand to rub at the sting it leaves behind. Red smears my fingers. I stand up slowly and turn to her, my palms raised. 'It is me – Elizabeth, your friend.' She stares, disbelieving, and I realise how I must look. A tall man, weatherbeaten and dusty, clothes poor and covered with the dust and grime of many weeks of walking. She holds the trembling blade out before her, her face stern and uncertain, but then her eyes travel up to mine, she puts her hand to her mouth and gasps. The knife drops from her hand and clatters on the weed-strewn path.

'Elizabeth? Is it truly you?' She moves towards me and raises her hand to my face, running it gently over my cheek, cupping my chin, as her eyes fill with tears. She smiles thinly through them as she gazes at me. 'Oh, Bess, you have come back to me' Her voice trembles, then she looks behind me and back into the dark of the cottage, her eyes searching. 'Priscilla – is she with you?' She turns and sees pain pinch my face. 'Oh, no! We heard that those taken to Bury had been hanged in a rush, because of some sort of alarm ... Thomas Spatchett has been trying to find out the truth of it but no one seemed sure.'

I take her hand and it is small and warm in mine.

'Priss was not hanged, but she is gone. Aubrey, I am so sorry ... here, help me light the fire, and I will tell you everything that has happened. I need to get the cottage warmed through, find some food and ale ...'

Aubrey wipes away her tears with the back of her hand and becomes herself again. 'You get the fire lit and I will go home and get some food and ale to tide you over. I have plenty. Then you can tell me what happened to you both. But – she is truly dead?' I nod and her face clouds. 'Then may her soul rest in peace.'

'Amen.'

She bends and picks up her knife and tucks it into the band of her skirt then turns and reaches out, taking me in her arms. Her embrace warms and comforts me and we stand there for a long time, emotions overwhelming us, before I pull away.

'We must not be seen like this. What would people say, you with a strange man in your arms outside a derelict cottage?'

She laughs softly.

'Indeed! I would be hauled before Master Spatchett if anyone were to see me.'

My heart lurches at the name.

'He is still in Dunwich? I had hoped that maybe he had gone back to Cookley.'

'No, he remains here and has become ever more powerful. He has tried to catch me out many a time, for he has not forgotten that I escaped his accusations when you and Priscilla were seized. He would bring me down in the blink of an eye if he could. You will need to be very careful, Bess, for his spies are everywhere and the whole town seems in his thrall. That man sees and hears everything, and that which he does not see, he will imagine.' She looks me up and down. 'But being a man suits you – I barely recognised you. It may be best for you to stay like that while you are here, safer. For now, let me go and get some food. Light that fire, sit and rest, and I will be back shortly I promise. I must know what has happened to you all these months. And I want you to tell me about Priss – were you there with her . . . at the end?'

'I was.'

'Then you must tell me all.' She turns and walks away into the evening gloom. In the half-light, Priscilla dances before me like a ghost, as she was before the pain, the imaginings. Thick blonde hair swirling around her face, blue eyes sparkling, her smile warm, her arms outstretched to me. Our friend, dead in a ditch of gaol fever. She haunts me still.

I FIND SOME DRY KINDLING IN THE BACK OF THE COTTAGE, ENOUGH TO charge the damp wood, and flames eventually come. I am coughing with the smoke, flapping it out of the open door with an old apron, when Aubrey returns. She is holding a large basket of food and I remember when she saved me once before with such a gift, after Mother had died. I take the basket from her.

'It seems you are saving me once more.' I glance down at the contents. It is the same meal that I remember then – cheese, wrapped in cloth, fresh bread, butter and a small jug of ale – and I smile at her.

She steps inside and looks around.

'I have come by here each week to make sure things are as they should be. I kept people away, 'though 'twas not hard, for most feared to come anyway. They call it the witches house and tell their children that the Devil would get them if they venture near . . .' She falters.

'Thank you for keeping it safe for me.'

I dust off the two chairs at the table and we sit. We unwrap the cheese and, using the cloth as a plate, begin to eat. The food is fresh and delicious. We eat in silence, then Aubrey pours two mugs of ale and looks at me, waiting for me to speak. I take a deep breath and glance down into my mug, as if I will find the right words in that sweet darkness. The fire crackles and spits as the room warms and Aubrey reaches for my hand.

'Tell me of Priscilla. And then of you. All of it, do not leave anything out.' So I tell her of the journey from Dunwich, the others who were taken up with us, the bumping of the cart, the heat and dust. I tell her how our friend withdrew into herself, confused by the many people stuffed into the barn, how she was made ill by the foulness of the gaol. How the court was in uproar and so confused when the alarm came that they did not know what to do with us all. And I speak of how James helped us escape, how Priscilla died, burning up with fever in a ditch. How she forgave me at the end and sent her love to Aubrey, that our long friendship was in her mind as she faded, and how much it had meant to her before the bad times came. Then, when we had sat in silence thinking of her, I told her of my own journey, of James and his plans, of how we had travelled as man and wife for safety.

'Were you not afraid, Bess?'

'No, he is a good man. I was very lucky . . . it was his bravery and cunning that saved us.' His face shimmers before me, smiling, and I smile back. 'He asked me to go with him to Halesworth, to be his wife. I nearly did. But I wanted to come home.'

Aubrey leans forward and cups my face in her hand.

'Do you miss him?' I nod. 'Well, I am glad you came back. I knew you would. I just did not know when.'

She is smiling but the soft conviction in her voice causes a shiver to run down my spine

'How did you know?' Aubrey's face looks startled at the urgency of my tone. 'How did you know, Aubrey? Please don't tell me . . .'

'It was a feeling, only that. Nothing else.' She sees the fear in my eyes.

'As long as that is all it was. You must never speak of such things to anyone else, even your friends. There is still much fear in this land, I have seen it on my travels. People still look to accuse others as witches, the trials are not ended. The slightest suspicion will be good enough reason for them to seize you, and you have said yourself how Thomas Spatchett has eyes and ears everywhere . . . you must take very great care, Aubrey, promise me?'

She looks at me shrewdly and I see something in her eyes that was not there before.

'I am careful, I promise. It was just a knowing inside that I would see you again. I am not afraid when the townsfolk draw back from me, for it is their fear that keeps me safe.'

'Why do some fear you so? You have lived here all your life. You have only ever been good and kind...'

'I was the one who escaped trial when you and Priscilla were taken. I am the witch that got away. Thomas Spatchett and his like have convinced the people that the Devil had his hand in it. They all think that Satan protected his own and I am content to let them think it. Their fear gives me some little power.' I nod, although I am not sure I fully understand. 'But what of you? What will you do, Bess, how will you live?'

I HAVE THOUGHT OF LITTLE ELSE SINCE I LEFT FRAMLINGHAM AND James, and now the answer comes to me.

'I am no longer Elizabeth, she is dead. I am her cousin, who heard that she had been hanged for a witch, and I have come to claim her cottage. I am a pedlar too, and I will carry out my trade from here, as she did, home in the winter, travelling when the weather warms.'

Aubrey's brow furrows.

'You will need to be very careful, for Thomas Spatchett is not convinced that you died. There was no list of names, no confirmation, and Master Spatchett still questions anyone who will listen about this.'

'There was too much confusion and no records were kept. The court was in disarray, we were moved quickly, without preparation. If you tell this to anyone who asks, people will come to believe it. They will think that I died on the journey to Ipswich, or I died in the gaol there – everyone knows what a fearful place that is, rife with disease and vermin.'

'The talk of witchcraft has not died down here, Master Spatchett sees to that. He is obsessed with it. He spies witches and imps around every corner, points his finger at all and sundry until they are so afraid they dare not even leave their homes. Some say that the blows to the head he has had have affected his mind, but they still seem happy to promote him to higher and higher office, to have him represent them. He is strong-willed, good with words and persuasive, and he has the money to go with that power. It makes him dangerous. You will always be in great peril if you stay here.'

'I had to come home to Dunwich. You do not know what it was like; it was an ache, the longing, and I could think of nothing else. I know it will be dangerous, that I will have to be very careful, but I need to be here. And I wanted to see you. I have long wished to sit here like this, talking to you. I dreamed of it so often and now I can hardly believe it's real.'

I clasp her hand and she squeezes mine in return, then looks me up and down.

'Fortunately, you no longer look like Elizabeth Southerne. Even I did not recognise you. She was not so sun-touched, so thin. Those britches, they make you look even taller. And you seem older, your face and eyes tell of troubles and time. So, Bess's cousin, what is your name?'

This is the one thing I had not thought of, but when she asks it comes to me in an instant. I look at her and smile broadly.

'James. I am called James.'

CHAPTER 19

So James I am, and I pray that my namesake is safe and well in Halesworth, brewing a better type of ale, that he found his niece, and that he is happy. I think of him often and what might have been, but I made my choice and must live with it. The tiredness and pains of the watching never leave me, nor does the fear of being discovered. At first, Aubrey brings me food and ale but slowly, as winter bites, I become braver. Aubrey has given me a winter cloak that belonged to William and I wrap it tight around me, over my man's jerkin and boots, as, with hat pulled down over my face, I venture out to the lane and then down into the town. There are whispers behind hands, and I am sometimes looked at with suspicion, but Dunwich has been a port for centuries, strangers are familiar here, and gradually I am accepted. I become known as a recluse, for I only answer questions when I have to and do not take part in conversations and gossip. One or two remark on my likeness to Elizabeth but, as family, this is not thought unusual and generally I am left alone. The only one who comes to my cottage is Aubrey, and whether people comment on her visiting me, a strange man, I do not hear. As the winter pulls in, my life settles and becomes almost normal. Until they seize another witch.

. . .

Aubrey comes to me in the dead of night with the news. Her red hair is wild under the hood of her cloak, her face drawn with fear as I usher her in, peering around outside in the blackness to see if she was followed, then shut the door firmly behind her.

'They have seized another.' Her voice breaks and she starts to shake. 'Bess, it is starting again. What are we to do?'

I grasp her shoulders.

'Who have they taken?'

'It is the old widow who lives by the shore, the one whose mind has gone. Dorothy Clarke. The men seized her this afternoon, they have taken her to the gaol.' I think of my time in that place – it is winter now. The cold and damp will eat into her frail frame. I shudder.

'I knew her. She was a friend of my mother's, they were young women together. She has lived all her life in Dunwich – she must be very aged.'

Aubrey nods.

'It is she. Her mind has been going for a long time and now she is no longer of this world.'

I think of Widow Clarke's great age, remember her stooped back and thin white hair, her tiny bird-like frame, and I wonder what they are doing to her now. It is as if a ghost walks over my grave.

Aubrey's voice shakes me out of my dream.

'She has been begging from door to door and I have heard that she has recently taken to wandering at night, that she mumbles and curses. It is Thomas Spatchett himself who has accused her. He has whipped up fear in the town and has told the magistrate that she sent a plague of lice to torment him, then an imp, and it was this imp that caused the pains in his head. And they believe him . . .' She pauses then stands straight and looks at me. 'He will search for others, there will be no stopping him now. I am afraid for you.'

Fear is spiking through me as she gives voice to my thoughts. I am still seen as a stranger here and it is known that I am related to

Elizabeth Southerne. They seize men as witches too, and if they seize me and I am searched they will find . . . I gaze back at Aubrey. She stands before me, a flame-haired warrior, small and proud, her worry all for me, and my heart clenches with love for her.

'But you, Aubrey. They may also come for you.'

She laughs grimly and shakes her head.

'I doubt they will take me again, they are too afraid of me. I am not elderly or confused. I am respected, amongst the fishermen anyway. I can speak up for myself and people will listen, I am sure of it. But you – you are different. You have taken great care, but people have noticed you, and there has been talk . . .'

I reach for her hands.

'Let us wait a few hours, see what happens. They may yet let Dorothy go.'

But we both know they will not.

THE NEXT DAY I GO DOWN TO THE MARKET PLACE – I HAVE TO KNOW what is happening. The December air is bitter and I pull my cloak around my face, keeping my hat low on my brow. Despite the cold, there are many people about, and all they are talking about is the seizing of the witch. They cluster around the stalls chattering and gesturing towards the gaol. I move closer to one group, huddled around a small trestle table, trying to hear what is being said, then the wares on display catch my eye. Blades glitter in the low winter sun. The knife seller watches me with beady eyes as I pick one up after the other, feeling their size and heft.

'Are you looking for a knife, Sir?' He stares at me. 'Do I know you?'

'I don't think so – I am not from these parts.' He leans closer, peering at me, and I pull my hat lower. There is a slim knife on the table and I test its edge with my thumb. It is sharp, its handle fits cleanly in my palm, its heft is right.

'How much is this one?' He names a price far above its worth. I look at him hard. 'What is the real price?' The figure comes down, and I pull my purse from under my cloak and count the coins into his grubby palm. The price is still too high but I cannot risk his curiosity any longer.

'You've heard about the witch seized here, have you?' He is leaning towards me now, over familiar, his face gleaming with gossip. 'Well, they have just announced that she is to be put on trial at Aldeburgh. Master Spatchett is to go there and bear witness. Nothing is to happen here.' He spits on the ground, his disgust at this obvious. 'I'm told that she will be examined there, and by no other person than the Witchfinder himself!'

My heart stops dead in my chest and I think my legs will fail me.

'The Witchfinder? Hopkins?' His reputation has grown, and these days his name is muttered behind hands that shake with fear. His power and reach have spread such that no one in East Anglia is safe. Towns now clamour to invite him to search out witches in their midst, willing to pay high sums, and his methods are copied by others. If he is in Aldeburgh he could come here. No one will be safe.

'Matthew Hopkins, yes, the very same. Apparently, the Aldeburgh bailiffs invited him to search out witches September-time, for they had already seized one for themselves. He had such success they invited him back. He will be there this week. So our town has arranged to have the Clarke witch taken there.' He steps back in satisfaction. 'Saves them money I suppose, and we will be seen to be cleansing our town of the sin of witchcraft. Examinations and trials are an expensive business – but I would like to have seen her tried here. Never seen a hanging.'

'No – nor me.' But I have heard one . . . I look down at the knife in my hand, then pull back my cloak and tuck it into my belt. The knife-seller looks at me again, his gaze sharp.

'I *do* know you. You're the one who is living in the cottage that belonged to the witch that was hanged at Bury. Up on the track past the Leper Hospital.' His accusation rings clear in the chill air and I see people stop and look. I step back, touching the brim of my hat. I do not know if I imagine people beginning to mutter behind wool-clad hands, or the word witch hissing in the air. But I know that eyes are following me as I move hurriedly away and I go cold. I am no longer safe here.

AUBREY IS WAITING FOR ME AT THE COTTAGE WHEN I GET BACK. She knows. She always knew. My clothes and belongings are already folded into my pack and she has wrapped some food in a cloth. She sits at the table, hands clasped in her lap as I look around me for the last time.

'Everything is ready for you.'

'Aubrey . . .' The words dry in my mouth.

She stands and embraces me, her tears mingling with mine as we hold each other tightly.

'Where will you go?'

I have been pondering this constantly since I left the town but as she asks, all becomes clear. I will do what I should have done earlier.

'I will try to find James in Halesworth, see if he will still have me. If he is not there, well, I will do as I have always done – survive on my own.'

Aubrey smiles at me.

'Go in peace, Bess, find him, be happy, and may God be with you. I will never forget you, or Priscilla and our friendship. I will keep you in my heart always.' She fumbles in her skirts and brings out the blade she held against my throat a few months earlier. 'Here, you may need this.'

I push her hand away gently.

'I bought my own blade, for I could feel the danger coming, but thank you. You must keep it, you may have need of it yourself.' She tucks it away as I move to the hearth and pull at the loose brick. The purse I had hidden there remains; it is untouched. I look up at my friend.

'I was happy for you to have this...'

'I know but it did not feel right, taking what was so hard-earned.'

I reach into the depths of the purse, fingers sliding against the slubbed leather, and hear the cold chink of metal. I pass Aubrey a handful of coins. 'Here, take these.' She hesitates and I close her fingers over the silver. 'Please – you may need them.'

Her eyes sparkle with tears.

'Thank you.'

I hoist the pack onto my shoulders. 'What will you do? Surely you are not safe here?' I look down at her small face. 'Come with me? Please? It is not safe here for you. We can travel as man and wife, as James and I did, no one will...'

'Bess, I cannot, but I thank you for the thought. This is my home, I was born here. I cannot leave. All I know is here. I make a good living with my nets, people have known me all my life, there is little danger here for me.' She reaches for my hand. 'You know how it feels when you belong to a place.'

I nod.

'But I fear for you, Aubrey. I wish you would come with me.'

'You returned to Dunwich because this is your home. It is in your blood. Well, I am the same. But I am not brave as you are, I do not know where to go, nor how to be. I have not travelled like you – I've never even been out of this town. No, I will not leave, not of my own doing. Now, go, quick, before they come for you.' She pushes me towards the door and I step out. I turn and hold her tightly once more, breathing in her smell, her warmth, knowing this will be the last time I see her. I look around my cottage, drinking in its familiarity, fixing it in my memory, then I step outside and walk the short way up the path and into the lane. I look briefly towards Dunwich, saying a silent farewell, then turn away, finding my feet and my courage, and begin to move swiftly along the sandy track. At the bend in the way, I pause and turn back to gaze at the small figure of Aubrey standing in the doorway. Forcing myself to smile, I lift my hand and wave goodbye to her and all I know.

Then I walk away.

PART IV

Aubrey

CHAPTER 20

I watch Elizabeth wave goodbye, then stare at her retreating back as she strides away towards Westleton, unable to stop the tears that stream down my face. I hope she finds what she is looking for. Through my tears the ghosts of three girls slip, dancing away from me, hand in hand. Now Priscilla is dead, and Elizabeth is gone. There is only me left.

I walk back into the cottage, step inside and look around – our friendship is pressed into every corner and crevice. I dig out a kerchief from my pocket and wipe my face, breathe deeply, gathering myself. There is little left here. Elizabeth had very few belongings and I made sure she took those with her. The cottage is poor and run down for she did not have time to make it whole again, she could not stay long enough. They have forced her out and now they will come here, Spatchett and his men. They will bring large, loping dogs to sniff and track her. He will tear this cottage apart looking for any shred of her, and I know he will not spare his anger when he finds she has gone.

I cannot bear to have this last piece of her treated so cruelly. There is a pile of kindling in the hearth, for she had laid the fire before she went down into the town for the last time. I take the logs she has put aside and heap them into the hearth, on top of the kindling, then go outside to the woodpile and bring in more, spreading them out from the hearth and across the floor. I work swiftly until my arms burn with the effort of carrying. There is a candle, half burned, on the window sill, so I spark my flint to light it, then stoop and hold the flame to the kindling. The dry wood begins to crackle and burn. It takes hold quickly, flames dancing ever higher, as I move swiftly to the bed and touch the candle's light to it. The flame darts serpent-like up the bed curtain then envelops it; the bedding catches, the straw in the mattress twisting and glowing as the blaze spreads. I open the window and door, and the rush of air causes the flames to dance higher, licking the rafters. The heat is growing, the whole room aflame, so I step quickly outside. I hope it is enough. I hope that it will destroy all trace of my friend so that the dogs cannot find her.

OUTSIDE, THE CLEAR AIR SHIMMERS BEFORE ME AND I RUB MY EYES against the pricking of the dense white smoke. Then, a shout in the distance, a deep bark, and I see the dark figures of men, coming towards me with torches and ropes. They are a little way off yet, but they will have seen the flames and may have seen me. I duck around the back of the blazing cottage, out of sight. I had intended to hide in the woods and then make my way back towards my own home. But as the men draw closer I freeze, pulling back into the shadows as they stomp up the track, voices raised, fierce dogs straining on long leashes, keen for the chase. It is a large crowd, they are milling and thinning like a shoal of herring, moving ever forwards, their pace increasing as they spy the flames rising into the dark night and hear the dull roar and crackle of the fire. They charge towards it, torches bobbing, and I hear their cries of fury as they see the cottage burning. It is starting to collapse in on itself now, smoke billowing and flames leaping, as the walls crumble and the thatch smokes. They surround the blaze, black outlines wheeling and turning like dancing imps, as if the Devil himself has possessed them.

Then I see him. Standing alone, further back on the track, detached from the fire and fury. Thomas Spatchett. He is looking around, searching, his face flickering orange and yellow in the firelight, and I duck down out of sight, peering through the grass at him. He knows I am here, I can tell, but he cannot see me, and I watch as he stands stock still, rips his hat from his head, and raises his face to the sky. The jagged scar ripples his forehead as he opens his mouth and bellows his rage into the night.

His cry causes the others to stop and turn, watching in surprise as he yowls his fury. He knows he has been outwitted. Elizabeth has escaped his clutches and I am glad she will be safe, wherever she is. The malice of this man caused my two friends to be seized, searched, and watched. Thomas Spatchett, a man of the church, of God, stood by and enabled his own cousin to desert his wife, to take her children from her, and he did nothing to stop it. What John Collit did to Priscilla was cruel, but Thomas Spatchett and his hatred of witches was behind it. And when she became deranged by all that had happened to her, when life was too much for her mind to take, it was Thomas Spatchett that had her brought into the church, had her body searched, and then held her for three nights and days without sleep, to force a confession from her, a poor damaged woman who had done him no wrong. He listened to her ravings and used them to damn Elizabeth. He convinced others that they were both witches, sent them to be tried and then hanged. Priscilla died in a ditch because of him, Elizabeth endured so much and came home, but now she has had to leave forever, and it is because of him. He is the cause of all of this, he is obsessed, and I know he will not rest until he has seized me as well. So I curse him. I mutter the words silently to myself and they are powerful and strange. I damn him with my whole heart for what he has done to

Elizabeth and Priscilla. But he will not break me. I escaped his venom before, and I will escape it again.

Dawn is breaking by the time I dare enter my cottage. The room is chill, the fire in the hearth almost gone out, so I feed it with kindling, coaxing it back into life, watching as the flames grow, remembering all I have just done. I put a pot on the fire, pour a bowl of water and gather some vegetables from my store, pull out my knife, and start to prepare them for a broth. All must appear normal.

And this is what I am doing when they come for me again.

I see them from my window. Thomas Spatchett is leading a crowd which has grown in size since they went to Elizabeth's cottage. Townspeople have swelled its ranks, thinking to be there at the seizing of another witch.

There is the thundering of a wooden stave on my door and my heart hammers in time with it.

'Mistress Grinsett? Aubrey Grinsett? Show yourself.' Spatchett's voice carries over the crowd, now silent in anticipation, their excitement palpable. Slowly, my movements deliberate, I wipe my hands on my apron and place my knife on the table, then think again and tuck it into the pocket in my skirt. I take a deep breath and open the door.

'Sir?' I hold myself tall and steady, as I face him, but my legs shake in fear.

'The man that was living in the cottage. Mistress Southerne's cottage.' I keep my face blank. 'He has gone. The cottage is burned to the ground. What do you know of this? Tell me.' His whole body is stiff with anger, his voice harsh.

'I know nothing, Sir. I have been here, preparing my meal.' I push the door open wide to show him. He peers in but can see the place is empty. The water boils and hisses on the fire, the vegetables gleam wetly on the table.

'It has been noticed that you are frequently in the company of this man, you have been seen visiting him. It is not seemly, a widowed woman such as yourself.' He sees my face. 'I am told your husband went to sea and never returned. I nod, keeping my head bowed, all the time my mind racing. Thomas Spatchett has made enquiries about me, and people have talked – I should have known better than to think it was all forgotten. But, though I am small in stature, I am strong, and I will stand up to this man. It is as if Elizabeth has bequeathed me her courage. I stand square in the doorway and look him in the eye.

'That is correct, Sir, God rest his soul, for my husband has been many years gone. He is long dead.' A lump rises in my throat.

'But *if* he is dead – and we have no proof of that . . .' I look at him blankly, trying to think what he is suggesting, for it is long accepted that a man who is lost at sea and does not return, is deemed to have drowned. '. . . if he is, in fact, dead, as you have put about, it does not absolve you from your wifely state. A widow, like a wife, should remain seemly and modest, and you have not been. You have consorted with a man who is not your husband. And I am told other men are seen to visit your house. This conduct alone is a matter for the church. The punishment is whipping and a fine. What think you of that, Mistress?' His face is growing red now as his voice rises, and he scratches at his scar with gloved fingers.

'I am a net-maker, Sir. Men are seen coming to my house because they need new nets, or old ones mending. It is my living and all hereabouts know it.'

'But you have been seen, many times, coming from the house of a woman condemned for witchcraft. And this person is her kin, I hear? Well, we all know that the sin of witchcraft runs rife through families; man, woman and child, so it seems right to assume that this man, this stranger, was also of that ilk. And this is not the first time you have been seen to be consorting with witches, is it, Mistress Grinsett?'

I raise my head and look straight at him. I am not sure if it is imagined, but he seems to pull back a little.

'I was seized last summer, Sir, with others, but, as you well know, the magistrate let me go because no evidence could be found.' I narrow my eyes, trying to keep my temper in check. 'You falsely accused me then and you falsely accuse me now. I know nothing about a fire . . .' I cross my fingers behind my back and hope God will forgive the lie. 'I have merely visited the kin of my late friend to welcome him to the town and to make sure all was well with the cottage. I provided some food and ale and company. I have done nothing wrong, nothing *unseemly* or *immodest.*' I spit the words at him, then pinch the skin on one hand with shaking fingers, trying to keep my voice measured and calm. But fear is rising in my chest and my stomach turns and roils.

THOMAS SPATCHETT TURNS AND GESTURES TO TWO MEN WHO STEP forward, arms outstretched, ready to seize me. But I am not done yet.

'Who has accused me?' My voice rings clear in the morning air. 'What crime am I said to have committed?'

The men hesitate and Master Spatchett steps forward.

'The crime of witchcraft, Mistress, what else? The magistrate will decide if there is a case to answer. I have found three witches already in this town, he will listen to me when I deliver up a fourth, I am sure.'

I do not know where I find the courage but I bend closer so that my voice can be heard only by him.

'As he did last time?' Master Spatchett's face tightens. 'Are you sure of that?' He hisses at me through clenched teeth, his breath warm and stale on my cheek. 'Are you sure he will take your word alone? Has anyone truly accused me, or is it you, still determined to see me hanged? Well, if you wish to be dismissed by the magistrate a second time, then take me. Try.' I am shaking now. All I can believe in is the fairness of the magistrate, for he saw through this once before, he was not as quick to judge as Master Spatchett expected him to be. The man before me has been made to look a fool once, and I chance my freedom on his unwillingness for it to happen again. For Thomas Spatchett has attained great heights in Dunwich and I am certain he would not wish to fall to earth so publicly.

We face each other like cats, stock-still and bristling, their hackles risen, their fur greasy and fetid with anger and fear.

'So . . .' I step away and look at the two men standing behind him, confusion on their faces. '. . . am I to be taken?' I hold out my arms for shackles to be fixed and close my eyes, listening for the crunch of footsteps, the cold weight of iron on my wrists. This is how Priscilla and Elizabeth must have felt, waiting, waiting, hearts thundering in chests, breath coming short.

Then, a step, a scrape of earth underfoot and I open my eyes again. Thomas Spatchett has stepped back. He is shaking with anger, his words sharp and precise.

'I will make further enquiries about you, Mistress. I am going to turn over every stone, search behind every bush and tree. I will find out everything there is to know about you, and I will find the evidence that proves that you are a creature of Satan, to be reviled and condemned. You are a witch, Madam, I know it here.' He thumps a leather-clad fist to his chest. 'And as soon as I have found that proof I will return, and you will be taken, you have my word on this.' His distorted forehead is glistening with sweat and his eyes are black and narrow. He looks like the very Devil himself.

I step back into my cottage and slam the door, fixing the bar in place. Then I turn and rest against it as my shaking legs finally give way and I slide to the floor. I can scarce breath for terror.

On the fire, the pot spits and steams.

. . .

But I am soon forgotten, for word from Aldeburgh silences the town. The news is that the Witchfinder himself questioned Dorothy Clarke, that poor disturbed widow, who was plucked from all she knew in Dunwich and taken on a hard, rattling cart in the freezing depths of the harshest winter in living memory. That old and feeble-minded soul who never hurt a fly was kept in Aldeburgh gaol in the bitter cold. They say that she uttered no words, so he had his woman prick her, but still she did not confess. They tell how she was watched, and that it was a beetle, of a kind you often find in old buildings, that was her undoing, for it crawled over her foot, and that was enough for them to claim that her imp had come to her and suckled from her. It was Matthew Hopkins who carried out this cruelty and it was Thomas Spatchett who travelled to Aldeburgh to give evidence at her trial and declaim her as a witch. It was Thomas Spatchett who returned to proudly proclaim how she was taken, with others, and hanged in the bitter cold.

It is the carter, charged with taking Dorothy Clarke to Aldeburgh who tells the rest. He describes how the bodies were left on the gallows in the marketplace as an example, so that all could see what the law does to witches. And that the leaden skies finally broke and snow fell gentle on their corpses.

CHAPTER 21

I live a quiet life. My house is small, made of wood, blacked with pitch to withstand the storms that batter this coastline, and there is plenty to do keeping it repaired. It is full of nets now, leaving scarcely any space for me, but I am happy like this, for I do not allow anyone inside – my business is transacted in the open where people can see and have no cause to gossip. I go to the market only for necessities, do not speak to strangers and keep myself close. But I watch Thomas Spatchett, as I know he watches me. And he rises even further. He is given the post of Chamberlain for Dunwich, and the next year he is made one of the ruling twenty-four. The year after that he is appointed as coroner and rises to the highest position of Bailiff of the town two years after. Thomas Spatchett becomes Dunwich. He holds it in the palm of his hand. Then, as if this power is not enough, he finds God. He cleaves to him, as a drowning man to flotsam, and begins to travel the countryside preaching the gospels, so much so that folk begin to mutter about his lack of attention to the administration of Dunwich. He is well-known now, revered as much for his bible preaching as his authority and status here. He rules over all but, as his star ascends, mine plunges. People turn away from me in the street and I know this is his doing, that he has made it known that I am to be feared and reviled. As I walk by now, I often see people make the sign against witchcraft, thumb clutched between fingers in protection. I sometimes find I am talking to myself, for mine is a solitary life, but I pull myself up quickly; people will not hesitate to suggest I curse them with my mumblings. I long to keep an animal for company but I dare not, for fear it would be seen as an imp or familiar. I am careful, I tread lightly in the town so as not to cause a ripple on its glassy surface.

But all changes and the ripple comes, rising and roaring like a spring tide, high and fierce, though none of my doing – for Thomas Spatchett is taken ill. It is the baker's wife, a kindly woman, one of the few who will speak with me, who tells me.

'It happened here in the marketplace only days ago. It was as if he left his body. Never seen the like of it . . . he stopped, stock still, his eyes went black and it was as if he was absent from the world. They sent for his servant, who took him away, but I hear that now he is like this for hours at a time, unseeing and unhearing. And when he is present, he complains of severe pains in his head, so much so that they fear that his mind will be damaged.' I nod at her and take up my bread, saying nothing. Days later, worse tales reach my ears. Stories are flying around the town of how he has become seized with wild distortions and shakings of his body, foaming at the mouth, his eyes turned in his head, his limbs twisting at unnatural angles. I remember the small boy on the day of the play, how he fell to the ground in a fit – it was in him then. But it seems that these fits have increased until twenty times a day or more he shudders and convulses, his body flailing, his mind gone. He is no longer able to preach, no longer able to carry out his role as Bailiff. Out of the blue, he has become incapable and ill, and gossip is alive with thoughts of why this has happened to such a God-fearing and worthy man such as he. So I look to my nets, keeping myself close, knowing that it will not take long for people to remember and talk, and that talk will become denunciation. I do not leave the house but wait in terror for the finger to point at me.

. . .

IT DOES NOT HAPPEN. MASTER SPATCHETT CONTINUES ILL BUT I AM left alone. But when the only food in the house is stale, and there is nothing to drink, I have to visit the market, I have no option. I go early, when fewer folk are about, my hood pulled close over my eyes, my willow basket on my arm, and I keep my head lowered. I pass the market stalls swiftly, buying bread, and cheese, handing over the coins, avoiding the gaze of the stallholders. Then I pause by the butcher's cart. My mouth waters at the thought of hot roast meat, a piece of pigeon or a rabbit. I point at a small chop, hand over the coins, and take the paper-wrapped parcel, putting it in my basket with a nod of thanks. A gust of wind rattles the awnings and I look out to sea. Dark clouds are forming; a storm is coming. I am ready to rush home before it hits us, but then, amongst the stalls, I see a barrel of herrings and I stop to look. Silver shapes glisten, staring moon-eyed at the sky, and I remember that day on the beach, how Priscilla's eyes shone when she saw the crabfish. How Elizabeth had come back then and we were together, three friends who loved each other. Before she met John, before...

It is as if I conjure him from thin air. I turn to go and there he is – John Collit, with a woman in tow, staring at me with a sly grin on his face.

'Aubrey Grinsett. Well, well. It has been a long time since I have seen you about in this town.' I drop a curtsey, head lowered. 'All alone, now, I wager.' I look up sharply. He is older but as handsome as ever. His dark curls are flecked with grey, his face browned and lined by the sun, but he is still the type of man that women stare at under their lashes. He is dressed soberly in solemn black, but I can see that the cloth is good, the cut fine; he looks prosperous and healthy, but I sense a hardness about him that was not there before.

'Good day, John. What brings you to Dunwich?'

'I am here to visit Cousin Thomas. He is sorely afflicted, and none seem to be able to find the cause. He has been seen by the best doctors, but no one can stop his fits. They bleed him and purge him but nothing helps. It seems to me as if he has been bewitched.' I look around frantically, trying to remove myself from his presence, but then the woman with him, who has been standing back, steps forward and takes his arm. She looks up at him in enquiry and he pats her hand.

'Martha, this is Aubrey Grinsett; she was known to my late wife.' He says the words with contempt and I bristle.

'Mistress Grinsett.' The woman barely curtseys, her wariness and disdain clear. She turns to John. 'We must be about our business, Husband.' His eyes narrow and I see that, just below the surface, his temper still simmers.

'I will come when I choose, Wife, and not before.'

She pulls her hand away from his arm as if burned.

'Of course, I meant nothing by it, merely . . .'

'I would speak with Mistress Grinsett. Go, buy your meat, and I will find you shortly.' She flinches under his words, her face flushing, then scuttles away.

JOHN TURNS BACK TO ME AND LOOKS ME UP AND DOWN.

'I am surprised to find you still in Dunwich, Aubrey.' I see the hardness in his eyes and begin to back away. 'I thought you to be seized by now, like those other whores of Satan.'

I know I should not rise to his bait, but I cannot let this rest.

'You know that is not the truth of it. Elizabeth and Priscilla were falsely accused. Priscilla was your wife, John, mother of your children. She was ill, her mind . . .'

'Was gone, yes, and that is why I had rid of her.' He stops, as if he has said too much, and I feel the blood drain from my face.

'What you did to her was cruelty itself. She could not help her illness, it was brought on by childbirth, as sometimes happens. You knew that.'

John shrugs and I think of how he took her children, how he left her without a word, making her homeless.

'She could not work, nor carry out the simplest task, she just lay there, useless. The children were neglected and I was afraid for them after what she did to poor Edward, may his soul rest in peace. Cousin Thomas offered to take them in, then he offered me a good position on his farm in Cookley but he told me that I must come alone, that I was not to bring her in case she brought that village into disrepute. I was to ensure she stayed in Dunwich. His offer was generous. What I did was a small price to pay for an opportunity such as that.'

I am breathing heavily now, my heart juddering in my chest. Fear takes me over and I cannot make sense of what he is saying, his words are jangling and clattering in my ears.

'What you did?'

He draws closer and looks down at me, his body large and imposing.

'Cousin Thomas told me that to seize a witch would raise him up in the eyes of the Lord, and with the great and the good of Dunwich. He offered me security and a new life. In return, I was to give him a witch.'

'But . . .?' He looks down at his feet and shuffles. It is as if his conscience finally pricks him and I am to be his confessional.

'Priscilla was getting weaker after each birth, her mind failing more and more, you saw that, we all did. So I began to whisper in her ear at night, or when she slept. I told her that Satan wanted her for his own. Over and over I breathed it, until she believed me when I told her what she must do. She truly thought it was the Devil speaking to her.' He straightens. 'Small words dripped into her ear in the dark of night. Moving her belongings so she could not find them, making her think she had misplaced them. Telling her she was nothing, that no one cared for her. I kept her away from you and Elizabeth, for I knew how you would have wanted to help her. I made her think you were no longer her friends, that what was happening to her was the work of the Devil. I made her believe that no one loved her.'

JOHN SEES THE REVULSION ON MY FACE AND PAUSES. I CAN BARELY speak for shock.

'But what of Edward? Surely you did not tell her to harm...?'

He looks at me, appalled.

'No, how can you think such a thing? To tell her to murder our babe would have been evil. It took little to make her believe that she had entered into a covenant with Satan, but to murder our son? No, I never thought she would do such a thing! That poor child, to see him suffer like that at her hands . . . but it was none of my doing. The Devil must have entered her after all, for she was weak, sinful. It was the Devil who made her do it. After, I told Priscilla that she could only be made whole again if she confessed her sins. I left her and went to Cookley, and Cousin Thomas told me that Elizabeth took her in – 'twas guilt, I have no doubt of that, for why else bother with one whose wits had gone such as she?'

'And Elizabeth? What of her?'

John snorts at the memory.

'What of her? It was so easy to seduce her – great cow-eyes she'd been making at me for years. No, she raised her skirts as quick as a tuppenny whore. My wife was no use to me, just lying there, no chance of her carrying out her wifely duty. And a man has needs, and Elizabeth was always a fair-looking maid. No, she seduced me and I was weak . . . but I have repented and I know that God has forgiven me for my transgression. He has given me a godly new wife to tend to my needs, a home and a hearth, a good living. He has shown that I am truly forgiven. No, Thomas was right, I was best rid of her.' He shrugs his shoulders. 'Best rid.'

I am statue-still, frozen, like a rabbit caught in lamp-light. John looks down at me, smiling at the horror on my face, the old confidence returning now his confession is made. But we are no longer alone – people are stopping to see what is happening, ears pricked, curiosity bright in their faces. I step back, trembling. Part of me knows I should challenge him, stand up for myself, for poor sad Priscilla, and ill-used Elizabeth. I should speak of it to the townsfolk, loudly condemn what he has done to anyone that will listen. The town elders should learn of this. But then I remember that Thomas Spatchett is a Bailiff and I know that no one would believe me. John looks hard at me with narrowed eyes and I wonder how I had not seen before his cruelty and lack of compassion.

'Did you ever love Priss?'

He does not even look ashamed.

'Aye, I did, in the beginning, maybe. But she was a foolish fancy, she trapped me into that marriage. Satan was in her even then, it seems.'

I see it all now. My poor Priscilla; a beautiful face and willing manner, someone for him to bully and cajole. John wanted a wife, that was all, someone to raise his family but, even when she had borne three children who lived, ruining her health in the doing of it, he betrayed her over and over by persuading her that the Devil spoke to her. He took her children away and her home from her, just to further his own fortunes. And he made a whore of Elizabeth for his own gratification. He is a serpent and his darkness coils around me. The blood rushes in my ears and I think I might faint for lack of air.

His voice brings me back.

'She confessed eventually, though, didn't she? Couldn't stand the torment I suppose, although it took longer than I thought. She confessed and she took Elizabeth down with her and so Cousin Thomas had two witches instead of one. Nearly had three, eh, Aubrey? But you escaped, didn't you? By witchcraft, was it, for all know how the Devil looks after his own?'

The words rattle around the marketplace as silence drops like a stone. I stumble backwards as he lifts his arm and points a shaking finger at me, his voice rising. 'You are a witch, Aubrey Grinsett.

Cousin Thomas knows it, I know it, and soon the whole town will too. We are coming for you, mark my words.' He leans in closer. 'You will not escape again, I will make sure of it. I had rid of Priscilla and I will have rid of you.'

His words undo me. I spin around, my basket flying, the purchases scattering. I do not pause to pick them up but run as fast as I can to escape John Collit and his words, the shocked faces of the townsfolk, the mutterings and black looks. I fling myself through the door of my cottage, breathless and trembling, and slam it shut, dropping the bar in place, then look around wildly, thinking to gather my belongings and flee, but the realisation hits me in a cold wave that I have nowhere to go. I had my chance, I could have gone with Elizabeth, but I chose to stay, and now there is nowhere to hide. I did not fear this town, never thought it would turn on me. But I was wrong. And now I am trapped. I am not resourceful like Bess, not as worldly-wise. I have lived a narrow life and I would not know how to live anywhere else. So I sit down and try to calm my fears by mending a net. I work ceaselessly, like a demon, not pausing to rest, the needle flying through my fingers, tightening and knotting, the smell of the twine calming and familiar. When it is done and I am satisfied, I eat a meal of stale bread and hard cheese that sticks dry in my throat, drink the last of my ale, and all the time thinking, thinking about what to do, how to avoid an accusation.

And then it comes to me.

CHAPTER 22

The following day I dress carefully in my best skirt, a clean apron and coif. I tidy my hair and wash my face, making myself as presentable as I can for a woman of middling years who is in fear for her life. I summon all the courage I have, then walk down into the town and speak to the carters man. Coins change hands, and I am soon sat with the barrels of fish in the back of the cart, jolting and swaying on the road to Halesworth. My heart beats with fear – I have never left Dunwich before. The journey takes until midday, the sun high in the sky when I set down and begin the three-mile walk. I have brought bread with me, so stop by the side of the road at midday to eat, looking around me at the landscape. It is green and gold, corn ripe in the fields, the dust of July blowing in soft clouds over the track. I have never travelled so far from home and it is a revelation. There are no buildings around, no streets bustling with people. I had imagined a place like Dunwich, but there is no sea, the only view here is of rolling fields and woodland, the only sound that of birds singing high in the sky. I walk on, brushing myself down as best I can, until I reach Cookley.

I had expected it to be more. A small town perhaps, a village at least, but this place is a hamlet, with only a few cottages and a church. As I approach the lychgate, a man in the black garb of a preacher comes out of the church, closing the old oak door carefully behind him. He turns and looks me up and down. He is small and round, his nose red-veined and bulbous, that of a drinker. There is no kindness in his face. I know how I must look to him, so I bob a curtsey, keeping my eyes lowered.

'Reverend, I seek Master John Collit. Do you know of him?'

'You must mean Mistress Collit. If you are seeking work, I know of none there.'

My mind spins, then settles on a path.

'Yes, Sir, forgive me, I meant Mistress Collit. I do not seek work but wish to speak to her on a matter of some urgency.'

The minister raises his arm and points, suspicious and alert

'Down there, on the left. And God's blessings be upon you, Sister.' The words are uttered without feeling. I curtsey again and move away quickly, aware of his eyes on my back, following me.

The house he has indicated is much larger than I expected. John has done well for himself. Thomas Spatchett clearly looks after his own, and I feel a pang of anger for Priscilla, for what she never had. I go round the back, past a tidy garden of herbs, to the servant's entrance and ring the bell, going over my story in my head.

A young girl, a maidservant by her dress, answers the door.

'I wish to speak with your master, John Collit.' She looks at me, the amusement scarcely disguised.

'Go away old woman, we do not buy from the door, nor do we entertain beggars. Father is most firm about that.' I look hard at her and she meets my gaze with eyes the colour of the sky – Priscilla's eyes. I see pale blonde hair tucked into a spotless white coif, the bow of her mouth...

'Bess?'

She steps back, startled.

'How do you know my name? What do you want?' I have frightened her and I seek to reassure her.

'You are Bess? John Collit is your father, is he not? Your brother is Robert and your mother was Priscilla. She was my best friend...'

'I have no mother. She abandoned us.' The girl is shaking now and I know it will only be moments before she shouts for help.

'No Bess, she did not abandon you. She would never have done that. I was there, she was ill. She loved you and Robert above all things...'

'YOU LIE!'

'Bess...' She spits at me then slams the door closed in my face before I can say another word.

I STUMBLE TO THE END OF THE GARDEN, THROUGH THE GATE AND OUT into the road, sinking to the ground under the hedge. Those poor children, to grow up believing that their mother deserted them. What stories they must have been told. And poor Priscilla – she is lost to them completely. As I sit there, my sorrow gradually changes to anger and I clench my fists. I will not be turned away. I will do what I came here to do. I sit still, trying to breathe lightly and look around me, thinking. Birds chorus in the trees high above, and the hedge is alive with the small sounds of creatures. On the path before me, in a shaft of sunlight, is a brown shape, like a wet stick. It lies prone but, as I stretch my foot out towards it, it slithers away into the undergrowth; a serpent such as are often seen in these parts.

And then it comes to me. I run back to the house, my feet raising dust that clings to my skirt. I do not go to the back entrance this time, but run up the steps and hammer on the carved front door. A different maidservant answers, older, and I point behind me to the road.

'Come quickly, a serpent! You must come and see, for I never saw the like of it. It is large, bigger than I have ever seen before, and I fear for your safety, for it comes this way.' The woman looks perplexed, but then sees the urgency on my face and raises her hand to her mouth in horror.

She looks behind me then turns and shouts back into the gloom of the hallway.

'Mistress, Mistress, come quick. A great snake is outside, what shall we do?' The house comes alive with people rushing and calling. I am forced to one side, holding fast to the wall, as they push past me and out into the road. I see Mistress Collit, some servants, then Bess and Robert – they are the image of Priscilla and I stifle a sob, my hand to my mouth. She would have loved them so.

No one notices me in the confusion, it is as if I do not exist. They cluster around the gateway, peering up and down the road, holding on to each other, looking all ways for the serpent, shrieking and wailing when they believe they see it.

I WAIT, HEART THUMPING, BIDING MY TIME, AND THEN HE COMES. JOHN Collit stands in the doorway, drawn by the commotion, his face confused, and I seize my chance.

'John?'

He turns and sees me, and I hold on tighter to the wall for support as his face pinches with anger. Now my moment is here, my legs threaten to give way.

'Aubrey Grinsett? What are you doing in my house?'

I take a deep breath. I intended to ask him – nay, beg him – not to denounce me as a witch, on the lives of his children, for I have done no wrong. I planned to say that I would move away from Dunwich, disappear, that he would not be troubled by me again, if only he will not accuse me. I would promise anything if he will just let me be. But I can see now that I have badly misjudged the situation for his face blackens like thunder. He is shaking, beside himself with anger, and his fists are clenching and unclenching at his sides until I fear he will hit me.

His eyes bulge large in a blood-red face and his breath comes harsh.

'How dare you come here. Who do you think you are? You come and disrupt my household by some pretence and . . .', his eyes widen in horror, '. . . you think to damn me. That's it, you seek to destroy me with your curses, to be revenged in your friends.' He holds his hand before him, thumb enclosed by fingers. 'Go, witch. Cousin Thomas will hear of this.' I back away and turn. Four pairs of eyes stare at me from the road. Mistress Collit is white-faced and terrified, clutching the children close to her side. Bess and Robert gaze at me with open mouths, their eyes round, mute with fear. They must have heard John's words. I am not safe here.

I turn on my heel and stagger away, past the crowd, along the track, back towards Halesworth, my breathing tight with dust, dryness and panic. I clutch at my chest, trying to steady myself, but terror has me in its grip and I keep walking as fast as I can, away from this place. I should never have come. I have dug a hole for myself so deep, and I will not escape from it, once John goes to Dunwich and accuses me. And I know he will, for I have angered him beyond forgiveness and I know too much. He will denounce me to Thomas Spatchett, the mob will come for me, and I will be seized as a witch. I am crying now, sobs ripping through me for I know, with my actions, I have signed my own death warrant. I turn my face to the skies and weep, not caring who hears me.

I wait for days, trembling in the shelter of my home, for men to hammer on my door, expecting at any moment to see John Collit and Thomas Spatchett with the constables. I can already see the quiet satisfaction on their faces as I am seized and bound and they take me away. But nothing happens, no one comes. And I wonder if I dare to breathe a little more freely. That, maybe, after all, John has changed his mind.

. . .

THE KNOCK COMES ON MY DOOR AS DAWN BREAKS. I OPEN IT cautiously. The Reverend Browne stands there, a crowd of men behind him. I know them from the church. The Reverend has grown thinner since I last saw him and he has the haunted face of the zealot, though his eyes blaze with Godly fervour. I curtsey.

'Reverend?'

'Mistress Grinsett, there has been a laying of information against you. The magistrate has listened to the many complaints and you are to be taken for questioning.' He turns and clicks his fingers. 'Seize her.' Two guards spring forward and I flinch as they bind my wrists with coarse rope. I do not resist, my time is come, and, anyway, I have no strength left to fight.

I expect to be taken to the town gaol but, instead, they escort me straight to the magistrate. His house is large and impressive and smells of lavender, good candles and other people's labour. The man himself sits stern behind a desk in the parlour, a vast room heated by a crackling fire. I am held tight by the guards, the ropes cutting into my wrists. I know how I must look – hair flying, apron torn, coif lost, but I am not able to tidy myself, so all I can do is bring my bound fists to my face to wipe away my tears. The room is full of men, staring, examining me as if I were a piece of poor meat brought to their table. They are shuffling and muttering, a sound which rises as I am pushed forward into the room, and the magistrate has to call twice for order before they fall silent.

I stand before the magistrate, trying to make myself tall, to summon a courage that I no longer have. He pins me with a sharp look.

'You are . . .' He looks down at a parchment before him. '. . . Aubrey Grinsett?' I say nothing. 'Speak woman, is that your name? Or are you so stupid you do not remember?' He looks around, playing to the room, and the men guffaw in unison.

'I am she.'

'Better. And who here accuses this woman?' He looks around

expectantly and Reverend Browne steps forward. The magistrate nods for him to speak.

The Reverend opens his mouth and venom pours forth. He calls me witch. He says that I have harmed many others, that I have sent imps and consorted with the Devil, and, as each word damns me further, the men surrounding me nod sagely, saying nothing.

The magistrate straightens the gown on his shoulders.

'So, Mistress Grinsett, do you offer your confession?' He is shuffling his papers, not looking at me, as if I am not worthy of his attention, but I know he is quivering for my answer. I say nothing. They expect me to confess, but I will not bow to them. Inside me, a power begins to uncoil.

'Nothing?' The magistrate waves a pudgy hand behind him. 'Then we shall pray for your deliverance from the evil that possesses you, and pray that you admit your sins. Reverend Browne?'

The Reverend looks at me with sorrowful eyes as he opens his black bible and begins to read. I am made to stand whilst the men kneel around me, black crows surrounding their prey, heads bowed, mouths muttering, begging the Lord to forgive me and make me confess. But I do not. I stand firm, letting their prayers wash over me. I no longer hear the words, it is just a droning, like a bee buzzing around a dusty room. My back is aching now and my legs tremble, but I believe I will bear it. Reverend Browne walks forward, pushing his face too close to mine.

'You are in the presence of God in this place, for we are employed in His name to carry out His commands. You must speak the truth, for God looks deep into your soul and will find you out. You were accused of witchcraft once before, were you not? The Devil aided your escape then, although others did not fare so well? See, we do not forget.' His words are almost gentle, sorrowful, as if he despises what he is doing, and I see the preacher in him, genuine and fervent. But there are two parts to this man, one the Godly pillar of the community, the other weak and subservient. I think of Elizabeth, of Priscilla, of what they endured, and I turn to him, stronger now.

'Reverend Browne, you have been good to me in the past and I bear you no ill will. I am no witch. It is correct that I was seized once before but there was found to be no justification for the accusations and I do not understand why I have been accused again.'

The magistrate shuffles in his seat.

'You will be silent, Mistress. It is not your place to question. It is I who will decide the rights and wrongs of this matter, and whether to issue a warrant for your arrest.' He pauses as he regains his authority. 'You are summoned today, in the sight of God and your betters, to answer an accusation of witchcraft. Reverend Browne has accused you of bewitching Master Thomas Spatchett, of sending an imp to him in the form of a blackish-grey cat, and says that this imp caused him to fall into an apoplexy. He also says that this same imp caused pains to Master Spatchett's head that were so bad that he fell down in frequent fits. This could only have been caused by witchcraft, by someone who is in league with the Devil. Master Spatchett himself is too ill to attend and bear witness, so the Reverend is acting on his behalf. What say you to this charge?'

The magistrate sits back in his seat, fanning his face with his hand, sweat beading his forehead.

I hesitate, thinking hard, weighing my words.

'I am sorry for Master Spatchett's misfortune, Sir, but it is not of my doing. I know nothing of a cat, nothing of an imp. I have no animals, I am just a poor woman, living my life, such as it is, trying to get by.'

There is a pause, then Reverend Browne steps forward again.

'But you consorted with witches, Mistress, did you not? Priscilla Collit and Elizabeth Southerne, both gone from this place to who knows where, for they were not hanged as the law dictated, and no one can explain their absence.'

'They are dead. The alarm . . .' I realise, too late, what I say, and he jumps at it.

'How do you know that, Mistress? How did that news reach you and not the town? Numerous messages were sent to the gaol, asking for confirmation that they were taken there, that they had been tried and condemned, or that they had died there, but no reply has been forthcoming. So how can you possibly know this – unless . . .' I begin to shake. He has me now. I have made a grave error. His face pushes close and I see flecks of white in the corners of his mouth. His eyes are wild and for a moment I pray that he, too, will fall down in a fit and I will not have to answer, but God does not listen to me anymore. 'You have spoken with them, have you not? You know where they are. Are they back in this town, back to be revenged on us all?' He looks around wildly, spittle flying, looking as if he himself were possessed.

The magistrate rises to his feet and stretches out a hand.

'Reverend Browne, we will find out the truth, calm yourself. You do not wish to make yourself ill with the strain of this matter. Let me consider whether there is sufficient evidence, and then I will have this woman brought before me again, and I will decide what to do with her. You may carry on.' He waves his hand soothingly and the Reverend returns to his seat, dabbing at his mouth with a clean white kerchief, still shaking. The magistrate pulls his gown over his shoulders, gathers his papers and stands. It is clear we are all dismissed. I breathe a sigh, for a moment thinking that the magistrate does not wholly believe the charge, else he would have me taken to the gaol, but then I go cold as Reverend Browne stands and turns to the guards at his side then nods at me.

'Escort this woman back to her home and stand guard outside. She is to be searched. Orders of Thomas Spatchett.'

CHAPTER 23

I am taken back to my cottage. The power that I felt when I first faced the magistrate is gone and I can do little except sit beside the fire, shivering with fear. After a while I make myself get up. I find a nub of bread and some ale and set them on the table, but I am unable to eat or drink, for my throat is tight, my stomach lurching.

It seems but a moment before they come for me again. I hear a disturbance outside and peek through the window to see Thomas Spatchett and the Reverend Browne, surrounded by guards, escorting two women, cloaked, with their faces hidden, coming towards my cottage. I do not move from my chair by the fire, I will give them nothing. My door bursts open.

'Aubrey Grinsett, these women are here to search you for the marks of the Devil. Make your confession now and I will save you this pain.' Thomas Spatchett's voice trembles, whether through illness or excitement, I know not. I say nothing. 'So be it. Reverend, we will pray for the immortal soul of our poor sister while this task is carried out.'

The two women shuffle into my cottage and the door is firmly closed behind them. They look around as they push back their hoods and remove their cloaks. One I recognise instantly, the town washer-woman. I have often watched her red-raw arms and sturdy body hard at work, scrubbing and wringing. She has always had time for a kind word and a smile, but now her face is hard and set. There is no longer any friendship in her eyes, and I try not to shudder. I turn to the other and, with a jolt, I realise that it is Mary Spatchett – Elizabeth told me she was at their searching. I have never spoken to her but now, close to, I see she is younger than I had thought her to be, and there is a glitter of fear in her eyes. She does not catch my eye, but looks to the floor, white hands folded neatly in front of her. The older woman takes the lead and, with a nod to Mistress Spatchett, they move as one to undo my clothing and strip me to my shift. The washer-woman sweeps aside the remains of my meal from the table and I watch as my precious plate topples from the table edge and falls, breaking into sharp shards on the packed earth.

'On the table. Lie still and it will go the better for you.' Her voice is hard and, behind her, I hear Mistress Spatchett give a small gulp. I clamber onto the table and lie facing upwards, trying not to shake, breathing deeply, and think of what Elizabeth told me; how she thought of better times, of sunlight and leaves and the endless throb of the sea. I squeeze my eyes tight shut and try to make myself small, to leave this room and this ordeal.

The women are not rough, but their touch is firm and I do not wish to anger them, so I lie as still as I can, flushing with humiliation as they prod and poke my body. I know what they will find – a nub of skin by my right breast, like a small teat, worn hard with the chafing of my bodice over the years. The kind of blemish that every woman has when life and childbirth and toil have left their marks. A natural thing, a normal thing, something that is noticed and then forgotten. I feel fingers probing and smoothing my skin, moving from my feet, up and between my legs, over my stomach to my chest, as I pray to a God that doesn't listen, begging Him to make it end.

. . .

IT DOES NOT TAKE LONG.

'Here.' There is an intake of breath.

'Yes. Pass me the bodkin.' I bite my lip against the pain of what is to come, but cannot stifle a gasp as the sharp point sinks into my flesh. Tears flood my eyes. The pain is fierce, and a great sob rips my throat as I open my eyes and turn my head to one side. The washer-woman pulls the needle out and I brace myself for the next. 'See, it is as your husband described – she does not bleed. This is what we were told to look for, a true mark of the Devil.' Mistress Spatchett moves forward, her hand pressed to her mouth and nods. The washer-woman pauses. 'Must we continue? Is this not enough? For I have no taste for this task, Mistress, truth be told. It is your husband who has instructed us to search thoroughly . . . the decision is yours.'

Mistress Spatchett's face is grey, she looks as if she is about to vomit, and I stare at her, finally catching her eye. I plead wordlessly with her and she studies my face. She hesitates and I blink the tears away, willing her to speak, to have this thing done with. Time stands still in that moment. The tip of the bodkin glitters, clean and damning, poised in the washer-woman's reddened hand. The white aprons and coifs of the two women gleam in the half-light, while the voices of the men outside drone ever on, as if this were an ordinary day.

'This will be sufficient.' Mary Spatchett speaks softly but firmly. 'My husband has said we should search for a witch's mark and that is what we have done. We need go no further. I will tell him what we have found and I am sure he will be satisfied. There is no need to put ourselves through any more . . . distress.'

The washer-woman nods her agreement, putting the bodkin down, and I let out the breath that has been held in my thudding chest for what seems like an eternity.

'You may get up and put on your clothes, Mistress.' Mary Spatchett is business-like now the thing is done, but a shadow remains on her face. She will not forget this day. I push myself to sit as she passes me my clothes and I struggle to put them on. The washer-woman glances at me once, to make sure I am decent, then opens the door and calls to the men outside. I lace my bodice and straighten my clothes hurriedly, aware of the leers and looks of the guards as they bustle through the door, Thomas Spatchett at their head.

'You have found proof?'

The two women nod but it is Mary who speaks.

'We have, Husband. She has a teat on her body that does not bleed when pricked, but her body is otherwise whole. This mark is what you instructed us to search for, so there can be no doubt of her guilt. As you thought, the woman is a witch and must face justice.'

Thomas bows his head as if it pains him. He rubs at his scar with his hand.

'One mark? Only this? Did she not confess? '

'She did not, Husband.'

Thomas drops his head.

'I must be sure . . . she must not escape again. She is a witch, and for that she must hang. She must . . .' His words drop to a mumble and no one can hear what he says. Then he glances up, sees the guards and the troubled face of his wife, and composes himself. 'I must be certain this time. There can be no room for error. She must be made to confess. She will be watched.'

THE GUARDS CLEAR THE FURNITURE TO THE SIDE OF THE ROOM AS I look wildly about me. This cannot be right. The magistrate did not say this should happen. The washer-woman and Mistress Spatchett press themselves against the wall, hands over mouths in shock, watching me fight the guards all the way as they seize hold of me. One brings a chair and places it in the centre of the small room, then they thrust me down hard onto it and bind my arms to the back. The ropes cut in so I try to sit still. I think of Elizabeth and

Priscilla, how they must have endured the same torment, and the thought of them warms my heart and gives me a little strength. I flinch as one of the men approaches and lifts my skirt over my knees, exposing my lower legs, and I shy away from him in shame. Thomas Spatchett's voice looms large from the dark corner.

'We do this only so your imps can clearly be seen when they come to you, so they cannot hide from us in your skirts.' He looks around and then nods with approval as the other guards take their places around the room. 'Men, you will be relieved after three hours, I will arrange for others to take your place. She must not be moved, must not be untied for any reason, and you must watch carefully at all times. Imps come in all shapes and forms, some as cats and dogs, some as mice or insects. She has a teat under one breast which does not bleed and her familiar will try to reach it, to feed from her. If you see such a thing you must send for me immediately. The witch will not escape judgement this time.'

He takes one more look around and then offers his arm to his wife as if they were merely walking home from church. Her hand shakes as she takes it. They step outside into the evening air, the washer-woman following behind, and I am left with the guards, bound to my chair, hardly daring to breathe.

During the first hours, I manage to aid my aching limbs by moving my hips from side to side to ease the stiffness, but the chair becomes harder and, increasingly, I cannot find relief. My legs and arms grow cold with lack of movement, and my stomach rumbles, although I could not eat anything. Then, a twinge, deep down between my legs, and I know I need to relieve myself. I put off the thought for as long as I can, but the harder I try to put the feeling from me the worse it becomes until I have no option.

'I need to use the privy.'

The guards heads lift as one.

'What?'

'I need to relieve myself.'

They look at each other, unsure.

'We are not to untie her for any reason – Master Spatchett was clear...'

'He is not here though is he? It is not him that will have to sit with the stink if we do not let her. I say we untie her and two of us keep close watch as she does her business.' There are nods of agreement and one draws a sharp blade. 'We will untie you, Mistress, but you must not make any attempt to run. Are you clear? If you do, I will use this.' The blade flashes as he points it at me. I nod my agreement. I just want to go outside, the need is getting more urgent by the minute. It is as if he reads my mind. 'We are not taking you outside though. I do not doubt that you will flee if we do that and we cannot risk you escaping. You must have a chamberpot here, you will use that. Where is it?'

My voice is cracked and rough with lack of use.

'Under my bed.' The guard goes over and stretches under the wooden frame, his hand pulling out a metal pan. 'This? You use this?' I nod again, and he brings it over and sets it down before me. One of the others reaches behind me and struggles to untie the ropes. As they come loose my arms fall to my sides and a sharp pain shoots up them, stabbing at my shoulders and neck. My hands are blue and puffed and I rub them to get the feeling back, then fumble under my skirts.

'Will you at least turn away?'

'More than my job is worth, witch, be grateful I give you this much liberty.' There is no point in arguing with him, and my need is urgent, so stiffly, painfully, I hoist up my skirts and crouch. The splashing sound seems to fill the room and the stench thickens the air but the relief is so great that, despite my intentions, tears begin to fall. I stand and straighten myself.

'Sit down. Tie her up and no one will be any the wiser.' The ropes are tightened around my wrists once more, my arms bound sharp behind me. A guard opens the door and throws the contents of the pot outside, then returns it to its place under the bed. My skirts are hoisted over my knees once more and the pain begins immediately.

TIME STANDS STILL. GUARDS CHANGE IN A WHOOSH OF CLEAN AIR, and people seem to come and go, but I am no longer sure what is real and what is fantasy. I think I hear Reverend Browne's voice, asking if I will confess, but dark shadows block my mind so that understanding leaves me. The pain is all-encompassing now and, on the rare occasions when I feel myself slip into peaceful oblivion, they shake me, even untying me and making me walk around the room to wake me. They give me no water or food, and gradually my body begins to shut down. I can no longer feel my hands and legs and I become a solid lump of matter with no semblance of a human being. My mind flutters and fades, thoughts swooping like bats in the darkening. The room lightens and dims several times but I cannot work out how long I have been here. And all the time, voices raised, hard and angry, pressing me to confess.

'Did you bewitch Master Spatchett, Aubrey? All know you did it, so why not end this torment and confess?' A new voice cuts through the fug of my thoughts, clear as a bell, wheedling and gentle, and I struggle to listen. 'Confess, Sister. I know your pain is great. You have been here these last three days and nights, no one can endure as you have done. There is nothing to be ashamed of in confessing all.' It is the voice of the Devil himself and it writhes its way into my consciousness. He offers an end to this pain, an end to my suffering and I realise how Priscilla must have felt, for his words are tempting and seductive. 'You will be able to sleep again. You will be warm and comfortable, I will see to it you are brought food and water, if only you will confess your sins now.' I watch his hand stretch out to me, offering me release, and I cannot remember what is right and wrong anymore, what I have said or done. My mind is gone and all is rushing darkness, save for the lone voice, soft and beguiling. 'Aubrey, it is time. You cannot endure this anymore. You have done your best to protect me but now it is time to confess.' The words sink into my mind like water soaking through sand, slow and persistent. Soon they are all there is.

My face feels dry as parchment, my eyes burn as I force them open, my lips crack and bleed as I part them to speak. The voice has gone now and I am left alone. He is right, I cannot endure this anymore. If I just say the words it will end. I take a deep breath and the air is hot and expectant, but I cannot bring myself to do it. Then, from the corner of my eye, I see Thomas Spatchett nod to one of the guards, who walks slowly to the fire and pulls out the poker. Its tip glows bright as he walks back, holding it close to my face, brushing it against my hair, and I smell the acrid singeing, feel the heat against my cheek. I cry out in terror. It is the threat of burning which undoes me. A picture comes to me of Edward, newborn and innocent, his hollowed skin, the blackened hair. How he must have suffered when Priscilla, in her madness, set him on the fire. I remember the blaze I set when Elizabeth's cottage burned, its heat and crackle. I remember how I cursed Thomas Spatchett then, and know I am guilty of some things.

As the glowing poker edges closer to my face, the guard leering, his mouth wet and open, breath foul, I close my eyes and speak.

'I am all that you say of me.'

THOMAS SPATCHETT LEANS FORWARD, I HAVE HIS FULL ATTENTION now. He licks his lips.

'You confess?'

'Yes.'

He nods to the guard, who pushes the poker back into the flames. I watch it warily.

'How long have you served your master, Satan?'

'These past twenty years.'

'And how did you come to serve him. Who induced you?'

The thought of Priscilla's wedding to John jumps into my head, and the words are out before I have time to form them.

'It was at a wedding. I was enticed into it by a witch at a wedding.' I can think of nothing else. The words come out muffled, for my voice is dry, my throat burns and I cannot push them out further.

'I did not hear that . . .' Thomas Spatchett leans towards me, I can smell him. I blink hard to clear my vision – my eyelids are caked and gritty. 'Speak, woman, what did you say? Guard, bring her some water.'

A mug is pushed hard against my mouth and I suck at it gratefully. The water is stale and tastes of iron, but that may be the blood from my lips. It helps.

'I confess.'

'And what of the Devil? Do you confess to consorting with him?' I cannot. I have never had dealings with the Devil but I am sure it was he that just came to me, he that helps me now. There is a shuffling and, just as I am hesitating, the Devil's voice whispers once more into my ear. This time I can feel his warm breath on my cheek.

'Tell us, Aubrey, tell all now and you will rest easier for it.' I try to turn to see his face but my neck is stiff and will not move. And a vision of William, my poor lost husband, comes into my mind as if to bring comfort and I start to speak.

'He came to me one day on the Heath. He was such a pretty young man.' I remember William as he was, how he looked on our wedding night, his body lean and strong. I remember. 'He was dark and thin and he lay with me and it was wonderful.'

The room fills with a hiss of indrawn breath.

'And did he speak to you? What did he say? Tell us!' The voice changes, harsh. Thomas Spatchett. I think of my William's words of love that night, and after. He whispered them to me in the dark and I will not sully them by speaking them now. They are mine alone. I stay silent. 'Did Satan come to you again? In the form of a grey kitten? He did, didn't he, and the kit sucked on the teat my searchers found? Did it draw blood from you? Speak – SPEAK! Did you send your imp to torment me? Is this all your doing?' His voice is rising in rage.

'I bear you no ill will, Master Spatchett. I am a God-fearing woman . . .' I cannot speak more. Then the room blurs and I hear the Devil's voice again in my ear, soft and smooth and I close my eyes to listen.

'You are in the presence of God, Aubrey, you may speak the truth. If you did these things of which you are accused, then tell the whole truth, all of it, for God wishes you to bring the truth to light.' I am about to speak again, but then stop myself, my mind clearing. If this is truly the Devil whispering to me, then why would he say I am in the presence of God? My mind is confused and wandering, but this rings clear. The voice is still wheedling, low, almost loving. I squeeze my eyes tight and then open them sharply. I force my head to turn to where the words come from, wincing at the pain, and look straight into the face of the Reverend Browne.

CHAPTER 24

It is all written down. They go through my confession again and again, each claim exaggerated further. The clerk scribbles, pen scratching, until they have what they want, then they untie me and lift me roughly to my bed. I am dropped onto the hard mattress and cry out in pain. I do not know if it is day or night. The room bustles around me, men's voices loud and soft, coming and going. There are women here too. I am given water, bread soaked in ale, and I eat it cautiously. The feeling is slowly returning to my hands, but I cannot fend for myself. It is Mary Spatchett who tends to me. We do not speak, but I watch her face – her eyes are hollow and purple-shaded, but her movements are gentle. She holds a cup to my lips. The contents are thick and bitter, and I drink, then I lie back and sink into sleep, blessed sleep, all pain forgotten.

I wake at the first signs of a new day. I do not know how long I have been asleep and I am not sure where I am, but then the memories come flooding back along with the pain. I struggle to sit and there is a movement from the other side of the room. The washer-woman comes over to me, Mistress Spatchett behind her. I cannot read their faces.

'We have orders to search you again.' I am filled with horror, for

I cannot face more pain. I have confessed, is that not enough? But it seems that Thomas Spatchett wants more. 'I will clear the table, we will do it now.'

Mistress Spatchett sees my face.

'You will not be pricked, Mistress. We are to search your body again for further signs. You have been tossing and turning in your bed for two days, and my husband – Master Spatchett – wishes to ensure that the Devil did not visit you in that time.'

The washer-woman turns to her.

'She was watched, no one saw anything untoward. Surely this is not necessary? Your husband must have enough evidence by now?'

Mary Spatchett hesitates, then her face turns prim.

'My husband's orders are that we search her again. As his wife, I obey him in all things, as our Lord teaches. And so I will ensure his wishes are carried out. If you object . . .?'

The washer-woman shakes her head.

'No, no, Mistress, I only thought to . . .'

'We are not here to think. We are here to carry out the wishes of our betters, as good Christian women should always do.'

'Amen.' The washer-woman nods her acceptance and stoops to help me stand. She is strong, her grip firm and she half-carries me to the table, lifts me up, lays me back, and pulls my shift over my head. There is a sharp intake of breath but I am made blind by the cloth, I do not know what it is they see, but I feel a tingling and stinging over my skin now the cold air has touched it.

'It looks as if she has been through a thorn patch, look, her arms and legs – it is all over her body!'

They roll me onto my front and exclaim again.

'My husband must be informed.' The washer-woman helps me to sit up and pulls the shift back down. As she does so I see what has made them exclaim. Red marks and scratches cover my arms and legs as if made by briars. How? I have not been outside. The washer-woman turns to Mistress Spatchett.

'Her skin is dry, Mistress, it flakes and itches, so she has been scratching in her sleep. I have seen this before. Her own nails will be the cause.'

No one heeds her.

They make haste to take me back to the magistrate, Thomas Spatchett and Reverend Browne, aquiver with anticipation, faces flushed, clutching papers in their hands. I stand again before the empty desk, my hands bound in front of me, trying to contain my fear, for my heart leaps in my chest as if it will burst. The magistrate keeps us all waiting a suitable time to enforce his superiority, then strides into his parlour and settles himself at his table. The same men are assembled, watching and waiting. The very air crackles with excitement.

'Master Spatchett, I see you have returned with this woman.'

'I have, Sir, she has . . .'

The magistrate holds up his hand.

'And you have further proof that this woman is a witch?'

'I have her confession, Sir. She has been searched by two good women of the town, one of whom is my . . .' The magistrate raises his eyebrows and narrows his eyes.

'A searching? I did not order this.'

Thomas clears his throat.

'I had the opportunity to speak with the Witchfinder at Christ-tide, in Aldeburgh, when I was chief witness at the trial of the Clarke woman. Master Hopkins told me then, in no uncertain terms, that a suspected witch must be searched by women of good character, to discern whether she carries the marks of Satan. She must then be watched to see if her familiars come forth to suckle from her. As Master Hopkins is a man of excellent reputation where the searching out of witches is concerned, I had no doubt, Sir, that this would be in the best interests of the town – for surely we should not allow a suspected witch to evade justice?' The magistrate glares at him, piqued by this challenge to his authority, but says nothing, just waves him on irritably. 'The search-women found a teat on her body which fails to bleed when pricked. This is the sure sign of a witch, but I did not consider this to be proof enough, so I have had her watched.'

The magistrate sits up at this.

'For how long?'

Thomas coughs and wipes his face with a spotless white kerchief.

'Four days and nights, Sir.'

'Man, do you consider that to be fair and reasonable? To deprive someone of sleep and comfort for that time. Even your Master Hopkins has said that two to three days and nights is sufficient. We do not want to be accused of undue force. And I gave you no authority to . . .'

'She has confessed, Sir. She was searched a second time, after the watching. She was covered in scratches, and this was by no human means. She admits to consorting with the Devil, fornicating with him, sending her imp to plague me with fits and apoplexies. She has admitted all of this, I heard her speak the words myself, as did Reverend Browne here.' The minister nods in agreement. 'It is written down, clear, for all to read.' He pauses to draw breath, then passes the paper in his hand to the magistrate. 'And now there is something even more serious. This morning I have been told that she has bewitched two men to death. This is murder, Sir!' The room breaks into noise at these latest accusations, and it is all I can do to remain on my feet. Murder? I know nothing of any deaths.

The magistrate closes his eyes and is still. Then he opens them and looks at me.

'Mistress Grinsett, these are most heinous crimes. You have already confessed to witchcraft, but what say you to these new accusations of murder that Master Spatchett has just brought to this examination?'

I hold his gaze.

'Sir, I do not know of what he speaks. I know of no murders.'

Cold chills me to the bone.

'Master Spatchett?'

'Sir, I understand that two men have died these past few days. One is Henry Winson of Walpole...' I shake my head. I have never heard of this man. '... and the other is known to the accused. It is my cousin and trusted employee, a good and Godly father of two orphaned children...'

I was wrong to fear John Collit's words. It is his death that damns me.

MY SHOCK MUST SHOW ON MY FACE, FOR THE MAGISTRATE LEANS forward and stares at me.

'You know this man I see. Explain how.'

I struggle for words, terror is ripping through me like fire through thatch.

'He was... John Collit was the husband of my friend. He left her after her mind became unbalanced by the birth of her children. He took her children from her, Sir, it was cruel, and she was never the same again. But I did not murder him, I swear on all that is Holy.'

'And where is your friend now?'

I hesitate.

'I believe her to be dead, Sir.'

'Tell him how she died, Mistress Grinsett.' Thomas Spatchett's voice is sharp and hard. 'Tell him, for I am sure you know.'

I take a deep breath – I must choose my words with care.

'She was seized as a witch and taken to the assize in Bury St Edmunds. I do not know if she was hanged there, but I have heard that many who stood accused were removed to Ipswich Gaol because of an alarm. The King's men were said to be marching on the town...'

'I remember this alarm. The courts were in chaos. But Mistress Collit? What of her?'

'I do not know what happened to her, Sir.' I cross my fingers in the folds of my apron. I am sure God will forgive my lie.

Thomas Spatchett strides across the room and pushes a sharp finger into my chest.

'You lie, Mistress! You know full well what happened to her. I have reason to believe that she is dead, that you have knowledge of the circumstances, and because of this, because of what you allege my cousin John did to her . . .' He is becoming blinded by rage. '. . . you held a grudge against him and, when you saw an opportunity, you cursed him and caused his death and that of his friend, Master Winson. You are lying and I will have the truth from you or else . . .'

The magistrate bangs his hand on the table.

'Enough! Master Spatchett, you will control yourself. This is my hearing and I will draw my own conclusions from the evidence before me.'

He turns his gaze on me.

'Mistress Grinsett, you have confessed to witchcraft. How do you plead to the further accusations of murder?' He holds up his hand for silence and the room stills in an instant.

'I did go to speak with John Collit, that is true, but I do not know of Henry Winson. I have never heard the name . . .'

'You see, she confesses.' Thomas is beside himself. 'Ask her about the scratches my women found on her body when they searched her for a second time. It was the Devil, tormenting her for her confession, all could see it. I have her now. She has confessed to witchcraft. She has confessed to murder. She must hang.'

THE ROOM ERUPTS, MEN TALKING AND SHOUTING, AS I STAND, WITH my head down trying to make myself invisible. I am not sure what I have said and what I have done, the word 'hang' is all I recognise.

The magistrate bangs on the table and shouts for silence, but he is not heard over the hubbub. Then, a loud crash, as his bailiff comes to the front and thumps his stave onto the desk. The room quietens in an instant.

A voice from the back of the room splits the silence.

'Sir, if I may?' The magistrate looks around. One of the men has come forward from the back of the room, his head lowered, submissive. He is tall and thin and nervously turns his cap round and round in his hands.

'Yes? Speak, man. Do you have any light to shed on this matter, before I issue a warrant for this woman's arrest and detainment?'

'I may do, Sir. Correct me if I am wrong but surely, if it is Master Spatchett who accuses this woman of bewitching him, he cannot then bear witness against her. Does the law not require other witnesses to her crimes, those not directly affected by her actions? And was this woman not sent home once before as there was no evidence against her? Master Spatchett may have once had the ear of the Witchfinder, but that man's methods of interrogation have recently been viewed by those in authority as excessive and . . .'

The magistrate holds up his hand, his brow furrowed.

'I am the authority here, Sir, but you are correct in what you say.' He turns back towards Thomas Spatchett who stands, his face ablaze with anger. 'Master Spatchett, many in Dunwich will bear testimony to your falling ill with fits and pains in your head, and no one would deny their existence or their severity, and you are to be pitied. You have accused this woman, Aubrey Grimsett of causing your dreadful afflictions by sending an imp . . .'

Thomas can contain himself no longer.

'It was witchcraft, Sir, that caused it, I have no doubt of it. I have been bewitched. This woman's two friends were tried for witchcraft and found guilty. Who knows what happened to them, no doubt their master, the Devil, freed them and is using them now in other places, but this one . . .' He points a long finger at me. It trembles with rage. '. . . this one escaped. But she will not get away this time.

Perhaps she bewitched those present at the first hearing, certainly the Devil came to her aid then ...'

The magistrate holds up his hand for silence. His face is set.

'Master Spatchett, can you produce others who were witness to your bewitching? Your wife maybe, your servants? Someone else who will testify to this?'

I hold my breath, for I see doubt written on the magistrate's long face.

His words hang in the silent air and there is a shuffling of feet. No one looks up. Thomas Spatchett looks around him as if expecting someone to come forward, but no one moves, no one catches his eye, for all are looking at their boots. Then the Reverend Browne steps up and stands before the magistrate.

'I can speak for Master Spatchett, for I have witnessed the ferocity of his fits, their frequency. I have often sat with Mistress Spatchett, when she was at a loss as to what to do, for there is no helping him when he is taken like that. His limbs shake and his jaw hardens so much that he often bites through his tongue. His whole body judders uncontrollably and his limbs fly out as if he were indeed possessed. He cannot hear or see his fellow men, and does not respond to his wife's words, nor indeed those of God, for I often read passages from the Scriptures to him in order to bring him back to the Lord at such times. He is surely bewitched, Sir, for I have never seen such violent afflictions as torment this poor, good man.'

He stops to draw breath and I think of the power he has in his voice. He speaks today as if in the pulpit – at the watching his voice was soft and beguiling.

The magistrate gazes at him.

'Reverend Browne, I have no doubt that Master Spatchett is sorely tormented, and that many wonder at the cause of such a dreadful affliction. It may well be the result of witchcraft, but I ask you, Sir, were you witness to his bewitching by the woman who stands before us, Aubrey Grinsett?'

The Reverend bows his head.

'Not directly, Sir, but Master Spatchett assures me . . .'

'Again, I have no reason to doubt your word, but evidence must be provided to show that this woman was the direct cause.'

The Reverend looks up.

'I was at the watching, Sir. She confessed, I heard it with my own ears. Surely that is enough proof under the law?'

The magistrate sighs.

'I will need to consult as to the precise wording of the law in this matter. I will release the accused to her own home under recognisance, to return here tomorrow for further questioning. In the meantime, Master Spatchett, I would advise you to find witnesses who can add credence to your claims of bewitchment. And I warn you, Sir – this woman is not to be harmed. No more searching, no more watching. She should be guarded, but she is not to be touched. Am I understood?'

Thomas Spatchett nods, his look as black as thunder. He does not like to be bested.

For, like me, he sees a glimpse of freedom.

CHAPTER 25

They return for me at dawn. I have slept a little better and am feeling more rested. I have washed thoroughly and tended my wounds with honey and calendula. They will heal quickly. I have plaited my hair under a clean coif and have on my best skirt and bodice and a clean apron, for I do not wish them to see me as a witch again. They do not bind me this time, nor do they lay a finger on me, but the men who surround me are broad and intimidating, their cudgels held ready. They think to frighten me but I clutch hard onto the thought that maybe there is some doubt as to my guilt.

The magistrate sits at his desk expectantly, the others forming a row behind him, and this time he has a clerk by his side, smoothing paper out before him and scraping a fresh nib with a small, sharp knife. The white curls float upwards in a shaft of sunlight and I watch as they are blown away when the door opens. Thomas Spatchett is shown in. He looks as if he has not slept and I am glad, for he may be less dangerous if his mind is tired.

'Are we all assembled?' The magistrate's gaze sweeps the room. 'Very well, let us proceed. I will question the accused myself to try and get to the nub of this matter.' He looks down at the papers in front of him, his finger moving over the words set down there, then looks at me, holding my gaze.

'Mistress Grinsett, you have confessed to making a pact with the Devil and said that you were beguiled by another witch at a wedding. Is this true?'

I swallow but my eyes never leave his. The next words could seal my fate and I want him to see that I speak the truth.

'Sir, it is not true. These words were suggested to me by Master Spatchett and Reverend Browne. I had been watched for four days and nights, Sir, and I did not know what I was saying. My mind was disturbed by lack of sleep and sustenance, and my words were muddled and unconsidered. I do not know what I may have said. I am a Godly woman, Sir, who has kept herself to herself. I was widowed at an early age and have struggled sometimes to make my way in this world, for it is a hard place for a woman with no husband or father to guide her.' I see the magistrate nod at this. 'I would never send an imp to Master Spatchett or anyone else, for I am no witch. I am truly sorry for his affliction, but it is not caused by me. I have done nothing to bring harm to him and I bear him no ill will.'

'And what of your confession that you had a familiar spirit?'

'I have never had a familiar spirit, Sir, nor any animal that lived with me.'

'And what of the serious crime of murder? Do you confess that you caused the death of one John Collit and one Henry Winson? What say you to this?'

I keep my eye fixed on his face and stand up tall.

'I do not know of Henry Winson, Sir. I had not heard his name before yesterday. I know John Collit, but not well. It is true that I did go and see him at Cookley . . .' I hesitate. Many there could bear witness to my presence, the cart owner who took me, the household, the minister who gave me directions. I must speak with great caution. 'I went to plead with him. He had spoken to me in the market square here, threatened to denounce me as a witch, and I was afeared. So I went to Cookley and found his house, but they would not let me in, so I said that there was a great serpent approaching. I know this was a lie, Sir, but I could think of no other way to speak to Master Collit. And it worked, for the household all came outside to look and he came to the door. I spoke to him, Sir, and beseeched him, but he would not shift. He became angry and I fled. I did not cause his death, I would not harm any man in that way, for it is a grave sin to take a life. I do not know why he died, and I did not hear of it until yesterday, in this very room.'

THE ROOM RUSTLES AT MY WORDS.

'So you do not confess to the murder of these two poor souls?'

'I do not, Sir. I never knew of this matter before Master Spatchett spoke of it yesterday.'

Silence now, no sound but for the crackling logs in the hearth. Suddenly I long to be in my little home, sitting before my own fire, a mug of ale by my side, my nets on my lap. The thought pulls and drags at me but I dismiss it, and quickly, for I must keep my wits about me. The magistrate sighs and looks again at his papers.

'And what of Master Spatchett? Why do you think he has accused you of such a grave crime?'

I pick my words with very great care.

'I know Master Spatchett to be a Godly man, much given to preaching and good works. Indeed, when I was widowed he once took pity on me and gave me some coins. But when Master Spatchett took fits so badly, he changed. He became convinced that I and my friends had bewitched him, causing his illness. But we did not, Sir, as God is my witness, we were all innocent. But his accusations caused Bess – Elizabeth Southerne – and Priscilla Collit, John's wife, to be sent to the Bury assize for trial.' My voice gains strength and I stand proud before the men, whose eyes are all fixed on me. Power surges in me. 'I am not a witch, Sir, I did not murder John Collit or Master Winson. I did make some confession, yes, but I had been held for so long that I did not know what I was doing. I have not harmed Master Spatchett.'

The speech has exhausted me and my legs begin to fail. I wobble and the magistrate sees my distress.

'Bring this woman a chair.' One appears and I sink onto it gratefully. I have tried my best. I can do no more.

The magistrate clears his throat.

'Master Spatchett, what say you to this?'

'Sir, I am disturbed that the word of a woman such as this should be taken above my own, as a respected businessman, property owner and preacher of God's Holy Word. God will guide your hand in this matter, Sir, for His is the only judgement we should fear. As Ecclesiastes says in chapter five, verse eight "*if thou seest the oppression of the poor, and violent perverting of judgement and justice in a province, marvel not at the matter, for He that is higher than the highest regardeth; and there be higher than they.*" There is nothing I can say, save that God will judge you, Sir, as He guides your hand here. The Word of the Lord is my comfort and hope.'

I watch as Thomas Spatchett returns to his place, his head bowed, his hands clasped in prayer. All wait for the magistrate to speak.

THE SILENCE SEEMS TO STRETCH OUT INTO ETERNITY. MY CHAIR grows hard, the men shuffle and cough. My heart thumps so that I can barely breathe, and I grip the stuff of my apron firmly to stop my hands from shaking, although my legs continue their trembling under my skirts. I have done all I can, and the man before me holds my life in his hands. I close my eyes and we wait, wait . . .

Then the magistrate clears his throat, looks up and gazes around the room.

'I know that we all regard witchcraft as a scourge on our

community, something that should be stamped out with the most brutish of feet. Many have been accused in this county and many hanged for it, and rightly so, for evidence was supplied and accepted. Master Spatchett has mentioned the Witchfinder. This man was invited to various towns, Aldeburgh amongst them, and he was paid well for his services. Those towns did what they thought was right, but I find it telling that he was never invited to Dunwich, despite there being three women accused of witchcraft in our midst. And why was he not invited?' I hold my breath. 'It is because we are a tolerant town, we demand evidence before pursuing supposed witches through the process of law. Master Hopkins has been commended by some . . .' His gaze falls on Thomas Spatchett. '. . . for all he did to free our countryside of witches, but increasing numbers were accused and many were hanged, even though the evidence becomes less and less sure. Cases became less rigorously tested before being sent to trial. And that is why I have been rigorous here. I see the righteousness in sending a proven witch to trial and all that may come after, but I must also be convinced that a person accused is truly guilty, that there is a case to answer, and that the case can be proved, with witnesses and evidence. The woman before me now was kept from sleep for four days and nights. I cannot accept her confession as true, for I believe that her mind would be severely disturbed by such treatment. Even the Witchfinder did not keep a suspect under watching for that length of time, nor, to my knowledge, did he have suspects searched twice.' He pauses and looks hard at Master Spatchett. 'The only witness in this case is the victim himself. No one, even from his close family and household, who surely would have witnessed an imp or other such creature visiting him and causing such great harm, has been brought forward to validate his claim. Nor has anyone come forward to support the accusations that the deaths of John Collit and Henry Winson were caused by witchcraft, despite them, no doubt, having family and friends who witnessed their demise. As my esteemed colleague quite rightly said at this hearing yesterday, other witnesses are required by law. Whilst I believe that Master Spatchett has been afflicted severely, and all will testify to that . . .' I dare not draw a breath – my heart is exploding in my chest and I cannot stop trembling. '. . . I do not believe that there is enough evidence to send this woman, Aubrey Grinsett, to trial. I therefore will not issue a warrant for her arrest, nor will I commit her to gaol, pending the next assize. I am truly sympathetic to Master Spatchett, and I believe that he has been visited by something ungodly that has produced so severe an affliction, but I do not find it proven that Mistress Grinsett was the cause. I, therefore, dismiss the accusations. That is all.'

The magistrate stands and straightens his gown, gathering his papers. The clerk beside him continues to scribble and scratch, ink splattering in his haste, as Thomas Spatchett slumps against the wall, his head in his hands. His wife pulls at his arm, concern creasing her face, and the Reverend Browne moves to his side. They escort him to the door and the men step aside to allow him to leave, pity in their eyes. Voices are hushed, murmuring, and no one looks at me. I am left, sitting on the chair, confused and tearful, as the room gradually empties. Soon none are left, save for me and the clerk. He finishes his recording and sands the paper, blowing it in a soft cloud onto the floor. As he does so he looks up and sees me. He is younger than I first thought, his boyish features kind but harried. There is a smudge of ink on his nose and his voice is the first gentleness I have heard in this place.

'It is over. Go. Quick, before they change their minds.'

I stand, staggering slightly, then walk away, out of the room, through the great entrance hall, forward, until I step out into a sunlit afternoon. The air is thicker here on the outskirts of the town, where it does not have the sea to cleanse it. I stand still and breathe it all in before setting off down the road to Dunwich.

I am hot and hungry when I reach the market square and I am so busy fumbling in the pocket of my skirt for the coins I keep there that I do not look where I am going, and bump hard into a man.

'Oi, watch out . . .' The man pauses and stoops towards me, peering closely. I pull back, the strength of his gaze making me nervous. 'Get out of my way. What business have you, coming back here?' I am about to ask him what he means when I become aware that the bustle of the marketplace has stopped, cut off as if by a knife.

'I beg pardon, Sir, 'twas my fault entirely.' I step aside, intending to walk past him, but he places himself deliberately in front of me and, as I move, thumps his shoulder hard against mine, causing the coins to scatter from my hand. They tinkle to the earth and I stoop to pick them up, then I cry out in pain as a heavy boot thuds sharp onto my outstretched hand.

'We'll tolerate no witches here.' I look around me wildly, holding my damaged hand to my chest. A strand of hair escapes from my coif and brushes my face as I try to stand on legs that have turned to water, not looking at him, not wishing to do anything to encourage further blows. The townsfolk are stock-still, their faces hard and fixed. Then, into the silence, above the sound of the waves crashing on the shingle, a murmur, rising to a chant.

'Witch, witch, witch . . .'

I pick up my skirts and run, clutching my coins, along the streets towards the quay, to the shelter of home, to safety, the chanting growing fainter, but with the words still searing through me.

It is not over.

THE DOOR OF MY LITTLE COTTAGE HANGS LOOSE, ITS HINGES SMASHED. Stones and mud litter the ground around it. My herbs and plants have all been uprooted, my vegetables gone.

I step inside nervously.

'Is anyone here? Show yourself.' I pause, ears stretched, but all is silent. I move slowly into the room. The table and chairs have been taken, anything of use has gone, and all else smashed and broken. It is as if a winter storm has blown through it, taking all in its wake.

They had not expected me to be freed. They have stolen the coverlet from the bed, that I stitched with such love for my marriage chest; take my knife and spoon, my pots and pans. Even the kindling has gone. And the nets – they have stolen the nets, and with them, my livelihood. I sink down onto the mattress, straw hanging from great rips in its surface, as despair rips through me. I will myself not to cry but still tears come, trickling at first, then pouring, as I sob and sob as if my heart would cleave in two. I sit and let all the emotions of the last days and weeks flood over me and out, then lie stiffly down on my side and wait for it to pass, my whole body juddering with the sobbing. At last, it begins to slow and I am left, wrung out, my eyes swollen shut, my face puffy and tight. I clasp the edge of my apron between shaking fingers and wipe my face. I do not know what to do now. I had little enough before, but now I have nothing. My few belongings have been taken or smashed, and even my home will be gone soon, slowly, inevitably taken as the tide creeps up to my door and in. It will be lost to the sea as so many have been lost before it. This town is damned, God is taking it apart stone by stone, and I wonder how much will be left for the generations that follow. There is nothing left for me now. I knew it would not be easy to live here, being accused twice and then freed, but I did not think that their vengeance would be so thorough and so swift. If I stay here I will always be the witch that evaded justice. Memories are long and time is short. The bitterness and anger of the people in the marketplace will happen over and over again, and it will only be a short step to being accused for a third time.

I am as doomed to destruction as the town itself.

. . .

I LIE ON THE BED UNTIL THE COLD DRAUGHT FROM THE BROKEN DOOR stirs me into life. I drag myself upright, my body aching and heavy. I have never felt so desperate, so alone. I have lived in Dunwich all my life and now I am treated as an outsider, someone to be reviled and despised. Someone other. I move wearily to the chest in the corner. The clasp is scratched but, for some reason, it remains fastened, and it creaks as I lift the scarred oak lid and peer inside. My winter cloak is still there, and a change of clothes, old but serviceable. My best boots have gone but my battered and old pair, which I keep for the winter months, remains. It was men then, men that did this to my house, for no woman would have left items like that, which could be of use.

I gather what is left of my belongings up in my arms and take them over to the bed. The sheet is darned and thin, still wet with my tears. I fold the clothes carefully onto it, then gather the corners of the sheet together and tie them. I still have no plan nor any idea of what I will do next but as I stare at the bundle, it comes to me through a haze. Elizabeth. I once made a bundle like this for her. She too fled this town for fear of persecution and worse. My friend, who endured more than I did, who still came back to me, will welcome me, I know it.

Once the idea is fixed in my mind, the thought fills me with strength and purpose. I will be brave. I will leave this place and find her, wherever it is she has gone. She mentioned Halesworth when she told me of the man who helped her escape, and that seems as good a place to start looking as any. It is as if a new life is being offered to me, away from the anger and hatred of Dunwich, and I take it with both hands. I will do this thing. I will search out the roads, ask the way, and I will find her.

I sit on the bed and lace up the old boots, putting my shoes in the pack, then gather up my bundle of possessions and haul it over my shoulder. The pack is heavy but I will be strong – I will tramp until I find my friend, and we will not be parted again.

I step out of the door, leaving it to swing broken on its hinges in the brisk sea breeze. I take one long look at the sea, cresting and falling, white spume creeping ever closer, like the hands of ghosts, and then I begin to walk.

CHAPTER 26

Last time I made this journey was with the carter, that fateful day I went to see John Collit, but this time I choose the paths less travelled, for I do not wish to be seen. I sleep under the stars and wonder why I had not done this before; the air is clear and fresh, the nights velvet-black and silent, save for the scuffling of animals in the undergrowth, the rustle of wind in the trees. And in this solitude I find I am no longer afraid. It is as if all my fear has been used up and I am left with a sense of peace and acceptance. I faced my fears and overcame them. The power was in me all along, but I failed to recognise it but I do now, and it comes to me that I have been afraid all of my life, save for those few short months when William was with me. Now I am free.

I take three days to reach Halesworth, and, as I look around at the rows of buildings and clusters of shops, my heart sinks. It is so busy I wonder how I will ever find Elizabeth, or if she is even here. I walk slowly through the town, gazing at the houses and inns, drawn by a rumbling noise ahead of me. Then the road curves like a serpent and before me looms a hill, topped by a large and imposing church surrounded by tall railings, and to one side is the source of the commotion; a bustling market. It seems as if the whole county is here. Carts display meat, fish and flour, trestles show off bread, cheese, and household necessities. Awnings flap and crack in a stiff breeze and all around are the cries of the traders. I make my way from stall to stall, looking at the wares, searching for Elizabeth, pushed and shoved by the mass of people. But there is no sign of her and my stomach drops as I reach the last stall. I am turning to leave, wondering what I will do next, when I see a pedlar weaving her way through the crowds, carrying a tray of bright ribbons. Her hat is pulled low over her face against a sun which shines high in a washed blue sky. My heart soars. I push my way to her and grasp her arm.

'Elizabeth!' A stranger turns and looks at me. 'I am sorry, I mistook you for...' The woman smiles.

''tis easy done. Are you seeking someone?'

'I am looking for a woman, Elizabeth Southerne. She came here some time ago. She was my friend. I need to find her.' My voice wobbles and tears are close. The woman pats my arm. 'I am sorry, dear, I do not know of anyone by that name. She came here, you say, to Halesworth?'

'She too was a pedlar once...' I look at the ribbons in her tray. 'She sold ribbons such as these.' The woman looks down at the tray and back up at me. 'The person who sold me these was called Elizabeth, but she was More, not Southerne. Wife of the brewer that has a place down Cherry Bow? That the one?' I look at her, dumbfounded. The coincidence is too much, surely it cannot...

'It may be. Where can I find her?'

She points at a narrow road that runs away from the marketplace.

'One of the brew houses down there, I'm not sure which one though. There are a number in the town now.'

I clasp her hand.

'Thank you.' I look down at her tray. A dark red ribbon lies on top and I pull it through my hands; it is soft and warm. 'May I buy this?' Tears fill my eyes. 'It reminds me of someone I once knew – someone much loved.' I give the woman the coins, thank her again, and, holding the ribbon tightly in my hand, walk slowly across the marketplace and along the road she indicated. There are several brewers, their shutters open, ale-wands displayed to show their brew is ready. People have overflowed here from the market and trade is brisk. I peer over shoulders and around bodies at each window, searching, and then I stop dead. Behind one window, halfway down the road, is a tall figure. Her dress is dark and sober, her collar white and crisp. A brown curl, flashed now with silver, has come undone from a spotless coif and she brushes it back from her face with her arm in a gesture that is so familiar. She is busy filling jugs of ale and taking payment, and she does not see me. I watch her work, see her turn to greet a man who appears from behind her, shouldering another barrel. He sets it down beside her and pats her shoulder. She smiles warmly at him, mouthing her thanks, before turning back to her customers. I stare hard at her, willing her to see me and, as if she senses it, she stops what she is doing, her face lifting, the jug in her hands shaking as she slowly puts it down. She looks up, her eyes searching the crowds, then they find mine. It is as if a cord stretches between us, pulling her to me. For a moment she pauses, disbelieving, then a smile broadens her face and I see my name on her lips.

'Aubrey?'

'Elizabeth . . .' I cry out her name and people stop and stare as I push through the crowds towards her. She moves to the doorway and into the street, opening her arms to me as the distance between us disappears. Beside us, the ghost of Priscilla shimmers, a red ribbon around her throat, pale gold hair flying around a face which sparkles with life, then it fades. I move into Elizabeth's embrace and, as I do, I look down at the ribbon in my palm, remembering. Then I hold it high into the air, loosen my fingers, and set it free.

HISTORICAL NOTES

Elizabeth Southerne, Priscilla Collit and Aubrey Grinsett existed. They were all women who were accused of witchcraft. The only trace they have left behind is their confessions, which still exist.

Elizabeth, Priscilla and Aubrey lived in Dunwich and were all accused of witchcraft at different times, but by the same man, Thomas Spatchett. The confessions of Elizabeth and Priscilla show that they knew each other and had a falling out. Aubrey is not mentioned but, as she was later accused by the same man, I have assumed a friendship.

There are records of Southernes (spelt in various ways) in Dunwich in the 1500s but I could find no record of **Elizabeth Southerne**. Elizabeth's confession is linked to Priscilla's. (*Ewen, CL, Witch-hunting & Witch Trials, p 298-299*). Ewen's meticulous recording of the archived documents place their confessions amongst others who were known to have been sent to the infamous Bury St Edmunds trial in August 1645, including **Maria Clowes** of Yoxford and **Kathryn Tooley** of Westleton, so it seems probable that they were sent there to be tried (and thank you to Ivan Bunn, witchcraft enthusiast extraordinaire, for your help with this conclusion.).

As with Elizabeth, I could find no records of **Priscilla Collit**, apart from her confession (*Ewen, CL, Witch-hunting & Witch Trials, p 299*) which seems to be a work of madness. But when I read it carefully and saw that she had recently given birth, I looked further. It seems clear to me now that Priscilla was suffering from postpartum psychosis, a medical condition still around now and these days viewed as a medical emergency. Most strangely, even now, with our changed view of religion, it is not uncommon for women to believe that God or the Devil is speaking to them. Information on the website of the Royal College of Psychiatrists (*www.rcpsych.ac.uk*) was most helpful in researching what must be a terrifying condition to have.

The information about **Aubrey Grinsett** (spelt Abre in her confession) comes from a different and very strange source. A pamphlet, written by Samuel Petto (*A Faithful Narrative of the Wonderful and Extraordinary Fits . . .*' publ. 1693, available at *www.quod.lib.umich.edu/e/eebo/A54590*) is about the life and trials of Thomas Spatchett, who believed that he had been bewitched by Aubrey Grinsett. The pamphlet accuses her of witchcraft and the murders of John Collit and Henry Wilson, and gives details of Aubrey's confession. It is clearly extremely biased in favour of Thomas, and is written from a deeply religious point of view, so I have borne this in mind when trying to extract what actually seems to have happened. In it, Aubrey is described as 'a bastard' and, as seems usual, the emphasis is on the goodness of Thomas and the malice of Aubrey, but it contains a wealth of extraordinary detail. In real life, Aubrey died two years after the accusations and it was said that Thomas's fits ceased from that date. The double searching and the snake referred to in my novel are all recorded as fact. The only difference is that she was accused in 1665 – I have shortened the timescale.

Thomas Spatchett was the grandson of Robert Spatchett of Dunwich, who left a lengthy will. Held in the National Archives,

Robert's will is a fascinating insight into the status of a landowner of that time. He was hugely wealthy and owned many properties, both in Dunwich and outlying areas. Everything was left to his grandson, Thomas, when Robert died in 1625. Thomas was only nineteen then and so did not come into his inheritance until he was 21. There is a record of his marriage to Mary Back in 1633. The only other mention of Thomas is in the pamphlet by Samuel Petto (*A Faithful Narrative of the Wonderful and Extraordinary Fits . . .' publ. 1693, available at www.quod.lib.umich.edu/e/eebo/A54590*) and I have used this as an insight into his beliefs and character.

On Tuesday 26 August 1645, at the height of the English Civil War, the trial began of around 150 people, all accused as witches, in **Bury St Edmunds,** There were so many that some had to be kept in a barn as the gaol was full. On the first day ninety cases were considered by the grand jury, the first stage of the process, and around sixty were approved for trial. These people were tried the next day before a jury. Witnesses were brought forward, among them Matthew Hopkins and his fellow witchfinder, John Stearne, and all gave evidence against the accused. Some were cleared, and some had their case carried over until the next day. One of these was **James More of Metfield** (see below). But before the court adjourned for the day there was a message to say that the King's Army was nearby. The assize was suspended and prisoners were hurriedly transferred to the gaol at Ipswich, but not before those who had already been found guilty were hanged. The hanging was seemingly done in a rush and many did not die quickly. There is a harrowing account of this in Malcolm Gaskill's book Witchfinders (*Gaskell, M, Witchfinders: a Seventeenth Century Tragedy, publ. John Murray, 2003)*

Unlike Aldeburgh and the Chamberlains Account book (featured in my research for 'The Unnamed'), there are no records to show that **Matthew Hopkins** ever came to Dunwich. It seems more likely that, as it is known that he went to Aldeburgh, someone from

Dunwich may have spoken to him about his methods, especially as we know that a Widow Clarke was taken from Dunwich by cart to Aldeburgh (*Suffolk Records Office, EE6/3/3*). Given the timing, I have assumed that she was taken to stand trial there, and her story is told in 'The Unnamed'.

James More was put on trial at Bury St Edmunds. He was connected by marriage to the Everard family, brewers of Halesworth, who were accused of using imps to destroy crops, killing a child and sending an imp to aid the Royalist cause. They were also accused of bewitching their beer. **Mary and Thomas Everard** were hanged at Bury, their daughter Marian may have been cleared and, amazingly, James managed to escape in the confusion of the move to Ipswich.

The lost city of **Dunwich** was taken by the sea over the centuries. Very little remains from 1645, apart from the ruins of Greyfriars Priory, high on the cliff and, in the churchyard, what remains of an ancient Leper Hospital. This was in poor repair in 1645 and housed the 'aged and infirm', but was abandoned in 1685 due to its state. The church of St James which stands there today is much more recent, having been completed in 1832, but in the grounds stands the last buttress from the great church of Dunwich, All Saints, which crumbled into the sea between 1904 and 1922. The buttress was taken down and re-erected further inland as a reminder of how great the town once was. The marketplace, the church of St Peter and the gaol, all mentioned in my book, were taken by the sea between 1677-1715. Divers using sonar equipment have tried to explore the underwater ruins but the sea there is black and dark so nothing can be seen, although there is a story that, during a storm, the lost bells of Dunwich can be heard tolling. There is a wonderful model of the original town on display in Dunwich Museum, a fascinating place, full of local history and artefacts. (*Full info at www.dunwichmuseum.org.uk*). The whole village is atmospheric, full of history, and well worth a visit.

Lastly, Shakespeare's company, the King's Men, visited Dunwich three times while Shakespeare himself was a member of the troupe, although there is no evidence to show he came with them. His play, 'Macbeth', was written in c.1606 and so, with its links to witchcraft, I have assumed that this may have been the one performed in the town in 1614. (*www.bbc.co.uk search: Shakespeare 2016 On Tour.*)

ACKNOWLEDGEMENTS

Another enormous thank you to my husband Brian for his encouragement, help and support. I really couldn't do it without you.

A huge part of all my books has been the cover designs by Sandy Horsley so a very big thank you, once again, for another fabulous design.

My gratitude to Ivan Bunn, for the fascinating video calls about witch trials. His knowledge, common sense and enthusiasm have been invaluable in writing all three books, particularly regarding the intricacies of the trial system.

Thanks as always to Charlotte and Lynne at Southwold Library, who always go the extra mile; to the volunteers at Dunwich Museum for their knowledge and love of Dunwich; to Maybelle Wallis, Consultant Paediatrician, for her help with understanding the effects of burns on children, and to her and Melissa West for reading and commenting on the draft version of this book.

Thanks also to Mai Black and Suffolk Writers for their advice and encouragement, to Jerico Writers, and to Clare Harvey for her invaluable editorial report. And a big shout out to Phil and Sonja at Small Island Digital for all the tech advice!

Thank you to all those local bookshops who stock my books, especially Steph, Nina and staff at Southwold Books, Abbie and staff at The Halesworth Bookshop, and Andrew and staff at Dial Lane Books in Ipswich, Their enthusiasm, encouragement and support have meant so much to this unknown writer. I am so grateful to everyone who has read my books, talked about and recommended them to others, and to those who have taken the time to email me about them or write a review on Amazon and Goodreads. Thank you all!

This and my previous two books, 'This Fearful Thing' and 'The Unnamed', were written from a sense of anger at the treatment of those who were persecuted and tortured by others in positions of power who should have been protecting them. It seemed to me that history seems to have forgotten these victims, mainly women, and that they should be given a voice.

They were like us. My books are for them.

ABOUT THE AUTHOR

L M West lives in Suffolk with her husband. In 2020, during the first lockdown, she decided to have a go at writing a book. It was something she had always dreamed of doing and, at sixty-six, she thought she'd better get on with it! 'We Three' is her third novel.

When she is not writing she paints, gardens, walks and reads.

For more information head over to www.lmwestwriter.co.uk where you can sign up for a free article about Matthew Hopkins

ALSO BY L M WEST

An act of revenge. An accusation of witchcraft. A reckoning.
Southwold, Suffolk, 1645. Ann has fled from her past but when her childhood tormentor finds her in a busy street, she realises that the past she thought long-buried has come back to haunt her. When rumours of witchcraft begin she knows he will stop at nothing to destroy her...
Inspired by true events, 'This Fearful Thing' was published in May 2021

ALSO BY L M WEST

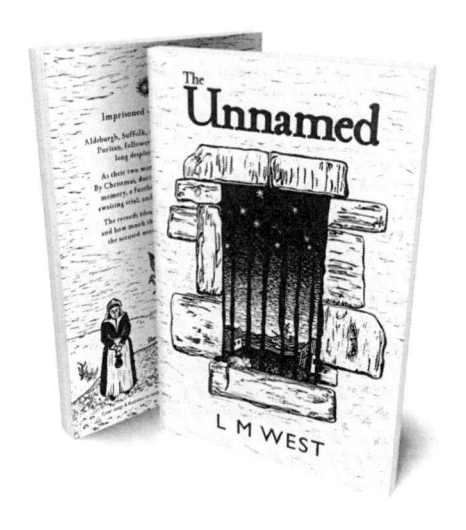

Aldeburgh, Suffolk, 1645. Mary Howldine, innkeeper, Puritan, follower of rules. Joan Wade, widow, long-despised, seized for witchcraft. As their two worlds collide the terror grows. By Christmas, during the hardest winter in living memory, a further six women are imprisoned, awaiting trial, and Mary's beliefs begin to waver. The records identify the many men involved and how much they were paid, but only two of the accused are named. This is their story.

'The Unnamed' was published in March 2022

AND LASTLY...

Look out for the fourth book by L M West...

'This I remember. The earthiness of his fingertips as he holds the cherries, one after the other, to my lips...'

In August 1828, a young man, William Corder, was hanged for the brutal murder of Maria Martin in Polstead, Suffolk. The ensuing media frenzy turned this case into one of the most celebrated and talked-about crimes of the nineteenth century. Known as the Red Barn Murder, the peep shows, ballads and broadsheets of the time proclaimed Maria as the poor village maiden, viciously slain by her callous lover. Until the end, William protested his innocence.

What if he was telling the truth...?

'The Red Barn' is underway, and will hopefully be published in 2024.

For updates pop over to https://www.lmwestwriter.co.uk